escape fro
amsterdam

escape from amsterdam

barrie sherwood

Granta Books

London

Granta Publications, 2/3 Hanover Yard, Noel Road, London N1 8BE

First published in Great Britain by Granta Books, 2007

The *manga* in the book were created by Richard Perkins.
See his oil paintings at www.richardperkinsarts.com
The sketches of flora and fauna were done by Mansho-*sensei*.
The photograph of *humuhumunukunukuāpua'a* is used with
the generous permission of photographer Jim Christensen.
See his work at www.uwphoto.net

The author would like to express his gratitude to the
Canada Council of the Arts for their generous funding
of the research and composition of this novel.

The quotation from Pope's *Rape of the Lock* is used
by permission of Routledge Publishing.

A CIP catalogue record for this book
is available from the British Library.

1 3 5 7 9 10 8 6 4 2

ISBN 978 1 86207 958 8

Typeset by M Rules
Printed and bound in Great Britain by
William Clowes Ltd, Beccles, Suffolk

à Patou

Even in Kyoto,
I long for Kyoto

BASHO

speed of lightness

Mr Tak comes back from the toilet, flings his linen jacket over the seat next to him and loosens his tie. He leans across the aisle to tap my knee. 'Mr Fujiwara, do you know that Hiroshima is famous around the world?'

I'm trying to read my book, but there's no ignoring Mr Tak. 'Oh?'

'Oh yes,' he says, cool in his excitement. 'It has just occurred to me now what I've been craving for *days*.' He closes his eyes in ecstasy. '*Oysters*. Hiroshima has the *best* oysters any*where*.'

'Really? Why?'

'*Why?*' He sits back and spreads his palms. 'Why are they the best? They're *famous*. Everyone knows that. This train stops in Hiroshima for . . . how long now?' He whirls around and digs through his Vuitton laptop case for the train schedule. 'Only *eleven* minutes? How inconsiderate. Only eleven minutes to find some oysters.' He tosses the schedule back and stares at his chunky blue-and-gold Breitling chronograph as if one of its ninety-nine functions can solve his problem. 'Still, you know, it *might* be possible,' he says with a widening grin. 'Acts of great faith are often accomplished in short time. If I try, would you like to come along for a bowl of deep-fried oysters too?'

This man I hardly know is proposing that I risk my onward journey to go charging through Hiroshima Station with him looking for an oyster shop that may not exist. And even if it does, there's no way we'll actually get served and be back to the train before it continues on its punctual way. *Eleven* minutes? Not possible.

What's more, I don't like oysters.

However, I *am* hungry. I could just go along and make some excuse to order something else. And it occurs to me that missing the train may not be a bad thing. I avoided trouble when I left Kyoto, but if there's anyone following me, a little detour in Hiroshima might be to my advantage.

'Sure,' I reply. 'Why not?'

'Yes!' Mr Tak slaps his knees. 'You are a traveller with heart, Mr Fujiwara. I could sense it the moment you sat down. We have seventeen minutes before we arrive. Shall we have another beer for added power?'

It wasn't my choice to sit across from Mr Tak. He was the only passenger in the cabin when I got aboard the *Speed of Lightness*. Though there were seventy-four other seats I could have been assigned by the ticket machine, my seat was directly facing his. I had the urge to take another seat further away, but I knew from past experience that the embarrassment of having to move seats when the train filled up at the next stop was not worth it. I sat down and fished in my rucksack for my book.

Nippon Rail probably figured if they could make the *Speed of Lightness* fast enough, they wouldn't need to waste money on passenger comfort. The bench seats faced each other like the subway trains and the only windows were two perfunctory strips of horizontal glass, one concealed behind the headrests, the other too high to offer anything in the way of a view but high-tension lines skipping like a lunatic's cardiogram. I tried to concentrate on my book, *Golden Pavilions: Bid-Rigging in Japanese Construction*, but had to shift around continually to avoid going numb. I finally ended up kneeling on my seat, peering out between the headrests at what passes for scenery in this part of the world.

Going to southern Japan is supposed to be special. The light's supposed to change. The scenery and greenery too. But Kyoto becomes Osaka. Osaka becomes Kobe. Kobe becomes Okayama. Entire neighbourhoods flash by; at 300 kilometres an hour it's next to impossible to focus on anything. Far in the background, the Inland Sea shines bright and inviting as drilled steel. Awaji Island is out there somewhere. And Shodo and Shikoku, but you'd never know it. The suspension bridges loop into the summer haze.

I slumped back into my seat.

The guy across the aisle wasn't the usual salaryman in a bin-liner suit. He was tall, well-built, and handsome enough to wear octagonal Porsche Design glasses without looking like a fop. (He reminded me of Chrono, the macho wristwatch in the *Metro-jin* comics.) He wore flash Italian shoes with double straps and silver buckles, a lustrous grey linen suit, a pink poplin shirt and a blue pearl necktie with an Escher-like pattern of interlocking ... what? Hard to tell without staring. He snapped his book, *A History of Kyushu,* shut. 'Another three hours,' he sighed.

I picked up my book again. *For those with an eye for opportunity, the Ministry of Construction is a veritable El Dorado of –*

'Still, it's got more ambience than the airplane,' he continued. 'So banal, the airplanes.'

I found a 'that's nice' smile for him in my repertoire of disingenuousness and tried to continue reading, but he didn't take the hint. The smile he gave me back was so wide and protracted it had to be held in place by Porsche Design clamps mounted inside his cheeks. 'I'm Takamura,' he said.

'Aozora,' I replied.

'Ah ...' He paused to prompt me for more information. 'And ... family name?'

'Fujiwara.'

'Oh, *Fujiwara*,' he said, putting his shoulders back, 'an old and honourable name. Yes indeed, you look like a Fujiwara. *Noble*, if you don't mind me saying so. Do you live in Kyoto?'

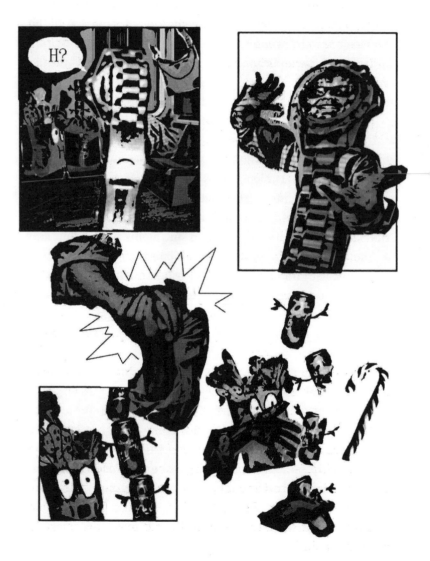

'That's it.'

'And you're going to Kyushu?'

'Right again.'

'May I ask why?'

There was no escape from the man's social ineptitude, yet neither was there a simple and honest answer to the question. *Well, in fact, I'm going to Marumachi to find my sister, whom I haven't seen in over a year and who is probably a prostitute indentured to the mafia and . . .* It didn't exactly roll off the tongue.

'Sightseeing,' I told him.

He beamed, his cheeks swelling like twin red globefish. His glasses rode up his nose. 'Ahh, *sightseeing*,' he said in admiration, as if I'd won the Nobel Prize. 'What better thing to do in Kyushu? It's a truly *wonderful* place. So full of history and tradition.' He picked up the book again. 'I've just been reading about the Satsuma Rebellion. Do you know much about the Satsuma Rebellion?'

I shrugged. 'Yeah, yeah. General Takamori?'

'Yes! A very romantic man. Did you know that his testicles were so prodigious he used to carry them in a basket suspended by a thong around his neck?'

Great, I thought. Never a dull moment with the general public. Because they're only general at a glance. Once you stop and watch, it's like twisting the knob on a microscope: that blurry apparition of faces becomes a very peculiar organism. I flashed him another 'that's nice' smile.

'Yes, he certainly did. And what's more, he marched fifty kilometres with a burst hernia *and* a bullet in his groin so he could kill himself overlooking Kagoshima Bay. Have you ever had a hernia? It's bad enough, I tell you. Imagine a bullet too. A Meiji Period bullet. Round like this. If you go to Kagoshima you must visit the site of his death and make the effort to relive his pain.'

5

Yeah, of course. I'd be *very* sure to do that. 'That'll be first on my itinerary for my next time,' I told him. 'But I'm just visiting Marumachi this time.'

'Of course, of course,' he said, leaning back and crossing his legs. 'Nightlife, bars, clubs. Just like the old "floating world" of Yoshiwara. I'm sure you'll pay Amsterdam a visit too, no?'

'The theme park?'

'Oh, it's very respectable, family entertainment, of course, *yang* to Marumachi's *yin*. But the Dutch have a long history in Japan. Very interesting.'

I shrugged. 'Hadn't thought about it.'

'Well, a young man such as yourself, alone on a trip . . .' He smiled knowingly. 'I can understand if a history lesson isn't your first priority. While you're in Marumachi perhaps you'd like to pay a visit to one of my seminars? You can come and have sex with one of my daughters.'

He said this in such a reasonable, matter-of-fact way, I thought I'd misunderstood.

'You're embarrassed,' he observed, pointing at me with an index finger and smiling.

'Not at all,' I replied, annoyed by his confidence.

'Really, Mr Fujiwara, it's not an uncommon feeling.'

'Uncommon or not, Mr Takamura,' I felt obliged to point out, 'I'm not in the habit of pre-arranging for . . . you know. Well, these daughters of yours, how *old* are they?'

'Here, my card, my card. Please, call me Mr Tak.' Smooth as a magician, he flicked out a business card – heavy cotton weave with a crepe-like gloss – that featured a Warhol take on an old Edo Period print – hot-pink man with a lime topknot sucking a pointy little peach breast with a blue nipple. 'I manufacture sex,' he told me. 'Facsimile companions and other therapeutic and recreational items. I'm holding an introductory seminar at a hotel in Marumachi.'

6

On the back the card read:

> *Cin-Cin Inc.*
> *Masturbation Lifestyle*
> *Facsimile Companions*
> *Naniwa, Harbin, Monty Carlo*

'Are you familiar with facsimile companions?' He opened a pocket in his laptop case and handed me a leaflet covered with pictures of girls in polka-dot minidresses or red lingerie, all in provocative poses. Only when I looked closely could I tell that these 'girls' were actually dolls. Half the leaflet was covered in photographs, the other half was devoted to technical data about the various available options – lubricant reservoir, fibre-optic pubic hair, moaning and *mots doux* in six different languages.

'Those,' he said proudly, 'are the best facsimile companions in the world. They're not the old mouth-permanently-open doll that broke a seam so easily, you remember, no matter how gently you treated them. Nowadays, my daughters weigh up to twenty-six kilos – solid as Akebono, I like to say, but much prettier. Do you know the famous English poet, Jonathon Keats? He wrote "*And what is Love? It is a doll dressed up, for fondling in corset, nurse or dancer.*" This means that true love comes in many distinctive forms. He was a very imaginative poet. He masturbated a great deal.'

A pneumatic wheeze came from the other end of the car. The doors opening. I spun to my right to see who was coming in.

Two young stewardesses in mustard outfits with gold buttons were pushing a refreshment cart up the aisle. I sighed and turned back to Mr Tak, who was now squinting at me, wondering why I was so jumpy. 'Perhaps you could use . . .' he began. 'Perhaps you would *like* to drink a beer with me, Mr Fujiwara?'

It was an obvious tactic to prolong a one-sided conversation, but as long as he was buying I wouldn't take the trouble to discourage him.

The uniform the girls were wearing was part parka (the furry sleeves), part burnous (the copious hood) and the rest a cross between a terry-cloth robe and a Chanel business suit. It was like some kind of fungus that had grown from the thigh up and left a ghastly white film on their legs. They wore matching summer hats with white hatbands and were exquisitely made up. If one of them had sat down instead of offering me nuts, I'd have thought she was a pop star. With her candied eyes nictitating wonderfully, the first one emitted a spiel in a high-pitched, almost synthesized voice. 'Welcome aboard the *Speed of Lightness*? The *Speed of Lightness* Express Service to Hiroshima? Hakata? And Marumachi? We have now reached cruising speed so why not enjoy your journey? A selection of refreshments is available from our refreshment cart? We have a fresh range of bento boxes? And canned drinks available?'

She had the most grating high-rise terminals I'd ever heard, but I was enraptured. She was easily a 7 on the Kasane Scale . . .

The Kasane Scale

A Romantic Interlude

Eight months ago my girlfriend Kasane left me. She was the greatest. This is why:

A. She had a pretty face and was physically well proportioned.

B. Once a week she made my favourite rice balls, arranged them in a bento box wrapped in brown paper, and paid 1500 yen to send it by Yamato same-day delivery to my residence at the university. She must have spent a fortune on bento boxes because I never returned them, and her rice balls, though she never knew it, kept half my floor fed. The guys would wait for the courier to pull up in his green van and then hover around my door. (When they started leaving me orders for cucumber rolls and potato croquettes, I had to tell her to stop.)

C. She was laissez-faire. I never had the impression she would get upset if I slept with anyone else, so I never did. The same went for drinking, gambling, all-night binges of Sega Rally. None of that got out of hand until she left.

D. Most of the girls I've known treat my penis something like a lobster in a fancy restaurant: it's a special occasion and they're looking forward to the whole experience in a general sort of way, but they'd prefer not to have to grapple with the thing. The following is not an exaggeration: Kasane prayed at the altar of my groin.

E. I really really liked her. More than that even. At least, I think I did. But who knows, right? And so what?

9

Kasane studied Japanese literature at Kyoto Women's College, but her dream was to become a snowboard instructor. When she got a job in Hokkaido, that spelled the end for us. It was sad, sure, but you can't get all romanchikku *when your dreams are at stake. Still, for a long time after, I saw her everywhere. The most incongruous, ugly, dissimilar people would feature components of Kasane – her clothes, her knees, her walk, her hair, ears, perfume; I even caught a glimpse of her 'Lucky You!' panties on an escalator in the Gap – but most unnerving of all was just that faint, indefinable resemblance, that air of Kasane. Every time I perceived this Kasane-ness out there in the world, I was debilitated by nostalgia and regret. This torture continued until, one afternoon as I was watching the Miss Universe pageant in the residence with my floormate Kuwahara, I conceived of the Kasane Scale. Instead of fighting this tendency to measure the girls I met against my memories of Kasane, I'd accept the psychological necessity of it and standardize the process. 1 would be the least Kasane-like on the scale, and 10 the most (with Kasane herself floating, as if on a velvet throne, just above and to the left of this staircase in lights). I have yet to find a 10, but the significant number of 7s and 8s I encounter gives me hope.*

What I'm taking unnecessary pains to get around to is this: for several heart-wrenching moments when she was at the far end of the cabin, this *Speed of Lightness* girl in the yellow outfit *could have been* Kasane. She had Kasane's eyebrows and nose – that much was striking – as well as smallish breasts, and shoulders that were perfectly wide and square (though this could have been the effect of the uniform). Once she got closer and my inspection more detailed, however, the façade crumpled. The skin of her cheeks was ever so slightly pebbled, her eyebrows pencilled in and the back of her neck hairy. She had pigeon toes too. And Kasane couldn't have spoken like that; she would have lilted her lines, insouciant, with a levity bordering on disrespect.

'Grolsch lager,' said Mr Tak. 'Two.'

'I'm sorry, sir? We have Sapporo today?'

I watched the girl's lacquered fingers pour the beer into plastic cups, her wrists adorned with platinum jewellery. I smiled, thanked her, gave her a 5.

Mr Tak took his cup and apologized for, as he put it, 'this sliced-bread-canned-tuna-cup-noodle of a lager'. (And now that he mentioned it, the Sapporo did taste faintly of both bread and canned tuna, though it's always smelled like urine.) I was wary of more Candy Girl sales pitch, but now that he'd bought me a beer, I felt like it was more or less my duty to humour the guy. I listened and nodded and drank my beer and learned more about love dolls than I'd ever admit to wanting to know.

malpeque

The train's bombing into Hiroshima, though the unrelieved urban ugliness doesn't exactly distinguish Hiroshima from anywhere else this corner of the planet. (Only the oysters do that, apparently.) The evening sky, however, is a perfect original, full of scrambled egg altocumulus and some flourishes of white cirrus higher up. As the train decelerates on approach to the station, the door lights start flashing and the public-service voice comes on.

'*Hiroshima Station. Hiroshima Station if you please. Please remain seated until the train has come to a full stop. Please watch your step when exiting the train. Please be sure you have taken all your possessions with you when exiting the train. If you have young children, be sure that they are accompanying you before you exit the train. Please allow the elderly and families with small children to exit the train first. Please check for connections on the connection board in the central concourse. To reach the concourse, please follow the yellow signs that read Central Concourse. Thank you for travelling aboard the* Speed of Lightness. *Hiroshima Station. Hiroshima Station if you please.*'

The train is well and truly stopped but we're standing there for a full minute of our mere eleven before the voice finally shuts up and the doors open with a hiss. Mr Tak leaps out and I'm right behind him. It's a good thing we're travelling light because we've got to weave through the crowds; my army surplus rucksack leaps and thumps on my back like a homicidal monkey, Mr Tak runs with his briefcase clenched to his gut like it's an American football. We dash for the underpass beneath the platforms and race up the stairs. We look left. We look right. Mr Tak grabs me by the shoulder and points. Right there in the shopping arcade beyond the turnstiles is a classic *ramen* bar, just the kind of place I was envisioning. It has a big red-and-white sign out front that reads HIROSHIMA OYSTER & RAMEN. Everyone inside is seated on stools in front of the bar, sucking up noodles from red lacquer bowls.

Mr Tak's already making the order as he goes through the front door. 'Oyster *ramen*!' he yells at a girl in a pink-and-white hospital uniform who's just getting up to leave after finishing her meal. She jumps back in alarm and whispers through her fingers: 'I – I beg your pardon?'

Mr Tak makes a quick bow. 'Sorry!' He eases past her – 'Very sorry' – and leans between two businessmen at the bar, flourishing a 10,000-yen note. 'Two-Hiroshima-oyster-*ramen*,' he barks at the chef. 'Go on, take it. We need oysters. *Quickly.*'

The chef snaps up the note and throws two handfuls of noodles into a wire basket that he plunges into the steaming soup pot. From the glass refrigerator case that runs the length of the bar he takes a square plastic tub full of shelled oysters, dips them one by one in batter, and drops them into the fryer. 'Hiro,' he calls out to the young blue-haired waiter, 'get these men some beer.'

'No, thank you,' Mr Tak retorts. 'We can get beer anywhere.' He checks his watch. 'Quickly now. We have a train to catch.'

Everyone at the bar is watching us, but I'm easy. I'm just playing sidekick to Mr Tak. He turns to me with a grin. 'We've still got *five* more minutes. *Yasu-yasu.* No problem!'

The chef pulls the basket from the pot and, with his great long chopsticks, fills two plastic bowls with noodles, then ladles in the broth. Just when he's placing the golden, crispy-fried oysters on top, Mr Tak leans forward and puts both hands on the glass case. '*Hmm?*'

He lifts his glasses and peers into the cabinet at the red chunks of tuna or the octopus legs, I can't tell exactly what. '*Malpeque?*' he says. 'Hey you, show me that container.' His manner is terse. Something's up. 'Yes, that one, the oysters.'

The chef frowns but does as Mr Tak asks. He takes the tub out of the refrigerator case and places it on the counter. The blue label reads, in English, *Elvira's Genuine Malpeque. Prince Edward Island, Canada.* Mr Tak reads the English out loud, slowly, incredulously, then spreads his hands and looks at the chef. '*Hiroshima* oysters?'

'Hiroshima *style*,' the chef replies.

With his hands still outstretched on the counter, Mr Tak takes a deep breath to steady himself, then pushes his glasses further up his head. 'Do you happen to have any *Hiroshima* oysters on the premises?'

'These oysters are the very best quality –'

'No, please,' interrupts Mr Tak, '*origin* is the issue. Do you have any *Japanese* oysters here? I've invited my respected friend Mr Fujiwara of Kyoto to your establishment for some *Hiroshima* oysters.'

If there's anyone who hasn't been casting long glances our way, Mr Tak's sarcastic vibes have got their interest now. The two businessmen on either side of us have their faces pressed into their bowls as they wolf down their noodles, glancing furtively out at the scene that's developing. And the chef is no geek. He's got a wide mouth and swarthy skin and it looks like his placid nature could be prone to sudden squalls. I lean towards Mr Tak and whisper: 'You know, we could just get some *tonkotsu*-style noodles once we're down in Kyushu.'

'I fully expect to, Mr Fujiwara,' he replies without looking at me, 'but for the moment I'm more intent upon oysters.' He puts his finger in the chef's face. 'What kind of ruse is this? *Hm?* Are you serving pancakes and maple syrup too? Is that what I'll get when I ask for *okonomiyaki*?'

Looking Mr Tak in the eyes, the chef lifts the two big red bowls onto the glass case, and eases them forward. 'This *is* what you asked for.'

Mr Tak gently eases the bowls back again. 'Oh no, in fact, this is *not* what I asked for.' He picks up the plastic tub, pinches one of the slimy grey oysters between thumb and index, and holds it up. '*This* is a fake. *This* is a parasite. *This* is a . . . a *Malpeque!*'

With that, he flings the oyster over the counter and onto the floor. The chef blinks in amazement. As if in a trance, he reaches up to wipe oyster juice from his cheek.

Mr Tak goes to throw another.

And that's pretty much when the scene erupts. With a growl the chef barrels forward to take a backhand swipe at Mr Tak. He misses, but his elbow connects with the two steaming bowls of *ramen* on the case and they cascade over the glass onto the bar. The two businessmen sitting there leap backwards, dancing around with boiling soup on their laps. The waiter-cum-punk rocker makes a sprint for the action but slips on the soup and takes me out along with two girls perched on stools near the window. One of them comes down right on top of me and I find my hands wrapped around her as I fall. It's not my fault, but when she goes to get up she puts a retaliatory stiletto heel in my crotch and the whole restaurant goes flash-bulb white. Men are shouting. Women are screaming. The whole scene comes back to me through a kaleidoscope of testicular pain. Mr Tak is sidestepping through the tables, picking out oysters from the tub and hurling them at the chef, berating him with perfect grammar and his teeth clenched tight: 'If-you're-going-to-*ad*vertise-*Hiroshima*-oysters-I-would-su*ggest*-you-sell-*oy*sters-from-*Hiroshima!*'

Both of us end up in a police cruiser, the chef standing outside making a statement to a constable of the Hiroshima City Police, and the *Speed of Lightness* long gone into the night.

father

A couple of fraught days before my culinary high jinks with Mr Tak, I was on my way from Kyoto back to my home town, Inaka.

I'd had some trouble in the city.

There was the matter of a gambling debt to a bar-owner from Ikoma named Mr Uno. His place was called the Shark Attack (sand on the floors, surfboards for tables, improbable cocktails with names like Great White and Hammerhead) but he also ran an illegal mah-jong parlour upstairs that I frequented for a six-month stretch of sheer bad luck, the last two months of which were made possible by kindly Mr Uno's heavy-interest, unlimited line of credit. When my gambling debt to Mr Uno finally came due, the string of figures in my bank account was found two decimal places short. With great calm, Mr Uno voiced his displeasure. I made grovelling promises, buying some time, and promptly disappeared. I emptied my room at the university residence of all personal documents, bought some dark glasses and started growing what I optimistically called a beard. For more than a week I had been sleeping in disco foyers, karaoke parlours and capsule hotels, only paying the occasional furtive visit to my room to pick up clean clothes.

It was during this short, regrettable period of personal flux that I received the news that – six months after she herself was put in a jar – my Aunt Okane's will was finally ready to be executed and, moreover, that my sister and I had been named as the inheritors of her estate. What it amounted to my father wouldn't tell me, but all that was necessary to claim it was to come back to Inaka to sign the forms . . .

The NR Inaka Line brochure will tell you that in one truly memorable hour, its historic, yellow, single-car diesel climbs out of picturesque Kyoto into the heart of the country; up many a lush tea field and sleepy cedar forest, through the jaws of the Kikui Gorge, down past the roaring rapids of the Shirakawa River, and along the neat, pleated rice fields to the head of the valley. Here we find the authentic and charming hamlet of Inaka, huddled at the base of majestic mountains!

In fact, the trip takes three sides of the Red Hot Chili Peppers' double-disc *Greatest Hits* and three Asahi beers (there is time for a fourth before arriving but it's lukewarm by then). They say it's beautiful in Inaka, a village from another century. Since leaving home for university when I was seventeen, I'd done my best to stay away. Unless, of course, there was cash involved. As the train approached Inaka Station, I reminded myself over and over why I'd come back: '*Cash, cash, cash.* Just think about *cash.*'

My father was standing at the centre of the platform in a green cotton apron, black rubber kneepads and a Yomiuri Giants baseball cap with black and white stripes. He'd been waving at the train from a great distance to make sure that it wouldn't pass by. He took me by both elbows as if he were going to hug me, then looked searchingly down the platform. 'And your bags?'

'I may not be here long,' I replied, easing away from his embrace. 'I've got studying to do.'

This was a complete falsehood, of course, but one that the father of the Kyoto University student was forced to accept. The undergrad prospectus said so: *The parents of the Kyoto University student will be very proud.*

'Of course,' he said, blinking repeatedly. 'Of course.'

Inaka Station. Two massive blocks of concrete next to the tracks with corrugated-iron awnings and a white wooden hut with overturned flowerpots on the windowsills. That was all. To the east, the rice fields and sulphurous swamps stretched away to the horizon; in every other direction the steaming bamboo hills hemmed us in. I followed my father across a parking lot that was cross-hatched with weeds and strewn with snails baking in their shells. Dragonflies did geometry above the rice paddy. The sun was a bunch of needles and a thin veil of cirrostratus only spread the glare. Ten o'clock and I was already wishing I were back in the cool, fragrant lobby of the Mitsukoshi department store downtown.

'The Sex Machine Guns, aren't they?' Father remarked, nodding at my T-shirt.

'I didn't imagine SexMachineGuns was one of your favourites.'

He laughed. As usual, it had more to do with self-effacement than humour. 'Oh, of course not,' he said. 'I just watched a show on the television recently, that's all. What they play is called "metal", no?'

'Yeah, metal,' I groaned.

'An interesting sub-genre of hard rock.'

'Yeah, an interesting sub-genre.'

'So I thought,' he said, nodding contentedly. He pointed at the dragonflies. 'I'll bet they don't have many of those in the city. Do you recognize them?'

I did, but I shrugged and said, 'Damselflies?'

He sucked his teeth as if I'd made a serious *faux pas.* 'Dear me, Aozora. Damselflies don't *prowl*. Those are *dragon*flies. Japanese common dragonflies. Don't you see their blue eyes?'

'Yeah, I guess,' I said. 'Whatever. They still look like damselflies.'

'Only because you don't know what you're looking for,' he harrumphed. 'What did I always tell you?'

Yeah, yeah. How could I forget? 'What doesn't have a name,' I muttered, 'doesn't exist.' It was better just to humour him now and get it out of the way. His Mitsubishi Proudia was sitting in the shade of a willow with the engine still running. It was the same car he'd been driving since my birth. It sported a chrome grille and upright mirrors in defiance of anything so ignoble as aerodynamics. Inside, the seats were covered with white lace antimacassars and the air-con was turned up to triple snowflake. Once Father had put on the white gloves that were tucked under the sun visor, he manipulated the levers and knobs, gripped the wheel firmly at four and eight, and we set off along the Yakyu Road.

Inaka may be isolated. Inaka may be the end of the earth.

Backward. Bumpkin. Uncouth. It may disappear beneath the snows of winter and steam in the summer like an old soldier's Borneo nightmare. It may reek of sulphur from the thick marshes beyond the river, the hot springs bubbling through the bamboo hills, and the thirty-seven matches it takes the original clerk at Inaka Station to light one bent cigarette. It may be full of good childhood memories tinged by the bad ones when Mom ceased being Mom and then outright died. It may be so unnervingly silent as to accuse your conscience for the evil things you did to insects, quail chicks or the Thalidomide girl in your class when you were ten – enough to make you take refuge for hours each day with Sky TV . . . Inaka may be all this, but Inaka is *safe*. I was *alone* on the train. The Proudia was the only car on the road. A stranger – a coconut-smelling, *natto*-eating, batik-sporting mah-jong-cheat of a bar-owner from Ikoma for example – would stand out in Inaka like a Caucasian. For the first time in days, I relaxed. I put my head back and closed my eyes. All was well, for the time being.

'So how much was Aunt Okane worth?' I asked, by way of conversation.

Father sucked his teeth again. 'This is something we need to talk about.'

'Fire away.'

His eyebrows, slowly greying and unravelling as he got older, dipped over his eyes. 'You need to understand that the monetary value of Aunt Okane's possessions isn't nearly as considerable as its cultural value.'

My hopes wilted. I'd come all this way for a homily on Inaka culture? 'What *exactly* did she leave us?'

'She left you her house, for a start. It's *shinden* style, you know. Very elegant and –'

'Old and run-down.'

'It needs attention.'

21

A house like my aunt's would have been worth a fortune in Kyoto just for the land it was on, but in Inaka there were dozens of similar houses abandoned and rotting beneath the pines. After selling it, paying the inheritance tax, the income tax and the realtor, then splitting the proceeds with my sister, Mai, I wouldn't have half my debt to Mr Uno.

'Apart from that there's her Daihatsu and –' he coughed '– I beg your pardon, her Daihatsu and a large collection of farm tools, some old *ukiyo-e* prints, and some pottery. There's quite a splendid bowl, actually, with a cracked pink finish.'

'What about these prints?'

Father ran his hand over his head. 'Well, there are several Eizan pieces and . . .' He turned to look at me and frowned. 'You're not familiar with Eizan, are you? No? Good. He's a minor artist really. And there are some later Meiji Period pieces and "floating world" themes –'

'Geisha girls taking a piss?'

'Oh please, Aozora,' he said. 'There are some toilet scenes, if that's what you're referring to. There's also some paraphernalia, you understand, some of the blocks, mostly half-burnt stuff, and several advertising posters of the period. There's a list of everything at home if you want to see it. It's quite lengthy and I've already been through it. Really you won't need to . . . won't need to look into it.'

I think there was a rice paddy floating by outside, but all I could see in my glum mind's eye was Mr Uno. 'Sure, fine, whatever.' I'd just have to get used to being a fugitive. Father and I slipped back into our usual, comfortable, stony silence.

I once saw a woman touch the tip of her cigarette to her daughter's neck outside a Mister Donut. It was very nonchalant. There was nothing violent about it. She took another drag and checked her mobile phone. The girl, perhaps twelve or thirteen, spun away with a hoarse cry, as if the burn had caught her vocal cords mid tremor. Her older sister was wearing a fichu and immediately covered the girl's head with it to deny her mother the pleasure of watching. There was never anything like that in my family. We're not particularly cosy, but there was never anything like that.

Just beyond Inari Shrine, the rice paddies and wheat fields gave way to plots of azaleas and sago palms and the sweeping roof of my old house rising like a turquoise wave above hundreds of topiary bushes. As many of the landowners in Inaka did, my father grew topiary – holly oak, box, cypress and privet – to sell to wholesale buyers from Osaka. He had, however, started a bit of a trend in Inaka gardening circles by cultivating an elaborate variety of original forms to suit both his botanical fancy and the market. Dinosaurs were a speciality, but clustered about the house were also dancing elephants, monkeys, giraffes, camels, humanoids, sphinxes and a squadron of low-flying Mitsubishi Zero fighter planes. All of Father's free time was spent in his garden training this slow circus. And his 'living sculpture', as he called it, sold rather well. The dinosaurs were popular with young parents. Zeros were a particular favourite of elderly men. The sphinxes were grown under contract for a chain of perfumeries in Nagoya.

'I see you're still playing ringmaster,' I said as we got out of the car.

Father shook his head. 'No, no, I'm very lazy. It's an absolute mess. Come, look here.'

I followed him down to a squadron of a dozen or more Zeros spread in perfect diamond formation beneath a troop of elephants. The dry soil crunched beneath our feet. Two bulbuls fought over something in a holly oak. Father kneeled down and took another pair of white gloves from the pocket of his apron. Standing above him, I was struck by how thick and unruly his hair had become, by his pendulous ears, and the chocolate blotches around his temples. The papery skin at the back of his neck was crisscrossed with wrinkles like ruined origami. He eased the little arboreal airplane over. Thick copper wire was twisted around the ailerons. 'Do you see where the wire is bruising the bark? It's time all these were readjusted. I hardly have a moment though. Between the Ramblers and the PTA Alumni and the neighbourhood circle group, and other things too, I can hardly keep up.' He let the little tree go and it sprang back into place. 'Still, son, it seems less a chore now than an art,' he said. 'And it pays well if you're assiduous.'

High above the steaming valley, two vapour trails led by tiny glinting airplanes crossed one another.

'*Well.*' Father got to his feet. 'You've come all this way. You look tired. Will we have some coffee together?'

The 'we' was almost insufferably condescending. My father only ever drank tea. But after the three-beer breakfast on the train, I was in need of something to wake me up. I shrugged. 'Whatever.'

We walked back up to the house. The roof of blue tiles that he had replaced by himself over the winter glistened and the golden devil's face on the ridgepole gleamed sharply in the sun. As we came to the front door, a greenish crab sidled out from beneath a loquat tree and slipped down through the grate over the gutter. I stopped and watched it go. 'I'd forgotten about those things,' I said, clenching my fists to repress a shiver.

I have a long-standing dislike of crabs, though it is not, I stress, a phobia, because unlike phobias it is not irrational.

Crabs *are* evil.

Evidence? An American film called *Vikings* that I watched when I was six, alone on a summer afternoon.

The scene: a wide bay at low tide. Gusts of rain sweep across the reach. Enter three blond-moustached, furry-booted thugs leading a shackled Celt towards a distant wooden piling. They strip him naked, lash him to the pole and leave him there, alone in the windswept bay. When the tide comes in later on that dreary afternoon, just up to his neck, dozens of crabs cluster on his body.

You can imagine where they began feeding. *I* didn't have to.

'There was one on my milk bottle this morning,' Father said cheerfully. 'Quite young. About this size. It would have fitted in a coffee cup.'

'I've never understood what they're doing so far away from the sea,' I muttered. 'They're an abomination. They should be eradicated.'

'Now, Aozora, what good would that do? They're *kawagani*, a *fresh*water crab,' he explained, lifting up the grate to see if he could find the little monster. 'You can find them just about anywhere there's water: gutters, drainage pipes, streams, rice paddies. They have a peculiarly mottled carapace and . . .'

I didn't want to hear any more; I knew it all already. But conversation with my father was seldom more than prelude to a lesson: Inaka 101. Lecture and seminar (primarily the former), frequent diagrams, frequent pop quizzes, comprehensive exams in my nightmares.

'Mind you, they're not land crabs,' he continued, replacing the grate. 'Land crabs live entirely out of the water. There's a species called the *Cobber* that eats coconuts in the tropics.' He slid open the front door. 'I have a superb National Geographic video I could show you some time, Aozora, about the migration of 10 million or more land crabs on Christmas Island. Here, we'll close the door all the way or they'll get inside. Of course, Japan has land crabs as well. There's a species down in Kyushu called *sawaragani*. Red, with yellow claws bright as bananas.'

'And as large, I assume.'

'No, no. Fit in a soup bowl. They're rather pleasant really. Here . . .' He took a Bottle World OK receipt from a pile of them on the windowsill and a pen from his pocket. He drew a rapid sketch on the back. 'There. *Sawaragani.* You can hear them clicking through the undergrowth if you listen carefully.'

I took the proffered drawing and pocketed it. He was always doing such annoying little drawings for my edification. 'Thanks,' I said beneath my breath. 'I'll treasure it.'

The anteroom that was once filled with rubber boots and bicycles was now arrayed like an arms magazine with tall brown saké bottles. 'I've been drinking a great deal of alcohol,' he said simply, by way of an explanation. What was even more impressive than my father's alcohol consumption was the reek of the place – a three-pronged assault on the nose: the yeast of stale saké, quickened by a whiff of the neighbouring drop-hole toilet, made near retch-inducing by Father's failed attempts at squid tempura in the kitchen on the other side.

I was expecting to find a certain genteel disarray in the house – my sister, who used to do all the housekeeping, had moved to the city almost a year ago – but the place was, in point of fact, a total disaster. The foyer floor was covered in newspapers and bits of string and balsawood, there was dust everywhere, and the kitchen counters were piled with dishes. We negotiated the shadowy, groaning corridor, littered with boxes and stacks of books and magazines and clothes and still more bottles, to emerge in the tearoom, a large open space fronted by floor-to-ceiling sliding glass, and the only room in the house that still looked as it did when my mom was alive. The ceilings, beams, and transoms carved with cranes had been polished to a deep shine. The still air was sliced with lemon cleanser and the green scent of new tatami mats. Father slid open the doors that give onto the garden and, apologizing twice for having to leave me, went into the kitchen to make coffee.

Tearooms. Another thing I've never liked.

The classical tearoom demands a certain compression of spirit that doesn't come naturally to me: merely entering this formalized emptiness is already a transgression of order – the most you can do is try to minimize it by affecting humility and keeping quiet. By playing dead, in effect. The Basho summer poem about the impermanence of impermanence written in almost illegible script on the gilt-edged scroll hanging in the alcove above the camellia floating in the hideously ugly cracked ceramic dish that Hideyori and Ieyasu fought a war over – it's all as cosy as a museum. (I once tried having sex with Kasane in this room but it was unsuccessful. We had more enjoyable sex on a toilet seat.) The only superfluous things in the space were a stack of newspapers topped by a wrench; several colourful, voluptuous potted plants – fuchsia, *Fritillaria imperialis*, hibiscus, guzmania ripstar (I read the little tags); a pile of brown, gold-tasselled cushions, and a diminutive rosewood chest with brass clasps in the shape of paulownia leaves. On it was a photograph of my little sister in an elaborate pewter frame.

A park in midsummer, windy and hot; perhaps a storm is building in the unseen 280 degrees. A deer noses into the frame at lower right, the grey-and-gold roof of Todai-ji Temple presides at upper left, but it's Mai who dominates the photo. Standing cock-hipped in a violet T-shirt with sparkly stars on the front and parrots perched on her huge hoop earrings, she is like a pop-star princess: brash, unreasonable, ecstatic – in every sense over the top. Her grin is bigger than her face. Her hair is a conflagration of wind and sun. Her hands are out-stretched to the camera, fingers in V's. I stared at the photo as if I were in the act of taking it, as if she'd move and I could snap at the apparition again. I wondered where she was exactly. I hadn't seen her in ages.

I went over to stand by the sliding doors that led to the TV room. This was where my mom transformed into an octopus when I was ten years old. Since then, I hadn't once entered the room of my own volition. She had been in an accident on the highway. I know the circumstances in detail now – all the technical minutiae of her injuries – but nobody told me much back then. So I invented my own solution. She became an octopus. It was magic, simply enough. After all, people had been turning into trees and stars and swords and *tanuki* for centuries. Suffice it to say, in my ten-year-old head, her meta-morphosis into an octopus was far neater and more comprehensible a transformation than the one she actually underwent. It was manageable this way. There was no guilt. No constant compulsion to fit this garbling, unmoving thing into the Mother-shaped void.

Still, Father always had to push me inside. 'Go on, go on. She likes this room in the afternoons. It's cool in here. You know how she dislikes the heat.'

In summer, the navy-blue curtains, pinpricked with sun-light, were always moving in the breeze from the open windows, expanding and contracting like a giant pair of lungs. And with their movement the light in the room was constantly changing, gleaming gold across the parquet, then ebbing away to leave the room in semi-blue darkness. She was on a special seat between the leather couch and the coffee table. I could hear her slight wheeze and the gentle pop of her siphon when she inhaled. One of her pale pink arms lay across the glass top of the coffee table and when the light came up again, I saw her head in a grey cotton cap, slightly listing to one side, shuddering upright with another breath and then subsiding again.

I was supposed to talk to her, Father used to tell me. Yet *he* never entered the room with me. *He* always had something *else* to do. I assumed that he had at least *some* interaction with her – at night, for instance, as they always had done – but perhaps this was simply not the case. Mai spent a lot of time with her then, and there was the nurse there to look after her too, because her octopus body was incapable of propelling itself about the house and sometimes she inked herself and couldn't clean up, so it was not inconceivable that my father could have avoided his wife for the seven entire months she sat there dying.

In contrast to the tearoom, the TV room was as cluttered as an English parlour. There were sofas and globe lamps, a glass cabinet full of china, a coffee table with violet silk hibiscus flowers entombed beneath its glass top, and my mom's crassula – her 'rubber bush' as Mai and I used to call it, unable to resist pinching the short, fat, rubbery leaves – which had now grown huge and lugubrious. An upright piano sat primly on a section of parquet near the door. On its dusty top were my mom's reading glasses; several framed photos she had taken of Mai and me as children; seven matryoshka dolls devolving right to left that she had bought at some theme park; three bronze judo medals with red, white and blue ribbons that I won in the second grade; a birch-bark canoe from Lake of the Woods, Canada; a glass box containing a minute Chinese scene carved out of cork (pavilion, half-moon maiden, suitor poling barque beneath willows); a pair of tailor's scissors; my first pair of shoes that my mom had had bronzed; and a plastic pouch of paperclips that Father would certainly never find when he needed them.

Father came back into the tearoom. 'Here we are, Aozora,' he said brightly. He was carrying a tray of coffee, Fig Newton biscuits and sliced persimmons. 'Try the persimmons. They're local. Very fresh.' He set two fancy, gilt-edged English cups and saucers on the tatami and poured coffee from a steel percolator with a discoloured glass bubble on the top. My cup had roses and stylized playing cards and a quotation in minute writing on the side:

> From silver spouts the grateful liquors glide,
> While China's earth receives the smoking tide.
> At once they gratify their scent and taste,
> And frequent cups prolong the rich repast

It was the kind of foreign virtu I knew my father hated, and which he kept around the house only because it had been my mom's, but he acted as if nothing was out of the ordinary at all.

As for the coffee, it was hardly gratifying, nor a rich repast. I knew at once that it was Key brand coffee bought for 500 yen a kilo at Inaka J-Coop, a 'blend so subtle' there was no discernible richness, robustness, sweetness, tartness, acidity, bouquet, colour, nose, aftertaste, equilibrium, suggestion, simplicity, complexity, aroma, roundness, *souplesse* or length on the palate at all. The Fig Newtons, however, were terrific. Amazingly fresh. The tiny seeds crunched between my molars and the rest was like cream. Father sipped his coffee.

Though impeccable in his old-fashioned manners, my father did have an odd way of drinking coffee. Instead of taking the saucer in his left hand and raising the cup by its handle with his right, he held the saucer with both hands and never touched the cup with anything but his lips. It was the kind of detail Kyoto or Tokyo people would have howled over. The bumpkin! Still, sharing humble coffee and Fig Newtons on the floor, I promised myself that I would never make an anecdote out of him.

'It is good to have you back,' he said. 'How are your studies going?'

Studies. How strange it sounded. Nothing in my father's vocabulary could describe how I spent my time at university. 'Fine,' I replied. 'You? What's this hospital visit about?' (When he called to tell me of Aunt Okane's will, he mentioned that he'd be going into hospital for an operation.)

'I go in on Monday,' he said. 'It's a gallstone. I've been having some laser treatment recently.'

I nodded.

'It's a gallstone,' he said again. And sipped his coffee.

So I sipped mine.

'But *you* look healthy enough, son.'

'I'm fine.'

It wasn't exactly scintillating conversation. It could have been us inside that Chinese box in the TV room, lively as cork. There should have been a radio playing in another room, traffic noise or a clock ticking. No such luxury.

'Where's Bengal?' I asked.

'He's with the vet. He damaged one of the sphincters in his throat choking on a hairball.'

I watched the pink tag on the hibiscus bobble in the breeze. 'So we go to see the lawyer about Aunt Okane's will tomorrow?'

'Yes.'

'And Mai? Where is she?'

With a pained expression he lifted the cup and saucer. 'Mn, I had hoped . . .' he began, then put the cup down again without drinking. He rocked back and forth slightly with his hands turned inwards on his thighs. 'Have you not spoken to her recently?'

It took me a moment to consider. My sister and I were hardly close. It could have been in the autumn, but I wasn't sure. 'Perhaps last September? She was taking dancing lessons in Kyoto, wasn't she?'

'Singing,' Father said, looking somewhat disappointed. 'Yes, singing lessons. I had hoped you had heard more from her, living in the same city.'

'It's a big city.'

'Yes, of course, very big.' He ran one palm from forehead to crown. (What I'd mistaken for a hairstyle was simply the path his right hand had worn over the top of his head.)

'How about you?' I asked. 'Have you been in touch with her?'

'Oh, in touch, I suppose, yes. Though not recently.' He rocked backwards and pushed himself to his feet. With his back bent and hands still upon his thighs, as if the ceiling were very much lower than it was, he crossed the floor to the rosewood chest, came back and handed me a tiny silver telephone.

The glowing blue screen read: ALIVE?

'That's the message I send every two weeks,' he explained. 'Now press Inbox.'

One word: YES.

'That's how we communicate,' he said. 'The last time she replied was three weeks ago.'

I shrugged. Three weeks wasn't so long. When we lived in the same house, Mai and I could go months without exchanging a single word apart from *Telephone!* 'Do you think everything's all right?' I asked.

'I've tried dialling her number several times, something she forbade me to do before, but someone else has her phone now, a very rude young woman. She answers, but she won't tell me anything and always hangs up.'

'Have you tried tracing the telephone through NTT?'

'Only the police can do that, and they won't unless she's declared an Official Missing Person. That won't happen until twenty-eight days after her last communication.' He closed his eyes and massaged an eyebrow with a thumb, trembling slightly. 'Can you imagine? Twenty-eight days? What could happen to a girl in twenty-eight days? Tell me, Aozora, why would she give her telephone away? I know how girls love their telephones. Why would she give her telephone away without changing the number?'

I drank my coffee and chewed on another Fig Newton. Mai was still there over Father's shoulder, hands in the air, for victory or peace. When Father caught my eye and glanced back himself, I got up and went in the other direction to stand in the open doorway. Beyond the bamboo fence, a tyrannosaurus rex and a giraffe peeked into the rock garden. 'What are the spikes on the back of a stegosaurus called?' I asked.

'Sorry? Oh . . . ossified plates.' He heaved himself up from the floor. 'Yes, that reminds me, there's something I'd like to show you. I've started a pterodactyl and I'd like to have your opinion.'

Father spent the rest of the day in the kitchen doing passable versions of *goma-yaki*, *chawan-mushi* and *katsu-don*. He ended up cooking enough food for the entire village and put the dishes down before me as if he were afraid of losing a Michelin star.

'You didn't happen to make any linguine, did you?' I asked.

'*Linguine*?' he repeated in disbelief. There was no way he could make such a thing. 'Is that like spaghetti?'

'Spaghetti's round,' I said. 'Linguine's more squared off.'

'Oh,' he said, and nodded, taking this information very seriously. 'If I can find it at the J-Coop tomorrow, I'm sure –'

'Nevermind. Nevermind.' I took a piece of *goma-yaki*. The cooking was decent for an old bachelor. I grunted at appropriate moments. After dinner we watched baseball in the TV room and drank Yebisu beer. The Carp were destroying the Tigers by the fourth inning. When I switched stations to watch *Serie A* football – Inter vs Fiorentina – it was as if Father had been waiting for this least movement on my part as an excuse to speak.

'Aozora?'

'You wanted to see that out?' I asked. 'They're already nine runs down. It's a totally foregone conclusion.'

'Oh, no, no.' He waved dismissively at the television. 'Please watch what you like, I don't mind. I was just wanting to say that, seeing as it's *o-bon* festival, I'll be going down to Inari Shrine soon.'

'Sure,' I said. 'Don't worry about me.' Just then, Batistuta shaved the outside of the post with a swerving free kick. I clenched my fists. 'Damn, that was close! Is there any more beer in the fridge?'

He left the room and came back with a can of beer and three paper globes on sticks. Turned out he'd made paper lanterns to take along to the temple, one for himself, one for Mai and one for me. He haunted the room for a while, looking for an excuse to break my concentration again, but finally left. I could hear him mumbling in the next room, 'Just tired . . . just tired . . . long journey . . .' I pushed the curtain aside and watched him go down the driveway, off to pray for Mom, and for Aunt Okane, and for all our dead relatives and forefathers and ancestors back to the beginning of time. Long after he himself disappeared into the darkness, the three yellow orbs decorated with red script continued to bobble along through the trees like a trio of glowfish in a nocturnal sea.

humuhumunukunukuāpua'a

And speaking of fish, Aunt Okane's lawyer looked like one. Yes, he was morose and pedantic, a typical stereotype for a lawyer, but at least he was morose and pedantic in his own particular way. To be precise, in his black suit, pale-lime shirt and orangey tie, he looked like humuhumunukunukuāpua'a, a Hawaiian pig-nosed reef trigger-fish. (Snapped this one through the glass on a date at Osaka Aquarium.) His head was so thin it was almost 2-D and his eyes, one on each side, were bulbous and watery. His cheeks extended out to his lips in an unintentional pout and, what's more, he never once looked straight at me for long enough that I could actually see both eyes at the same time. He was always looking at something on his desk or in a drawer or in the glass cabinets behind him.

'Is Miss Fujiwara on her way?' he asked, peering out of the door behind us when we arrived.

My father spread his hands apologetically. 'I'm afraid that my daughter won't be able to attend today.'

'We're just going to take care of my share,' I explained. 'Mai's gone shopping.'

'Oh?'

'Yes. In Singapore.'

Now he looked pained. His head tilted and it actually appeared for a moment that his ear was fluttering like a pectoral fin. 'I'm afraid this is not possible,' he sighed. 'Not possible at all. What a terrible waste of your time, Mr Fujiwara.'

'Is there a problem?'

'Please, sit down. To redeem the inheritance, Mr Fujiwara, *both* you and your sister will have to sign a set of documents before myself and the local magistrate. I cannot remit proceeds to one party. The will as it has been worded is *one* legal document, one contract between the deceased and the *two* parties named thereon. It is *not* two contracts pertaining to each of you respectively. As such, it cannot be executed without the authorization of all parties named thereon, you and your sister, as it is.

'I suggest you make an appointment to see me the moment Miss Fujiwara returns from her trip.'

My father just nodded. There was no way he was going to push any further.

Looked like I'd have to do it myself: 'What – just hypothetically speaking – what if one of the people named in the will were now a missing person?' I asked.

This set the eyes bulging and pectoral fins fluttering. His head turned from me to my father to me again. 'I hope there's no problem?'

I smiled. 'No, no. Just curious.'

'Well, Mr Fujiwara, it's an interesting question. If one of the named were a missing person, police documentation to that effect would need to be produced and the entire document would need to be expedited before the local magistrate and then, well, let me see –' elbows on desk, hands clasped, staring past them with one great eye '– from there it would go to the Kyoto Prefectural Ministry of Justice, the only local institution which could break an existing contract into, as it were, two contracts, or more likely, institute something on the order of a judicial codicil. But [here comes the really ugly part] such an action would take up to a year [!], Mr Fujiwara, depending on the Ministry of Justice's backlog. And with commensurate costs, of course.'

Even my father, who relished all official procedures and any kind of red-inked stamp or extra expense, shook his head at this daunting process. I felt an anger flash of Aozoran intensity coming on and was ready to heave the desk into the air any second. I stared the lawyer straight in his one eye. *Look, my friend, I cannot wait a year for a commensurately cost-depleted share of the cash, okay? If I don't get at least three of the twelve million yen I owe to a guy named Uno within zero days my ass is sashimizukuri! You understand? Now why don't I just expedite my sister's signature onto that form there and get this done?*

Humuhumunukunukuāpua'a is a slow-moving, unresponsive creature. It has no known powers of telepathy. 'I say again, I do hope everything is all right with Miss Fujiwara?' He cleared his throat and looked at me. 'On another related matter pertaining to you and your sister, Mr Fujiwara, once the inheritance *has* passed into your possession, there is the question of what to do with the *ukiyo-e* prints –'

Father's hands did a flurry in front of him. 'Thank you,' he interrupted, 'thank you for your concern but we've already discussed the matter and we've come to the decision that it would all be better off left in the museum.' He looked at me encouragingly. 'There's no point in worrying about it, is there, Aozora? I understand we can quite easily perpetuate the loan.'

'Yes,' the lawyer replied, 'yes indeed, I'm certain the National Museum in Tokyo would be more than happy to facilitate perpetuation of the loan if that is the inheritors' wish. Still, I do think you should be made aware, Mr Fujiwara, that should you choose not to perpetuate the loan, there are other parties expressing an interest in the collection. Both your aunt and your grandmother before her were listed on the National Cultural Property Bureau's List of Lenders. As executor of her will, I have not been short of correspondences in the past four days.'

'Really, I do think –' Father started.

'National Museum in Tokyo?' I said. 'What's this collection worth?'

The lawyer turned to the cabinet behind him and took a plastic folder stuffed with waxy fax paper from a drawer. 'I have seven offers so far,' he said.

'What's the best one?'

Father was aghast. 'Oh, Aozora, really. Such a question!' The lawyer shuffled through the papers. Father leaned over to whisper in my ear. 'If you ever need a little money, son, you only need ask me. Please don't –'

'A hundred million yen for the three Eizans, the Utamaro and the blocks,' the lawyer replied matter-of-factly. 'From a private collector in Dubai.'

'Dubai!' Father started laughing. 'It really is too absurd. Imagine sending our patrimony to Arabia! Imagine that, Aozora. These people must be crazy.'

But he was the only one laughing, and not for long at that. The lawyer and I were finally on the same wavelength. I had sudden thrilling visions of conspicuous consumption: hotel suites, flash threads, Italian cars. He saw that Ferrar-away look in my eye and he was just waiting for the word 'go'. I turned to Father. *Crazy is right, Pops. And I'm going to get some of that craziness myself.* 'I suppose we better find Mai,' I said. 'Have you still got that number?'

freegirl

Other End of the Line: [Shuffling leaves, dogs barking,
   car horns, the crackle of pigeons' wings.] *Mm-hm?*

Aozora: Hello?

OEOTL: *Mmn?*

Aozora: Mai-Tai, is this you?

OEOTL: Yes, it's you. Is that me? [Laughter.]

Aozora: Who is this, please?

OEOTL: Your name?

Aozora: Aozora.

[The girl – not my sister, however much her voice may
   have changed in a year's time – understands the
   protocols of conversation as well as a parrot.]

OEOTL: Who's this then?

Aozora: I just told you.

OEOTL: You want a date? How did you get this
   number? Who are you?

Aozora: Yes. [Reticence is 90 per cent of tact.]

OEOTL: [Background noises hush abruptly. Door
   closing. The girl is suddenly composed, speaking
   directly into the phone.] Are you one of my new
   dads? When do you want it then? Tonight?

Aozora: Um, yes, I can make it.

OEOTL: One, two or three?

Aozora: O'clock?

OEOTL: Eight thirty.

Aozora: Um . . . Fine.

OEOTL: Well? One, two or three? Each depends.

Aozora: I'm not sure yet. How about one and a half?

OEOTL: Very not funny. If you want three it's only in a hotel. Not in the photo booth.

Aozora: Now I understand.

OEOTL: Okay, bye-bye –

Aozora: Wait! Where do we meet?

OEOTL: You know Kyoto Station?

Aozora: Of course.

OEOTL: You know Sagano-Shijo Station?

Aozora: I'll find it.

OEOTL: Wait outside the Mos Burger with a Coke and call me again. Bye-bye!

We were standing in the kitchen. I put down the telephone and told my father the first thing that came to mind: the girl on the phone was a news reporter and one of Mai's closest friends. They traded phones sometimes. For fun. Girls did stuff like that. It was a total lie, but at least it was spontaneous and well-meaning. I wasn't exactly going to tell him I'd just negotiated for fellatio.

'Is that true, son?' he asked, and the look he gave me – of concern, surprise and a glimmer of pride – almost undid me. I turned away and looked for something to do. Next to the telephone was a basket full of pens and Scotch tape, small change, business cards . . . 'Yeah,' I muttered, probing the contents of the basket just to keep from having to face him, 'the one on NHK News with the, ah, really short hair who does the sports.'

'Is that so?'

Chrome suitcase padlock with no key, pink hair clip, black die-cast Lamborghini I hadn't seen since I was twelve, a vapid school photograph of Mai with her hair back. 'Yeah, she's busy with her, um . . . NHK stuff but I'm going to see her this evening in Kyoto.'

'And she's in touch with Mai?'

'Apparently.'

The uncertainty finally dissolved. 'Well, well, *well!*' he cried, and slapped his thighs. He rushed off to the front room to check the train schedule in the roll-top desk and I pocketed the photo of Mai. It wasn't the best likeness, but I thought it might be useful. Father came back with the schedule and set it down on the counter next to the cutting block, but his trembling fingers couldn't get the thin pages apart and he licked his thumb over and over. An hour later, he drove me back to the station. When we got there he gave me 50,000 yen and the 1600-yen train fare, his JCB credit card for any emergencies and a bento lunch box that he had pulled from the freezer and which was still frozen solid. 'It'll thaw in this heat,' he assured me, and reiterated several times over that I was to call him immediately with any news. 'Oh and Aozora,' he called out as I was getting aboard the train. 'If you were to give Mai my regards ... that would be fine.' (This is sentimental coming from him.) 'Fine for her, I hope. And me of course. If you'd tell her.'

'I could do that.'

'You could tell her about Aunt Okane too. And remind her of *o-bon* festival. If she would like to come back, it's not too late. I've made a lantern for her. I could send her money for the train. Or I could take the Mitsubishi into Kyoto to pick her up.'

Sure, sure. I dropped my bag and fell into a seat. As he did when I arrived, he stood on the concrete platform waving until the train was gone.

The Sagano-Shijo Mos Burger was plastered with advertisements for spicy nan bread tacos and spicy nan bread chorizo. The photographs were hardly appetizing. They could have been deep-fried platypus tails for all I could tell. I wasn't intending to go inside but it occurred to me that if I didn't try a nan bread taco now, they might disappear forever. It's easy enough to say, 'Oh, I'll try one another time,' but maybe it's the special of the month, maybe this item is available in selected outlets only, maybe they get discontinued because no one ever takes a liking to them – and then you forget that nan bread tacos even existed. I don't give a damn about spicy nan bread tacos or their spicy chorizo and spicy satay varieties per se. It's the principle of the thing. Where would we be if nobody had tried the first hamburger or *nigiri*? You give nan bread tacos a miss now, rosemary ice cream tomorrow,

gazpacho or *natto* beans or maybe foie gras the day after that . . . pretty soon we're all eating out of colour-coded tubes. I took a snap with my phone camera for posterity's sake, then went inside.

The Spicy Nan Bread Taco Meal consisted of one cardboard cup of French fries, an M-size Pepsi and one spicy nan bread taco in a Styrofoam box. I don't want to make too big a deal out of it, but it was great – fusion cuisine gone right for once, if just a little too sweet. (I took two sachets of soy sauce from the front counter and drizzled it on. A definite improvement.) The nan was mottled brown and shone with a layer of real ghee. And the salsa? I finally understood why they named a dance after a condiment. When a waitress came by to clear the next table I said, 'This is delicious. I'm a big Mos Burger fan.' I thought she'd be pleased but she looked at her friend at the counter and rolled her eyes. So much for company pride. I tore the last morsel of nan in two and wiped up soy sauce and salsa from the Styrofoam box, then stuffed it in my mouth.

Outside, a monk in black robes and a coolie hat was standing on the corner in the midst of traffic clapping two sonorous teak sticks together at long, meditative intervals. *Tock!* I'd seen the type before, but they usually went out at midday when the streets were busiest. *Tock!* This one had chosen to see off the sun, now wedging itself down into the endless corridor of Shijo-dori Boulevard. I leaned against the wall, finished my Pepsi and watched a white guy teaching English behind the glass in a second-storey language school across the street. He wore khaki trousers and a shirt and tie and though he pointed at the sentences on the whiteboard, you could tell it was more of a show than a lesson. Maybe they're the same thing, I don't know. The housewives at their desks looked happy in any case.

The girl was late. I called Mai's number again.

'Where are you?' she asked right away.

'Mos Burger. What about you?'

'Mmn, maybe Gakuen-mae?'

Which was light-years away. 'But you said Sagano-Shijo!'

'I said *Coke*,' she replied calmly.

The girl showed up less than a minute later and introduced herself as Sumi. She was a classic *Loli-Goth*: huge auburn-red hair held back by a pink bow, tanned like a Hawaiian except around her eyes where the flesh was pastier than a geisha's. With Day-Glo green mascara, it made for a frightening, galago-like effect. She wore a short red plaid pleated skirt, a black Ramones T-shirt, a thin white crocheted cardigan, and huge black elevator boots with fifty-odd steel buckles and lacy white socks peeking out the top. She strode up the pavement and I thought: I hope some of this outfit is superfluous, because if she's evolved to suit the exigencies of her environment, what the hell does that say about Kyoto? I'm inclined to avoid *Loli-Goths*, but this one was my only, tenuous link to Mai. I dropped the Pepsi cup into the garbage bin. 'Hi.'

She stood directly in front of me, frowned, then looked around as if she were truly disappointed – as if she had been expecting Takuya Kimura or some other teenage heart-throb and was now sizing up other options in the vicinity.

Gimme a break, I thought. I'm not exactly rugged, but I'm handsome enough in an Aozorable way. Yes, when I buy sunglasses I have to choose ones that wrap around my head or else buy a regular pair and fold them almost in half. Yes, my nose, at a certain angle, looks like it's been transplanted from a Red Indian. But I'm the true Yayoi: noble, upright, body of a swimmer. My father traced our genealogy back to hunter-gatherers and obsidian traders. Anyway, forget the self-portrait. It's not like I want to be recognized anyway.

The girl turned back to me, chewing her gum. 'You're tall,' she said. 'You look familiar. How did you get my number?'

I looked at my Tigers, thinking of what my father would say, or couldn't say if he saw this blasphemy of a good Japanese girl. 'A connection,' I replied.

She laughed and shook her red hair. 'I'm getting to be contagious, I think. Did you want one, two or three?'

I shrugged again.

She held up one index finger and laid it into an open palm. 'One.'

She put the same finger into her mouth. 'Two.'

She made a V with index and middle finger. 'Three. Understand?'

I thought maybe I should just broach the topic of Mai right there on the street, but she could have walked away and left me with nothing. I needed to buy myself some time. 'Three,' I told her.

'You have to pay for the hotel.'

'Fine, as long as it's not the Hyatt.'

'Aw,' she whined, and set off down the sidewalk.

We walked past a Toys 'Я' Us and underneath the Kintetsu Line railway. I tried to make conversational inroads, but her default mode was indifference highlighted with biliousness. The neighbourhood we went through was decent: high-rise apartments, playgrounds with brightly coloured apparatus, *izakaya* pubs, a gourmet hamburger joint full of Americana, cubby-hole hairstyling salons. In a street full of video-game parlours and bars and yet more language schools we came to a nine- or ten-storey building with a faintly Moorish air: stucco façade, windows hidden behind white concrete latticework, deep red curtains with golden tassels hanging over the door and the entrance to the parking garage. A small brass plaque read: PLAISANCE DE TOUCHE.

The corridor was narrow and dark. It led through some confusion of video games and ancient vinyl furniture to the 'Front Desk', a mere portal in the wall between two thrumming beer machines. The window was mirrored and there was a narrow vertical slot to one side. Encased in plastic on the counter were descriptions of the available rooms, each with an accompanying photo of a room at the New Otani or the Ritz-Carlton, all cream and gilt. I chose the cheapest room and put 3,000 yen through the slot. The bills disappeared and a key came tumbling out.

As we were going up in the elevator, Sumi made a telephone call. Without any small talk she said the name of the hotel, 'three', the time, and hung up. The room I paid for featured olive-green linoleum floors, a chipped white wooden desk, a fluorescent lamp with green glass shade on the nighttable, one double bed with a burgundy cover that I would not for anything in the world turn back, and a window half-filled with a loud, grimy air conditioner. Money was the first order of business. 30,000 yen. A lot of cash. Once Sumi had it stowed in her Prada bag, I had to undress. Boys first. That was

45

the rule. Then I had to lie down on the bed and put on a condom while she tugged down her panties from beneath her skirt and without the slightest, most perfunctory foreplay, stepped onto the bed and tried to squat down on me. Her mascara glowed in the light of the bedside lamp.

'What's wrong with it?' she demanded at once.

Ahem. '*It?*'

'I think it's got some kind of disease.'

'Um, no, it doesn't actually,' I informed her, 'but it's not going to react without some kind of stimulus.'

So she began pulling.

I interrupted this crude attempt at a caress: 'Sorry, Sumi, but even Pavlov's dog got better treatment than this. Maybe for my 30,000 yen I might get to *see* something? Perhaps your breasts, for example?'

She had obviously never dealt with such a strange request. 'Why? Can't you just imagine?'

'If I wanted to imagine a girl's body I wouldn't have bothered leaving home, would I?'

Reluctantly, petulantly, the Ramones T-shirt disappeared over her head and her orbs bounced in the air in front of me. It was enough. She certainly couldn't act, but she didn't need a body double either. If I were going to have time to get any information from her, I had to slow things down. Conversation works wonders in this respect. 'So, Sumi, are you the only one who uses that phone?'

She stopped. 'What's the matter?'

'Nothing.'

'Then why are you talking?'

'I was asking you a question.'

'Why are you asking me a question?' She started rocking her hips again. 'I don't have to go on for more than ten minutes.'

'It isn't really your phone, is it? Isn't it a little odd that you've got someone else's phone?'

'I didn't steal it.'

'I didn't suggest you had.'

She leaned across me to take a piece of chewing gum from her handbag on the night-table. 'Why can't salarymen be quiet? You're ruining the romance.' She folded the white stick of gum through her black lips.

'For your information, A. I am the antithesis of a salary-man. B. I'd like to know how you got the phone. Did you get it from a girl called Mai?'

Now she looked concerned, not quite so nonchalant as she had just been. She started easing off me. 'Who are you? How do you know Mai?'

'Easy, I'm nobody to be afraid of. I'm her brother, Aozora. She probably mentioned me.'

'No, she didn't.'

'Oh. Well, I just want to make sure that she's all right. If she's got problems I want to help her.'

'No problems,' she replied.

'She's incommunicado with her family and friends, living alone in the big city and, if my guess is right, doing one, two, three for Prada money . . . call me conservative but I'd say that's a problem.'

She shrugged. 'Business as usual.'

'Please. I'm her brother. Are you sure she didn't say anything about me? Aozora? We got on well together, Mai and I. We never fought.' Sumi looked bored. 'Please, I came all the way from Inaka today. Anyone who'd admit he comes from Inaka has got to be genuine.'

She looked at me uncertainly, twisting her lips about. 'You've got that same foreign nose,' she said. 'Maybe she did mention you. Though it was probably nothing good. Can I please finish you off now? I'll need a cigarette in a moment.'

*

47

I followed her out of the room and up a flight of stairs. On the next landing was a fire-escape window propped open with an umbrella. Sumi hitched up her skirt and sat on the window ledge. Whatever, I thought, taking a seat on the stairs; if she was more comfortable on the landing than in the room that was fine with me.

She swung her legs over into the night.

I made a grab for her knees, missed and caught her by Joey and Deedee.

'Hey, let go!' She disappeared out of the window. 'It's a rooftop.'

The space was no more than several metres square and dominated by shiny aluminium air-conditioning units that hummed contentedly. I crawled out the window and stood at the roof's edge. There's no night, as such, in Kyoto, only iso-lated pockets of darkness between swathes of light. The street below was a tight, glowing crevasse in a volcano. It was driz-zling and multicoloured pixels were scattered all across the wet pavement. There were neon signs for Yakult Probiotic and Pachinko Mir 2 and Pinky Club and the giant red circle of Maru brand saké. Static golds, flashing reds. Oblivious to the rain, Sumi sat on an air conditioner and lit up the 'I'll tell you but in my own nonchalant good time' cigarette. She inhaled long and slow and it was almost gone before she began speaking.

'I suppose you're horrified that Mai's a *freegirl*, right? Want to save the family honour?'

I hadn't thought about it like that. And perhaps being a hooker wasn't exactly the world's most salubrious profession, but what Mai did for a living had nothing to do with me. I just needed money.

'She didn't wanna be a *freegirl* at the start,' she told me. 'I met her at opera school. We were both taking voice lessons. She's got a beautiful voice, Mai. Anyway, I was going on

48

compensated dates now and again, from the back of a magazine, you know?'

I knew.

'So Mai started doing them too, to pay her fees. We put this ad in *Pink Parsley* for a two-for-one deal. Men love to have their attentions divided. And, you know they're always *asking* for more than just a date. So one time we just named a ridiculous price and these two guys paid it like it was pocket money. The next time, we doubled the ridiculous price and it was still no problem.' She sent the cigarette butt spinning down into the neon gulch. 'But you can't work on your own for long, not in Kyoto anyway. Someone eventually catches on. One time one of the guys we went with turned out to be in a biker gang, a *bosozoku*. He followed us home afterwards and the next day we got a visit from a real slick *yakuza*. He said he'd bought our telephone number from this guy and now we owed him for protection "and other services". That was the end of the fun. He took 60 per cent from then on. I'm still paying off the debt, though he never told me how much it was.'

'And Mai?'

'She got sold again.'

'To whom? Where?'

I must have looked alarmed. It appeared for a moment as if she were reaching out to touch my arm. But she lit up again, her face ghoulish above the flame, then pointed at me with the cigarette, the cherry glowing in the dark. 'It won't do you much good, but I don't care, whatever, they sent her down to Marumachi.'

It figured. For a small town in Kyushu it had a big reputation (bad or good depending on your morals).

'It's really busy,' she said. 'All the men come over from Amsterdam when their wives and children are sleeping. They spend a lot. What I'd do for that Roman nose of yours,' she sighed. 'I wouldn't be here, that's for sure.' The dial of her watch glowed green a moment. 'Gotta go.' She jumped off the ventilator. 'Say hi to Mai for me. And close the window when you come in.' With that she straddled the windowsill, swung her great buckled boots over and thumped down the stairs, back into the urban mass.

A new entry in *56 Things to Do in Osaka–Kyoto When You're Lonely and Out of Love*:

There's a love hotel called the Plaisance de Touche some-where on the Sagano Line. Visit the neighbourhood after dark and you'll find it populated by large-booted, galago-like women of the night who, though they pander to male fancy in no discernible way, do allow paid access to their vaginas. Once you've been relieved of physical necessity and you're feeling like your depression could not be more profound, go onto the rooftop from the landing between the seventh and eighth floors for one of the more indeterminate and depressing night views of the city.

Here's the memory I try but fail to suppress at quasi-sentimental moments like this:

November of last year. I had just passed the Ministry of Construction's initial fast-track entrance examination with the highest mark. Now I knew what the plan was. I would do another year and a half at KU, finish in the top 5 per cent of my class, visit Europe for a summer, then go to work for the Ministry of Construction for the rest of my life (or my working life anyhow, which was all that seemed to matter). I'm not exactly sure that I actually chose this plan – between career counsellors, professors, MOC recruiters, my father and me, it just seemed to formulate itself. Plan B, however, which was entirely my brainchild, was to go to Brazil after graduation and write a hip travel guide for Japanese backpackers. *Let's Go Baka in Brazil!* I already had the research for Chapter *Uma* ('Surf's Up, Tomodachi!') and Chapter *Duas* ('Fio Dentale') planned out in my head. As the time approached to inform my father of my plan, however, I became less and less sure of its feasibility. None of the query letters I had sent to publishers had been answered. I had no money for an airline ticket. I had never surfed or done the samba in my life. My Portuguese was still *merda* (not your fault, Mrs Nascimento). One night I told Kasane about my misgivings. With instant resolve she decided on the spot that *she* would find a solution.

Why she was so excited by the prospects for my future, I hardly know, but from then on, at least once a week, she would sit on the bed in my room searching for jobs in newspapers and employment magazines. One night, splayed out in a green plaid dress, scrolling through job sites on the net, she came across a call for Japanese language instructors. 'What about going to America?' she said.

I was sitting at my usual spot on the windowsill drinking pungent Viennese coffee with Greek figs mixed into the grounds. The football pitch was covered in snow and the lights along the pathways glowed a deep yellow. It was windy and snowflakes rushed towards me like asteroids at light speed. 'The USA is not Brazil,' I replied.

'Same side of the ocean.'

'Oh, so you do know something about world geography.'

'*EOS Language School, San Francisco*,' she read out happily, kicking her feet as if she were swimming. '*Full-time Instructors of Japanese wanted.* You could go be a teacher in San Francisco and drive down to Brazil for holidays.'

'*Ha!*' My disbelief made a puff of vapour, whisked away by the cold night air. 'There are people who devote *years* to driving to Brazil, Kasane. It's not a holiday, it's a National Geographic assignment.'

'EOS is a big company. They probably pay well,' she said. 'How much?'

She searched around with the mouse. 'I can't find it. For the best jobs they don't tell you.'

'Yeah, right. Like a fancy restaurant with no prices on the menu, you just assume it's high? Those slavers pay 200,000 yen, tops.'

'You could have sex with all your Californian students,' she said.

Where did that comment come from? 'What kind of guy do you think I am?'

Kasane twisted around on her elbows. 'You think the guys on this floor don't talk?'

'Since when have you been talking to the guys on this floor?'

She turned her attention back to the computer. 'California's nice. I could come for a visit. We could go to Universal Studios.'

'Now I see your motivation. Well, no thanks. You just go back to the Brazil site, *capiche*?' And I went back to the cosmos of Kyoto. The lamps in the courtyard made three yellow galaxies and the footpath was slowly turning into the Milky Way. Just what were my floormates telling her about my lifestyle? I'd been narrowly faithful and was proud of it.

'You know, Kasane,' I said, 'I think it might be a good idea if you stayed clear of the other guys here. They're . . . some of them . . . How do I put this? They don't have the good Inaka values I've got, you know? Besides, if your mom found out you were hanging around here having sex with me every time you told her you were going to calligraphy—'

She spun around on the bed. 'Oh, that's *funny!* If *your* dad found out how you waste his money on beer and mah-jong he'd dis*own* you.'

'All right, all right, cease fire. Since when did you get to be so tough? I think I liked it better when you were a pushover.'

The next day I got up and went for lunch at the *ramen* place behind Demachiyanagi Station. I sat at the bar watching the steam coming up from the soup pot for an entire hour, then went back to campus and watched *La Dolce Vita* for 120 yen in the cafeteria at the student union. It was already getting dark when I came out. I got some 7-Eleven *yakisoba* for dinner and took it back to my empty room.

When I twisted the knob and stepped in, she bounded across the bed. '*I called them!*' she trilled.

My *yakisoba* leaped like a basket of snakes and landed on the floor in a clump, dead. 'Damn! Kasane, can't you . . . look at this. You could at least . . .'

'Oops.' She leaned over the edge of the bed and stared at the food on the floor. 'Didn't you bring some for me?'

'How was I supposed to know you were here?'

'That's all right, I'll eat at home.' She rolled over to the desk and flipped open her notepad, the one with the grimacing penguins on the cover. 'Look, I called EOS for you.'

'What, Frisco again?' I said, picking up the bits that looked the cleanest.

'Nope . . . Guess!'

'Inaka.'

'Brazil! They've got a school in São Paulo. This is it, Ao! This is your ticket to Brazil! Mrs Inagaki in the personnel office—'

'Who?'

'Mrs Inagaki in the personnel office. She says she would be happy to submit your application. They've never had an applicant from a national university before. She told me that you'd get an automatic pass on the employee exam.'

I tried the *yakisoba*. Decent, if a little dusty.

'Are you even listening?' Her serious voice.

'Sorry.'

'Don't you care?'

'Sorry, go on, I'm just hungry, that's all.'

'You've got an interview on Wednesday. Will you go?'

I did. They gave me the job. I accepted because it would have been awkward not to. They welcomed me to the EOS family, made arrangements to send me an initiation pack by mail, and the Chief of Personnel came to bow at the door as I left the offices. I walked out onto the cold street and, within five metres of their front door, called back to leave a message with the receptionist that Mr Fujiwara wouldn't be able to accept after all. I couldn't suffer the idea of taking work that was below me, even if it meant sacrificing my dream of *Baka in Brazil* to the Ministry of Construction. There was also the diversion of a healthy starting salary. And the trauma this foolish change in my career plan would have caused my father. And the fact that all the guys on my floor were going into the ministries as well. Oh, there were a lot of reasons not to. Telling Kasane of my decision, however, would be a delicate operation.

'*Well? Well?*' she asked over the phone, but I wouldn't let anything slip. I had to see her in person. We agreed to meet in Maruyama Park.

The *yatai* food stalls glowed red around the perimeter of the gardens and pink steam rose through the bare tree branches. I had intended to lie to her. It would have made things much easier just to tell her that I hadn't passed the interview, but when I saw her face, all bundled up in her navy-blue coat-hood and the ridiculous lemon-yellow scarf she had knitted herself in high school, I couldn't do it. Her eyes glistened in the cold and she was so sweet and earnest, I knew she'd see through the lie. So I told her the truth. I wouldn't be going to Brazil. 'Nobody turns down the MOC,'

I said. 'It's the most powerful ministry in government. Once I graduate, I'll be understudy to some chief policy advisors. Right from day one.'

Suddenly she wasn't overly talkative any more. She stated facts. 'So you'll go to work like all the other salarymen.'

'No way, Kasa, not like these bozos,' I said. In a nearby *yatai*, several men in grey polyester were seated on stools in the harsh light of a naked bulb. 'MOC's uptown. I'll be going in Boss or Yves St Laurent.'

'I don't mean *clothes*, Aozora.' She kicked at the hard crust of snow, peppered with bird seed, that rimmed the walk. 'I don't care *what* you wear. I mean you'll be doing the nine-to-eight every day, filling in forms, going to meetings, just like them?'

'Yeah, more or less, sure,' I said. 'But I'll spend my nights at art-house cinemas and rape you on the weekends. Sounds like a good life, no? I'll buy an Alfa Romeo.'

The mere mention of sex when she was around would always get me excited, though it seemed to have the opposite effect upon her. I was trying to loosen her up, shaking her by the elbows, but she stayed rigid, arms compressed across her breasts, her mauve woollen gloves curled into her armpits. 'What does the Ministry of Construction actually *do*?'

I shrugged. 'Put up big buildings, finance them, tear them down, pay my salary. That's the important bit.'

She frowned. As if to say: 'Is it?'

I shrugged. I tried to laugh it off. 'C'mon. Let's get out of the cold.'

It didn't seem like a turning point so I didn't make a special effort to remember it, but now every moment of that night seems pregnant with sadness and foreboding. Kasane never came to see me again. Not once. I would ask her why on the phone and she would tell me she was busy preparing for exams. Or that her mother was suspicious. That she really should start going to calligraphy after all. It wasn't long after that she got the job at a ski resort in Hokkaido. She hadn't even told me she was looking for one.

I left the love hotel and walked up the street through a maze of stationary, steaming cars. The yellow-and-black railway barricades on Maidashi Street came down to stop traffic as an outgoing train left the nearby station. The driver sat bolt upright in his grey uniform and matching black hat and I could see his impeccable white-gloved hands on the controls. The people around me raised their voices to be heard above the clanging of the bells as the last of the carriages rushed past the barricade and plunged into the mist and rain. The destination, Kyoto Station, was outlined in red against a pale-yellow lozenge of illuminated glass above the rear window, and it was still visible, wavering, blurring slightly, long after the rest of the train had been swallowed by the darkness.

Kyoto Kyoto Kyoto Kyoto Kyoto Kyoto *Kyoto*

The bells stopped. The barricades came up. I rushed forward with the crowds and traffic.

mr uno

On my way to the station to buy a ticket for Marumachi, I stopped in at the university for what I hoped would be a short visit, to pick up clean clothes, a couple of books and some different CDs. I took my usual clandestine route across the park from Ito-dori, under the camellia bushes and through the kitchen window with the broken latch.

I didn't remember leaving my room in quite such a mess: all the desk drawers were stacked on the floor, and the contents of my closet had avalanched. But my friend next door, Kuwahara, had a double of my key. Knowing him, he'd probably come through like a tornado on a mad search for condoms in the middle of the night. I emptied my pockets on the desk and paused a moment to gaze at the photos on the corkboard. Kasane wrapped in blanket next to campfire. Kasane biting gold volleyball medal. Kasane in kimono on eighteenth birthday. Kasane and happy Aozora at the top of Sky Building. And the last one, sent from Hokkaido with a letter saying how wonderful her new job was: Kasane in her white snowboard instructor outfit, grinning behind a pair of orange iridium glasses. I think I must have sighed. I shook myself out of it and put some Nirvana on the stereo.

With the music blaring, I couldn't hear the door opening. I was crouched down, digging for some clean underwear in the pile of clothes on the floor, and didn't notice there was someone else in the room until the guitars and drums and Kurt Cobain's rasping voice all of a sudden stopped.

In that moment I had a vision in my mind's eye of Mr Uno

as I had seen him last. He was wearing one of his Hawaiian shirts, birds of paradise on a cerise sunset; his hair was greased back to emphasize his flat-nosed, jut-jawed face; and the eczema-like affliction on his neck – a raw, desiccated patch of pink skin that stretched from his open collar to his ears – was glistening with sweat. The only difference was, in *this* vision he wasn't making cocktails; he was standing in my room, levelling a handgun at the back of my head. (Here's a page from a recent edition of *Diamond Back* that does some justice to the guy's grim mug.) I took the desk chair by the legs, heaved it into the air and whirled around, ready to knock him senseless. Kuwahara backed into the corridor with his hands up in front of his face. 'Easy! It's me!' he croaked, and fell into a spate of unctuous coughing, doubled over to his knees.

'Damn it, Kuwahara, can't you knock?' I tried breathing again, dropped the chair and went back to the pile of clothes on the floor. 'So what colour were her panties?' I asked. 'You didn't have to tear the place apart, you know. The condoms are right there on the shelf.'

He stopped coughing but didn't respond. His breathing was coming loud and laboured, unnaturally wheezy. Something obviously wasn't right. I turned around to face him again. He straightened up and I saw his lopsided, purple, blue and scarlet face.

'What the hell . . .' I muttered under my breath. '*Kuwahara?*'

It could have been a car accident. He could have fallen off his motorbike. He could have fallen off a cliff. But the way he was staring at me . . .

'Someone came looking for you tonight,' he said through bloated lips.

My stomach twisted into a Möbius strip. I wanted to retch but it came out as a strange, prolonged groan. I swivelled the chair around and tried to get him to sit but he backed away, waving one dismissive hand in front of him.

'He *said* he was your friend,' he continued grimly, half-heartedly raising a finger, 'but I *know* you, Fujiwara. You don't *have* any friends.'

'Slick hair?' I mumbled. 'Hawaiian shirt?'

He tried to nod, but his neck was stiff and his whole torso just sort of shifted to one side.

Poor Kuwahara, he didn't deserve this. He was a good-looking, happy guy at a wonderful stage in which his adolescent shyness was alternating with new-found over-confidence. He came from a nice family in Shimane. I met his mom and dad in first year. His dad – ill-shaven piano teacher in a turquoise Lacoste – took us out for steak and talked about all the girls he'd met in university and how much fun we were going to have. His mom was kind of appealing in an 'I could teach you the ropes' kind of way, smiling at her own never-to-be-revealed stories while her husband played the buffoon.

In my most solemn voice I asked Kuwahara what had happened.

Kuwahara leaned against the far wall of the corridor with arms crossed limply in front of him. I couldn't be sure if he was looking at me when he spoke. I couldn't be sure that he could even see. 'On my way for a bath,' he said. 'The guy in the Hawaiian shirt was in the corridor. He asked where you were. I said I didn't know.

'He didn't believe me. He says: "Come on now, you're a good neighbour. You know where he is."

'I just kept walking. I didn't want any trouble. But then he pushed me from behind and I ran into the stairwell. I got down two flights of stairs when I heard a door crash open below. I should have known he wasn't alone. I ran down the second-floor corridor to the elevator.'

I shook my head. Fool, I thought. Didn't he ever watch any action films? You never take the elevator. You're a sitting duck. The only way the hero makes it out of an elevator alive is to spread-eagle himself ninja-style across the ceiling with the unsuspecting villain standing right beneath and then drop on top of him like a ton of bricks. Unfortunately,

Kuwahara's musculature made this tactic rather implausible.

'They caught me before the doors closed,' he said.

I wanted to tell him how sorry I was but it would have been meaningless. He wouldn't have let me anyway. I grabbed my army surplus rucksack and shoved in a book and some clothes.

'How much do you owe him?' he asked me.

'Price of a house.'

'Really?' he said. 'A nice one?'

He was so genuine, Kuwahara. So *good*. Every word the guy said was making me want to cry. 'Sure, Kuwahara,' I replied, 'a nice one. A one-bedroom prefab in the burbs. Look, I'm going to disappear for a while. Perhaps you should make yourself scarce too.'

'But the guy with the shirt wants you to call him,' he said. He pointed in the general direction of his head. I now realized that what I had assumed was bruising or smudged grease across his forehead was, in fact, Magic Marker. A telephone number.

I didn't want to make the call, but I couldn't be responsible for Kuwahara getting killed if they came back. I decided to buy some time for myself. Gingerly, Kuwahara swept his hair back from his forehead and I dialled the number on my mobile. I stood at the window as it started ringing. On the floodlit soccer pitch outside, the Kyoto University team was having a late-night practice in Day-Glo yellow jerseys. The lamps along the walkway were spinning galaxies of shining insects. In the parking lot, a man stepped out of a car. He put his hand up to the side of his head. The ringing in my right ear stopped. The man stepped out of the shadows and looked up, directly at my window.

'Hello, my friend,' came his voice.

I snapped the phone shut. 'He's here!'

Kuwahara's eyes actually opened for a moment. He hobbled away towards his door. 'Don't take the elevator,' he said.

'Yeah. Thanks. Really, Kuwahara' – slinging the rucksack over my shoulder and making for the door. 'Been great knowing you.'

The door slammed behind him.

I wanted to run, but I'd never make it to the bottom of the staircase before Uno or his men got there. I needed another option. I'd climb down the outside of the building! I rushed back into my room, pushed the window open and looked down the outer wall. It was perfectly flush. Not a cornice or a drainpipe in sight. How had I never noticed this before? I ran back into the corridor. I thought of hiding in a toilet stall. Stupid. My blood would look all the redder splashed across the clean white tiles.

No one ever takes the elevator. But there it was, waiting on my floor.

I pushed the button.

The doors obliged.

There *is* another option: the hatch in the ceiling! The hero forces open the service hatch in the ceiling, climbs up and – crouching in the thrumming darkness of the elevator shaft – fits the light-cover back into place just as the villain enters underneath! Thank you, Bruce Willis!

I stepped inside and pressed 6.

The silvery plastic grid in the ceiling came out easily: a little gentle pressure and it eased up and away. With my feet on the handrails along the walls, I put my head and shoulders through the gap. Two fluorescent tubes were set into a white steel panel just above my head, but there was no latch between them. I ran my hands along the edges, feeling for a seam, then pushed as hard as I could. The bell chimed as the elevator came to the sixth floor.

The doors opened.

62

The doors closed.

The elevator moaned as it began to descend. There was no way I could control it now. Perhaps there was a latch behind the lights? With a sharp tug, one of the fluorescent tubes came out in my hand, the metal brace hot enough to burn my palm. But there was nothing behind it. The elevators must be different in Hollywood.

The bell chimed again. The display next to my head read 3.

The doors slid open. Mr Uno was standing in front of the door, hands on his thighs, heaving for breath. He put one hand against the open doors and called down the corridor. 'He's here. Go tell the rest of them to come up.' He looked up at me and shook his head. 'What *are* you doing, Fujiwara?'

Standing on the handrails with the fluorescent bulb in my hand, I was somewhat at pains to explain my actions with any convincing excuse. I started but he cut me off: 'Oh, just come down.'

My face has never once been struck by a weapon or fist; it is still as handsome as it was in those cherubic school photographs from the fourth grade. I have never suffered a broken bone, nor any lesion grievous enough to leave a scar. How then did I extract my pristine self from this situation? Did I mention that I still had the fluorescent bulb in my right hand? I am not a violent man. I made a little hop and dropped to the floor of the elevator. At the same time, I lashed the bulb down across Mr Uno's forehead. It made a dull pop. White dust and shards of glass showered down around him. He grunted and lurched towards me. Again, I should emphasize that my actions were very much out of character. I brought the jagged stub of bulb up into Mr Uno's face as he came at me. He reared backwards with a roar, hands on his forehead.

'*Ohhh!* Oh no. Oh no. Oh no. Oh, my eyes. Oh, my eyes. Oh, my eyes.'

I found the acoustics of his pain strangely plaintive and

moving, but only momentarily. I punched G and CLOSE DOOR on the panel and read Leo Tolstoy's *War and Peace* in its entirety waiting for the doors to shut. My last view of Mr Uno was of him stumbling, bloodied, towards the far wall, picking at the milky-white shards in his eye.

When the elevator came to G, I heard the cheerful *bing!* like a sprinter hears the starter's pistol.

I spent the night on a leather couch at the back of a Starbucks. They don't like it when you stretch out to sleep on their furniture so the waitress came around periodically to remind me to buy something. Whenever she woke me up I ordered another espresso that I didn't drink and went back to sleep. In the morning, when the place was filling up and I couldn't keep the couch to myself any more, I counted seven espressos on the table, an expenditure of just under 1800 yen, which is as cheap a night as you'll find in central Kyoto. Thinking that Mr Uno might be expecting me to leave town at the earliest opportunity, I hung around the department stores in Kawaramachi until the early afternoon, then made my way cautiously to the station to catch the *Speed of Lightness* south.

gandhi

The police officer comes back to the car and sits down behind the wheel. He takes off his hat, yawns, rubs his eyes. He's a friendly-looking guy, one of those pitiable cops who probably didn't know what he'd got himself into when he signed up. Jovial guy in a dead-end job. 'I'm Constable Hiyashi,' he says. 'The cook out there says you tore his noodle restaurant apart.'

Mr Tak leans forward, his face up against the perforated Plexiglas partition. 'I paid that shyster 10,000 yen for Hiroshima oysters and he had the gall to serve us oysters from *Canada*.'

'Canada?' The cop laughs. 'What, no good?'

'It's not the quality at issue. It's the origin.'

'Well, I admire your principles but you're still the ones in the wrong,' the cop says. A little green icon in the shape of a walking man blinks on his computer and he punches a few keys to make it go away. 'Anyway, he said you threw oysters at him. He could claim assault. If he were to do that, I'd have to arrest you both. And that would mean I'd have to sit at my desk until all hours typing tonight while you two sit in a detention chamber.' He lets this pleasant information sink in. The little green man appears again and the constable types him away. 'You could, how shall I put it . . . *defuse* the situation though.'

Mr Tak takes out his wallet, rolls a 10,000-yen bill and pushes it through one of the holes in the Plexiglas.

'It may not be enough,' Constable Hiyashi says without even looking.

Mr Tak shoves another two bills through. 'Think he'll go for that?'

Constable Hiyashi takes the three bills and goes back out to the chef who's standing under the station marquee. He writes out something on a parking ticket pad and hands it to the chef with the bills inserted underneath. The chef glances at what he's been given and nods. He looks over at us in the car and smirks, then walks back inside. Done deal. Hiyashi comes back and tosses his hat on the passenger seat. He taps a few more keys on his computer and sighs. 'So you two must be some serious seafood connoisseurs. You were looking for Hiroshima oysters?'

'Yes,' Mr Tak replies, 'the kind that come from Hiroshima.'

'I gathered that,' says the cop. 'I like oysters myself.' For the first time, he turns around in his seat to look at us. His voice is stern. 'But you've dropped 40,000 yen and you still haven't got any oysters, have you? That wasn't a smart move now, was it? You could have just asked for your money back when you saw they were Canadian oysters. But you didn't. Is that any way to act? Did you show any respect for other people's rights?'

'But the others in the restaurant, they were being duped too!' cries Mr Tak.

Hiyashi purses his lips. 'And did you ever think maybe they don't *mind* being duped? That maybe they're *happy* and that's enough? I respect your principles, but your actions were unconscionable. What kind of society do you want to live in?'

The guy could be my own father. But somehow it's kind of charming to hear that same old spiel come from someone new.

'What do you two do for a living anyway? Are you chefs or something?'

'I'm a therapist,' Mr Tak replies.

'Student,' I say.

'*Hm.*' He turns back to the wheel. 'So Mr Therapist and Mr Student, are you still hungry?'

'Yeah,' I answer.

'My cousin's got a restaurant on Heiwa-dori. You can't sit down or anything, it's just a stall, but if his oysters aren't genuine Hiroshima I'll arrest him myself.'

Mr Tak is practically up against the glass. 'We're ready.'

'Fine then, fine.' He starts up the engine. 'And you're in luck. There's a special price for oyster *ramen* tonight. He usually charges 750 yen but, only for you two, the price is 5,000. With that you get the ride over there and no records with the Hiroshima City Police Department. Sound good?'

Mr Tak slaps my knee and grins.

'Is there all-you-can-drink beer included?' I ask.

The cop guffaws and spins the wheel.

It's a long drive through the city in the night-time traffic. Mr Tak is as curious about Constable Hiyashi as he was at first about me. Hiyashi is somewhat more inclined to conversation. He has a family and a fifty-year mortgage on a prefab house in the suburbs, but the plastics they used in the construction make everybody sick. His wife's taken the kids to live with her mother in Shikoku. So now he lives alone in the house with the windows wide open. He catches the ferry across the Inland Sea every Saturday to visit.

'I know a lot about plastics,' Mr Tak tells him. 'What kind of odour is it?'

'My daughter said vanilla. I think it's more like coconut.'

Mr Tak scribbles his address on a notepad he takes from his briefcase. 'You send a sample to my R & D department, Constable Hiyashi. It may very well be a polyurethane mix, in which case . . .'

I lose track of this thrilling conversation. It's pretty entertaining riding in the back of a police car. At stoplights people glance over. And glance again. Children point. I grimace back and make a pistol with my fingers. The kids get a kick out of this but it sure scares the living hell out of their parents.

The oyster stall turns out to be a bit of a dive, but popular. It's outside on a street corner beneath an overhead railway where one city train after another goes over, gnashing and grinding the rails. You have to pay a deposit for the bowls, and the beer comes from a machine down the street that's been rigged to stay open all night. Everyone's either standing at the counter or sitting down to eat on the kerb. Hiyashi wolfs down some *gyoza* dumplings and talks to his cousin. Mr Tak and I drink three litres of Asahi beer between us. I put two bowls of *ramen* away, he knocks back three and then picks the oysters out of a fourth. Every time he takes another of Hiroshima's globular, glutinous finest from his slopping bowl, a fountain of grease wells out between his chopsticks.

Two *freegirls* in school uniforms with skirts rolled up to the ass, fallen white socks and Burberry scarves show up to give me something else to watch. They stand on the kerb eating French fries and talking to a couple of construction workers in blue peg pants and dusty white T-shirts. Mr Tak shakes his head. 'Those are people's daughters,' he says and then grabs me by the shoulder. 'Those are people's daughters. D'you understand me?'

Everyone glances over at the loud drunk. I try to keep him calm. 'Sure, sure, I understand, Mr Tak. You're very observant.'

He shakes his weary head. 'Looking for freedom. All they end up doing is shacrificing it. For every Candy Girl I shell, another one of these girls leaves the streets. Be like Gandhi to these people,' he mutters.

Constable Hiyashi gets a call. He bows to his cousin at the counter and goes to his car. He leans out the window as he starts it up. 'So? Didn't I tell you you'd eat well?'

I give him the thumbs up.

'*Gatsu-gatsu*,' says Mr Tak. 'Shtuffed.'

Constable Hiyashi laughs. 'Goodbye then,' he says. 'Stay out of trouble now.' The cruiser pulls away with a chirp of the tyres.

There are no trains going south from Hiroshima after midnight so Mr Tak and I walk back into the centre of the city looking for clubs. We end up dancing on the stage in a cavern-like place lit with candles. It's a wild, eerie sight – the dance floor crowded and pumping in a candlelit miasma of cigarette smoke. Mr Tak buys a bottle of Goldschlager that he and I and any girl within reach drink shot by debilitating shot. For a guy who sells Masturbation Lifestyle he's a real playboy. Good-looking, well-dressed, wealthy, and even stumbling drunk, he's attracting the attention of some very pretty women – he's either the perfect man for the job or the absolute worst, I can't decide which.

By the time we cross the Straits of Shimonoseki to Kyushu later that morning, Mr Tak is KO'd. He's sleeping on two seats, jackknifed over the armrest, one arm wrenched behind him, the other dangling to the floor, and his glasses levered over his head. His pink shirt is half open to display a bundle of gold chains nestled between his pectorals. He can't be comfortable, but he's totally immobile and snoring all the same.

Unable to sleep in a similar position, I get out of my seat and wander the train like a zombie. In the rattling anteroom between cars, the dawn ripples beyond the dark, convex windows of the train. One moment there's a blur of trees and concrete embankments and endless conurbations making my eyes sore, the next the hillsides slide back like stage props and I'm flying serenely, 200 metres above the water. The shores of Honshu and Kyushu face each other like opposing camps, neon propaganda glaring upon the water, giant red and yellow mobile cranes sidling along the docks with arms raised. Further away to the east, in the early sun glinting off the straits, an impossible number of cargo ships are perfected in their own silhouettes. Forget it, it's beautiful is what I'm trying to indicate.

When the train arrives in Hakata to take on more passengers, I go to use the toilet in the station and when I come back to the cabin there are two very blonde women seated near the door speaking what I take to be Russian. As if this isn't unusual enough, one of them is crouched in a ball cutting her cerise toenails with a razor blade. Across the aisle, next to the door, a thug with a head like a ball-peen hammer, wearing a powder-blue sweat suit, is sending text messages on two mobile phones at once. I apologize as I take a *Speed of Lightness* magazine from a rack above his head, then step gingerly over his outstretched Reeboks.

I think I'll vomit Ramen *à la* Goldschlager if I try reading, so I just leaf through the pictures in an article about Amsterdam: the towers and windmills and flower markets, swans on canals and big-breasted women in parades. It actually looks attractive. It might be nice to escape there for an afternoon were I not saddled with other problems. Mr Tak sits up and yawns. He straightens his glasses and checks his watch. 'Another hour,' he groans. He looks around and notices the Russian women. 'Eh, Fujiwara,' he whispers and nods to his left. 'Sex slaves.'

'Really?'

'It's no secret. Tell me,' he says, 'do you masturbate?'

I'm unsure if the question is serious.

'No need to be shy,' he says. 'I'm a professional.'

'I'm not a big masturbator,' I tell him. 'I'm not even married yet.'

Mr Tak claps once and shouts with laughter. One of the Russian girls, arms crossed, looks up sleepily as Mr Tak collapses sideways. '*That's* the attitude!' he sings out. 'I think

70

you would enjoy a therapeutic treatment with my daughters.' He points at my magazine. 'You like reading, that's a start. People who like to read enjoy masturbation. It's a proven fact. You're a peaceable man too.'

I have my Bruce Lee moments, and there was the light bulb, of course, but, sure, I suppose 'peaceable' could apply.

'Of course you are,' he says, 'I can see it. Men who masturbate therapeutically are less violent than those who don't. It's the imagination.'

As he's speaking, one of the Russian girls straightens up and takes a mobile phone out of her bag. Immediately, the thug gets up from his seat and in an ungainly, sideways shuffle, dragging the left foot behind the right, crosses the aisle to take the phone out of her hands. He holds it directly in front of his face with both hands, his huge forearms dwarfing the blinking silver thing like the claws of some predator around a tiny fish. Eventually he snaps it shut and tosses it back on the seat. The Russian girl picks it up, puts it back in her bag and closes her eyes again.

'The market will only be mature,' Mr Tak's saying, 'when buying one of my daughters is as natural to you as buying a Coke when you're thirsty.' He lowers his voice again. 'The only alternative is them. More sex-slaves, more crime, more misery'.

He goes on but I'm not listening. I'm wondering under what circumstances I'd feel compelled to get naked with a plastic doll. I still fail to come up with one that is at all probable. But maybe that's just a failure of my imagination.

marumachi

Marumachi Station is clotted with people and fumes and is sorely unkempt. The platforms are littered with chewing gum and cigarette butts, the high glass roof is coated with grime, and the unadorned H-pillars that support it are gnarled with a hundred coats of once-white anti-rust paint. Above the platform exit is a giant aerial panorama of Amsterdam and a computer-generated image of what elegant and efficient Amsterdam Station will look like when it's completed in a year's time, all pilasters, arches, frescoes, pediments and crystal chandeliers beneath a gilt cupola. The advertisements at ground level, however, are somewhat grittier: desperate-looking teenagers loom in the dim light handing out information cards, free drinks coupons and lewd brochures for Marumachi clubs. The central concourse beyond the platforms is roofed with corrugated green fibre-glass that casts a green pall over yet more brochure kids, playbills, a wall of cigarette and beer machines, and a newspaper stand.

In brazen contrast to the murky station, a row of fantastic taxis stands gleaming in the sunlight outside. They're tall broughams with two-tone bodywork – burgundy and black, silver and black, red and silver, forest green and lime – egg-crate chrome grilles and gondola-like fenders. They could be Deusenbergs or Bugattis or Lagondas (though a closer inspection reveals them to be studious Nissan replicas) and they're tended to by uniformed chauffeurs with straight collars and gold epaulettes and white gloves. Couples and families and all the well-heeled among the train passengers make straight for the cabs and are whisked away to Amsterdam, while cigarette-smoking men in jeans and polyester two-pieces from Mr Suit slouch across the street into Marumachi.

The guy at the head of the taxi rank is dressed like a beefeater (the fat man on the gin bottle) and has a red nose and a fairly convincing handlebar moustache to match. He dives for Mr Tak's Vuitton lap-top case as we approach. Mr Tak is holding his seminar in Marumachi, he tells me, but prefers to stay in a five-star hotel in Amsterdam. 'Will you come to Amsterdam too?' he asks me.

I'm tempted to follow him and put a suite on Father's credit card, but in my jeans and T-shirt, my rucksack over my shoulder, I'll hardly fit in with the Amsterdam crowd. 'I'll find something in Marumachi,' I reply.

He gives me a sly smile. 'As you like, Mr Fujiwara. I'm sure Marumachi won't disappoint. But if ever you tire of the demands of flesh-and-blood women, my daughters will be there for you. At your disposal. All dowries waived!' He steps into a cab and is gone.

The Nishiki ryokan is dim, decrepit, dreary, and leans like it's about to fall over and take the whole street with it. ('Picturesque' is the epithet in the dusty brochures on the front desk.) Owner and operator is Mrs Nishiki, a hunchback with white hair, a navy-blue cotton *yukata* covered with white hexagons, and a face like a cured plum. She walks like a low-tech robot as she leads the way to my room, insists she'll be right back with tea and rice cakes, and takes an hour. It's almost noon by the time I escape her hospitality.

The shops and houses in the neighbourhood are well past their prime and in need of nothing so much as a wrecking ball. There are at least three signs per metre pointing the way to Amsterdam, as well as stands arrayed with brochures and fliers and newspaper boxes full of the *Amsterdam Blad*, but all that's visible of the 'Folk Tale Kingdom' in the west are some palms and a blue steeple that juts into the sky beyond the high, grassy embankment of the estuary.

It's unlikely I'll find Mai this early in the day; if she's working as an 'entertainer', she'll be sound asleep until mid-afternoon. When the aluminium shutters on the shop fronts all start going up at once – one long, screeching, multitoned toothache – I cut down an alleyway in what I assume is the direction of the harbour. I've got an image in mind of a calm place next to the water where I can have a cappuccino and watch joggers on the promenade and fishermen going out to sea, or coming in to port, or whatever it is they do at eleven thirty in the morning.

Following the alley takes me left and right and right and left and down a flight of moss-covered stone steps onto another residential street. Crepe myrtle, hibiscus, kiwi and pomegranate hang from garden walls. As I turn in the direction, I'm hoping, of the local equivalent of Copacabana, a young woman in a blue-and-gold kimono carrying a basket of dried persimmons and smoking a pipe emerges from a black, slatted gate. Through the interstices, I catch a glimpse of a garden of moss-covered rocks and sand raked into elegant waves. She's dressed in tall, lacquered *geta* and white *tabi* socks, and there's the lustre of brilliantine in her hair. When she sees me, she takes the pipe quickly from her mouth and shuffles past with her eyes on the ground. I think of putting her on the Kasane Scale, but though the nape of her neck where the hair's pulled up tight would be good for a couple of points, she's just too old-fashioned to rate.

At the end of the street, just beyond a little Shinto shrine with a green tile roof and a tall, red *torii* gate, I come upon a hundred or more new concrete tetrapods in a gravel lot. I check to see that no one's around, take a snap with my phone camera and then enter this strange forest.

They're T-38 tetrapods – no mistaking them. Each one of these beauties stands three metres high, weighs five tonnes and has a predicted life span of 10,000 years. I clamber onto one of the legs and run my hand along its curves, more like plastic than concrete – smooth, minutely porous, finely seamed where the moulds came apart. The geometry by which they fit together is a science in itself, laid two or three deep in great DNA-like rows along the coast. Yes, I find tetrapods enthralling. Odd? Maybe, but I'm not the only one; molluscs, crustaceans, the Departments of the Environment, Construction, Fisheries, and

Highways, and all their crony contractors seem to like them a great deal, too. Although they were designed to interrupt wave action so as to prevent shoreline erosion, proof that they don't hasn't diminished their popularity in the slightest. They were invented without patent in the 1960s by Dr Suresh Narlikar, a pro-sterilization gynaecologist from Bombay, but regardless of their exotic origin, it's here in Japan that the tetrapod has been perfected. Whenever I see them, I dream of a god reaching down from curlicue clouds to pick them up by the handful and toss them like jacks into the sea.

And their crotches remind me of large women in tight jeans.

A radio's playing somewhere further ahead. Pop music in a language I can't quite identify until the DJ cuts in and his high-pitched rant, interspersed with twanging American English, reveals his origin. *'You're on the line, honey,' 'Get it on!' 'I'm lovin' it!' 'This is Raaaaadio Maniiiiiila 101.5!'*

I hop from one tetrapod to another. As I get closer, I can hear a chatter of voices beneath the histrionics of the radio, bursts of female laughter. There's a multicoloured beach umbrella set up between the rows and I can see the top of someone's head bobbing up and down. What's going on, I wonder, a party? I clamber over two more rows and peer down.

Three, five, ten Filipina women are having a picnic between the tetrapods. 7-Eleven salads, bottles of lemonade, Tupperware, books and magazines lie strewn across a large plastic Mickey Mouse blanket. Two of the girls are dancing together to the *Footloose* theme song. The rest of them sit in the shade of the umbrella eating fried chicken and laughing at photographs in the magazines.

Someone taps me on the foot. Startled, I spin around to see who it is and slide right off the tetrapod onto the ground. Standing above me is a guy with a green Mohawk, matching clamdiggers, a black-and-white Korn T-shirt, and a red leather jacket that should have gone out with Michael Jackson. 'Looking for someone?' he demands.

How does he know that? 'Um, no, I was just' – getting to my feet – 'just wondering where the music was coming from.'

He doesn't believe me. 'They're not for hire now. Come to Slack Alice tonight if you want a piece of ass,' he says, leaning back into the shade of a tetrapod and folding his arms. 'Open at seven. Cover's more expensive after nine.'

'Thanks,' I mumble and weave my way back to the street.

When I finally arrive at the bay, it's only to discover that the horizon is obscured completely by a system of seawalls and breakwaters, the layout of which is impossible to make out from the shore. There are people fishing far out on these concrete islands and peninsulas, and perhaps they can see the open sea from where they are, but there's no way of telling how to get there myself. Tetrapods, derelict shops, a canning operation, the fishermen's co-op, oily, rainbow-hued water slapping at stained jetties – Marumachi's harbour is purely utilitarian. It is not the place to people-watch and eat *biscotti*.

Back on the pedestrian street is the Pêche Délice, an old-fashioned coffee house on a corner, with a façade of dark faux brick, a heavy wooden door with inset stained glass, and a sign in the shape of one of those peculiar Chinese peaches that look like breasts. The place is almost empty. The only other customer, a man in his fifties in a sharp blue suit, is busy barking at someone on his mobile phone, something about electricity bills and Chinese talc. At least the doormat provides a sedate 'Welcome'. I take a seat near the window. The white paper place mats on the table read 'Welcome' too.

A sweaty red face, a stovepipe paper hat and a red kerchief appear in the window to the kitchen. The man bellows: 'Welcome! Come in, come in. Hiroko! Yumi!' He turns away and starts kneading something out of sight behind the partition. The kitchen door swings open and two waitresses skitter out, one young, the other not. They're dressed in beige uniforms with gold embroidery on the pocket that reads PÊCHE DÉLICE. 'Welcome!' they chime in unison.

77

The girl comes straight to my table. Tall, with a generous mouth, widely spaced eyes and bangs cut straight across her forehead, she's lost in her baggy uniform but she's not an ugly girl – kind of sexy in an awkward way. I give her a 4 on the Kasane Scale – a little of the sex appeal but none of the composure. 'What would you like, sir?' she says for the second time.

'Oh, sorry, coffee and a brioche.'

This she writes out laboriously on her pad. 'And what kind of coffee would you care for, sir? There are choices.' She points to a menu in a transparent plastic stand next to the salt and pepper. The 'Coffees of the World' menu has a stylized compass on the cover and different full-colour spreads for each 'vintage' with highlighted maps, 1:1-scale illustrations of the bean, 'connoisseur's guides' and photographs that look as if they come from a travel magazine: ziggurats in the sunset, palm tree leaning over turquoise beach, wide-eyed wildcat staring from tree branch, Sugarloaf Mountain, Barong dance, Diamond Head.

Kona AA	Colombia High Mountain	Jamaica Blue Mountain
Kauai Coffee Estate	Colombia Utz Kapeh	Pico Duarte Hispaniola
Australia Skybury Estate	Guatemala Margogype	Cuba Turquino Lavado
Kopi Luwak	Guatemala Elephant Bean	Burma Bourbon
Papua New Guinea Sigri	Huehuetenango	Yemen
Sulawesi Kalossi	Costa Rica Yaoco Estate	Ethiopia Harare
Mocha Java	Costa Rica Peaberry	Ethiopia Sidamo
Bali Hai	Antigua	Kenya AA
Saigon Golden	Brazil Bourbon Santos	Kenya Andare
India Monsoon Coast	Peru Chinchamaya	Rwanda Maraba

I'm impressed. It's my sincere desire that someone some-where has good enough taste buds to tell the difference between all these. 'What's best?' I ask.

She bites her lip. '*Mmm*, I think . . . Blue Mountain?'

So I thought, but at 1200 yen a cup, too expensive. 'What else have you got that's similarly fruity, with as rich a bouquet, but at a cheaper price?' She is clearly mystified. She begins to beg her pardon, but I cut her off. 'No, forget it. Cuba Turquino Lavado,' I tell her. 'I'll have the Turquino Lavado.'

She turns away slowly, writing out my order, and then smiles and stutter-steps back to her elder counterpart waiting at the counter. The woman speaks with her for a moment, frowns and comes back to the table herself.

'Pardon me, sir. I'm sorry, sir.' She has a gold tooth. 'Did Yumi-*chan* tell you Blue Mountain was the best coffee?' Yumi stands watching, biting her lip, half-hidden behind the massive silver-and-black espresso machine with its brass eagle on top. The baker kneads away behind her, smiling like the benevolent sun in a children's book. 'The best coffee is Kopi Luwak,' the woman explains, pointing it out on the menu again.

'Really?' This is news to me. 'Why?'

'It's very famous and expensive. It's digested by civet cats. Wouldn't you care for it instead?'

I'm impressed, if slightly disconcerted that I've never heard of it. 'Sounds delightful,' I say, 'but I'll stick with the Cuba.'

She gives me a sour smile, bows rigidly and returns to the counter to make my coffee. A strip of dough floats into view as the baker flexes and folds it.

The man in the blue suit – a nice gabardine with a gold YSL tie – turns to look at me. 'Should have taken the Kopi Luwak,' he says.

'Oh?'

'*Mn*,' he grunts. 'Better taste.'

He's heavy-set and dark-skinned and half-jovial, half-malicious. With large square glasses and a towering bouffant coif, he looks like a cross between Kim Jong-il and Liberace.

'It's a bit expensive,' I tell him.

'Your line of work then?' he asks, determined to use me to liven up his morning routine.

'I'm a student.'

He throws up his hands. 'That explains it. Why not work instead? Then you can drink Kopi Luwak, *ne*?' He looks to the baker and shakes his head, then takes a pack of Dunhills out of his jacket pocket. 'Why do kids these days not understand this?'

The baker smiles his round smile and twists the dough.

'What company you going into when you graduate?' the man asks.

'Ministry of Construction.'

His lips purse. He takes a pensive drag on his cigarette. 'I like the MOC.' He points at the seat across from him, inviting me to sit down. I'm comfortable where I'm at, but it won't do to make enemies on my first day here. I go over to the table just as Yumi is bringing my Turquino Lavado. The man motions her away. 'Bring another Kopi Luwak.'

Yumi stops and looks like she's going to cry. She stands there hesitating, picks up the cream from her tray like she wants to put it down, then puts it back and returns to the kitchen.

'MOC, eh? What'll you do there?'

I shrug. 'Rig bids.'

He's going to take another drag but he stops. The smoke rises in one slim blue plume. His face begins to transform, spreading out in every direction – brows up, cheeks out, chin down. His head goes back and he roars with laughter. 'Is-that-*so*!' And he roars again, doubled over on his seat coughing like he's already dying of lung cancer.

He may find it funny but I'm not kidding. Once he's breathing normally again, I explain how I've passed the MOC's pre-graduation selection. I'll start in the Osaka–Kyoto Municipal Concrete Policy and Construction Strategy Office next April on a promotion fast-track. I'm going to work my way up, make some friends in the private sector, rig some bids, channel some government subsidy funds to the wrong people, then retire onto the board of directors of one of Osaka–Kyoto's better 112,533 registered construction companies. All by the time I'm forty-five. It's as solid a career plan as any.

'You're an angel,' he says, coughing and shaking his head. 'Descended from heaven. We need more people like you. Is that a Kansai accent?'

'Yeah. Kyoto.'

He spreads his hands. 'No surprise. *There's* a city that's gone from the middle ages to the twenty-first century in less than four decades.'

Yumi comes back with my cup of coffee and the man watches me sip. 'The best, *ne*?'

Yeah. I've got to admit it, cat-shit coffee is something else.

'What's your name?' he asks me.

'Aozora.'

Again he looks over to the baker to demonstrate his incredulity. 'Young people! Living hand to mouth, *ne*? Whatever happened to teaching them traditional values? Never think they had anything so uncouth as a *family*.' He points at me. 'Your *name*. What's your *name*?'

'Fujiwara,' I reply.

'Fujiwara? Well, well, *well*.' He watches me with steady appraisal as he lights another Dunhill, disappearing for a moment in his own smoke. 'No such thing as a born gentleman,' he says. 'They teach you any philosophy in university these days?'

This would be laughable were he any less intimidating. I shrug. 'I was sick that day.'

With a deliberate drawl, like a villain in a western, he leans back and asks, 'What brings you to Marumachi, Mr Fujiwara?'

I tell him I'm on holiday.

'Right,' he says, and gives his cigarette some more attention.

This guy's silences aren't exactly putting me at ease. 'Well,' I say, 'holiday and a little research too. I'm looking for a girl.'

He watches the cigarette smoke rise to the ceiling. 'All men desire happiness,' he sighs. 'There are lots of girls in Marumachi.'

'It's my sister.'

'Name?'

'Mai.'

'And she invited you here?' he asks without a beat.

'No.'

'So you're not invited then,' he says summarily. His words may be a little obscure, but his demeanour isn't too hard to read. The message is: that's the end of this particular line of discussion.

His mobile phone rings. Just once.

'*Aii*,' he groans, and gets to his feet. 'Enjoy your trip back to Kyoto,' he says, and flips a business card onto the table. 'Take this with you. Maybe we'll do business some day.'

The nondescript white business card reads:

Gondo

That's all. I flip it over but there's nothing on the back. No address. No telephone. No email. It's less a token of his existence than a reminder that he knows of mine. I find it a little eerie, like the local equivalent of a Sicilian godfather's kiss.

The two waitresses bow as he leaves. 'Goodbye, Mr Gondo!' 'Please come again, Mr Gondo!' The baker is still there in the kitchen, the tendons in his neck straining as he heaves over another great wad of dough. The door jingles, even for him, and he thunders away in a hulking, black, twelve-cylinder Century just like the ones the *yakuza* and the Cabinet Ministers drive.

In the evening the pedestrian street in front of the Nishiki is even busier than it was when the stores were open. I lean out of my window and watch a steady stream of men come around a bend at the western end of the street and disappear down the alleyways to the east. When I go downstairs and follow them, it isn't long before I come to the Marumachi I'd been expecting to find all along, a maze of a neighbourhood where thickets of neon obscure the sky and the tight streets are lined with *izakaya* pubs, strip clubs, whisky bars, lap-dancing bars, Swedish massage parlours, cabarets and *soapland*s. Yolanda, Nite Moves, Wonder Soap, Caligula, G-Spot, Slack Alice, Pre-Coitus, Chantilly Lace, Bar Come, Bar Pink, Cream Bar. Most of them have slick façades of stainless steel, glass tiles and brushed aluminium, but I come across a Grecian temple, Wild West saloon, the Palace of Versailles. The one with the longest queue out front is a traditional Japanese place called, appropriately enough, Floating World. The pleasure quarter goes on and on. For a town of this size, it's huge, more like Tokyo's Kabukicho than a small-town 'amusement street'. It's the kind of neighbourhood I'd be happy to spend the night in with 60,000 yen in mah-jong winnings and a head full of booze – one bright flower of a bar after another, their alluring neon leading the worker bee down a corridor of delights. The men who come here are all on vacation. They wear chinos and polo shirts, and as their families sleep happily behind the garret windows of Amsterdam they stream from one Marumachi bar to another with child-like shrieks of hilarity. Everywhere the spruikers in their black and charcoal zoot suits mill around talking on their mobile phones or handing out coupons. The *mama-sans* watch television just behind the velvet curtains of their brothels while strident groups of their girls try to waylay passing men. Playbills and brochures are everywhere. I take all that is offered to me and inspect the posters carefully; I suspect I will soon find my sister's pout among the splayed legs, sequins and top hats.

And how would I react if she stepped right now out of Wonder Soap in high heels and a wrinkled minidress, with bloodshot eyes and smeared mascara and bruised thighs? A certain kind of brother would slap her. A certain kind would turn and walk away. A certain kind would hold her in his arms and cry. A certain kind would take her to the 7-Eleven for coffee and a steamed pork bun and somehow manage not to condescend. I don't know how I'd react. I'm that certain kind of brother that's an Aozora, that's all.

The logical way to go about finding Mai is to start at one end of the neighbourhood and check every single establishment. In the first two places I visit, I get an enthusiastic enough reception until I mention I'm looking for someone in particular. The moment I pull out Mai's photograph I get shrugs, impenetrable stares, turned backs. They don't even look. They don't want to know. In the Cream Bar I ask the bartender if he knows a girl called Mai.

'Sure!' he says, and points at a Thai girl on the catwalk. 'She'll be Mai for you. Or Aki if you like. Hiromi, Kana, Madonna, you name it!'

The fourth place is a strip club called Superpussy. I have to pay 3,000 yen admission, and once inside it seems like a waste not to take advantage of the cheap drinks and free snack bar while watching the show. Besides, if Mai's working as a dancer, I won't know until I see her on stage anyway.

Three hours later, I emerge with somewhat less single-minded purpose than when I entered. I wander streets where clutches of drunken men stumble back through old Marumachi towards their Amsterdam hotels. The seawall appears at the end of an alley. Though the wind is unrelenting, I climb up and walk along the parapet. Up ahead, beside the seawall, a light burns with such intensity that it leaves indigo dots and squiggles floating across my vision when I look away. A man and woman dressed in green plastic suits are seated in a small aluminium boat, fishing for squid in the choppy sea. The man's got the outboard motor turned around on its swivel and he's crouched beside it, steering with one hand and scooping up the light-besotted squid with a net he holds in the other. Several inches above his head, a magnesium lamp suspended from a pole steams in the spray. The woman sits opposite, picking up the squid that he flings back and dropping them into an aluminium icebox that's strapped down to the bottom of the boat. It's an odd fishing technique to say the least: the boat bucks and yaws, every wave threatens to pitch them against the seawall, fingers of lamplight gesticulate wildly across the water, and there they are in a haze of spray and engine exhaust, husband and wife, fully engaged in their imperturbable and surely unnecessary routine – squid costs less than bread at your local J-Coop, after all.

I don't know how long I stand there watching them. I feel proud of them somehow, for being so indifferent to the pleasures on offer in Marumachi. I *wish* it were me out there in the waves. I'm soaked with spray by the time they whine away around the point. I want to share some more of their hardship, if only vicariously, as if a mere soaking isn't enough to awaken my ultra-urban sensibilities, but I cannot follow them down across the dark and glistening, crab-teeming rocks.

weekend monks

Mrs Nishiki enters my room with a loud knock at six in the morning. The sliding door parts from the frame and she edges into my room with a tray, pushing it along the tatami floor, then shifting her weight onto her fists and sliding her knees forward. She repeats this motion four times to reach my futon in the centre of the room, pushes the tray forward one last time until it's next to my head, turns it parallel with the futon and retreats backwards through the doorway on her knees like a crab backing down its hole. The door closes wood-on-wood with a comfortable, sleep-inducing *tock*.

At eleven o'clock I roll back over and stare at what she's brought – steamed broccoli, grilled salmon, steamed rice, one egg sunny side up, toast, coffee and, *la pièce de résistance,* a *crème caramel.* I get up, dress, eat a piece of toast and flush the broccoli and salmon down the toilet to be polite.

Today I turn away from the harbour, straight back into the entertainment district. By day all the glamour has evaporated; gone are the flashing lights and the women in plastic skirts. All that's left is the grimy functionality of cheap architecture. The eye catches on everything. The streets themselves have gone from wet mirrors to asphalt toilets splotched with vomit – always the same salmon pink – and rayed with dried rivulets of piss that lead from wall to somewhere mid-pavement depending on angle of incline and original volume. Electrical wires hum in galaxies overhead.

A tall pimp with pimples calls to me from a doorway. 'Looking for a wake-me-up?' Even at eleven o'clock in the morning, Nirvana Club is open for business. '*Rajio taiso?* Some early-morning callisthenics, my friend? Sure fix for morning glory. A good feeling guaranteed!'

I am sceptical of 'a good feeling'. I have purchased, since I started keeping track anyway, a total of fourteen products and services that assured me of 'a good feeling' – a toothbrush, fruit chews, a malted milk beverage, a sponge, Kimtak brand safety razors (Yes, I identify you and your treacherous product. I'd say 'Do your worst!' but you already have), a bicycle, multicoloured condoms with nibs and ribs, a pen with a rubber grip, a gruelling hour of acupuncture, coffee, a Korean heavy-metal compilation from the Soul of Seoul label, cutlery, silk boxer shorts and asparagus. Apart from the coffee, the bicycle and the pen, none of these products functioned as advertised. My 'feelings', when I got them, were almost invariably bad.

However, it's quiet in Marumachi this morning. Mr Good Feeling looks bored. He might be inclined to talk.

'What's inside?' I ask.

He steps into the street. 'Empty,' he says, leaning into me as if we're already fast friends. 'But I can arrange something. What are you looking for?'

The right question. I tell him I was here once before. Can't remember which bar I was in but there was this girl . . . oh, this girl. To die for, you know? Like a rock-'n'-roll princess. Tall with a straight nose and legs like . . . 'Well, I just can't get her out of my mind. She said her name was Mai.'

Mr Good Feeling nods and stares past me down the street. He probably looks slick by night, but in the morning light his clothes are rumpled, his collar filthy. He needs to shave and blow his nose. 'I know her,' he says.

'*Really?*'

'I know everyone here. Been here longer than anyone.'

'So where does she work?'

He frowns. Rubs his jaw. 'Forget about her. She's not read-ily available, if you know what I mean. No? You gotta move in the right circles to see that girl. Make the right contacts.' He holds up both hands, with his index and middle fingers folded down into his palms. 'The clientele is se*lect*.'

I don't understand.

'No *fingers*, get it?' he says. 'Lots of ta*ttoos* and spending cash and big black cars?' He nudges me with his elbow. '*Yakuza,* man. You're not one of them. But you like those legs of hers? I can put you between another pair just as good.'

Funny, I have a very strong urge to flatten this guy. I know for certain my sister's a hooker. But there's some vestige of something brotherly in my psyche that's getting really hot and violent with every word that comes out of this guy's mouth. I don't know how to explain it. I have to look away from him. I can't stand his feigned rapport with me. 'So you can't tell me where to find her?'

'Like I said, man . . .'

I nod and turn away. It's with some relief that I find my way back to the pedestrian street of old Marumachi, back in the sunlight where the shop owners are sweeping the stone tiles and watering the zinnias in the flowerpots, totally blasé about the fact that Sin City is right next door. I shift a copy of *Amsterdam Blad* out of my way and take a seat on a bench.

If that villain was talking about my Mai, then at least I know she's here in Marumachi. Somewhere.

My mobile buzzes in my pocket like a giant trapped wasp. I don't recognize the number, or the voice: 'Mr Fujiwara?' a man asks. 'My name is Ishikawa, right? Is that clear?'

'Ishikawa. Sure.'

'Good. So. I'm a friend of Mr Uno. You know? So I'm call-ing you, all right, because he's asked me to, because to have a conversation with you would probably . . . so, how do I say this . . . make him physically *sick*.'

'You know, I actually feel pretty bad about –'

'Sure, sure, of course you do. Which is just what Mr Uno is counting on, yeah? He wants you to come here to Ikoma to apologize. He doesn't want to kill you. He's only going to inflict upon you the same damage you inflicted upon him.' His voice retreats momentarily from the phone: '*Was that right? Did I say that right?*' He speaks into the receiver again: 'You made a mistake and Mr Uno accepts that. You come back with the money, grit your teeth and all's well, yeah? Mr Uno still has his sight.'

'How about if I send him the money and his medical expenses?' I counter. Strangely enough, I don't mean to be flippant. I just want to find a painless solution to the problem. 'Maybe a card too. Do you think he'd be okay with that?'

'So' – Ishikawa pauses to inhale dramatically – 'the answer to that is going to be a no, yeah? You take off his eyebrow with a light bulb, he takes off yours. It's fair, yeah?'

'Yes, I suppose it is. I'll give it some thought. And call you back, okay? Bye now.'

I get up and start walking. It's hard to sit still when you know there are people out there intent on hurting you. Tonight I'll have to target the upmarket bars where the *yakuza* are likely to go. I'll lie in wait for unsuspecting mobsters and follow them to their exclusive lairs. Until then, there isn't much chance I'll find Mai by sitting around on a bench.

Apart from the prim white cars in the parking lot, with their aprons of shiny black paint and gold medallions on the grilles, and the 'Criminal at Large' posters on the front doors, Marumachi Police Department looks a lot like a bank or post office. It's not some loud and dingy scene full of hard-boiled types. There are potted red maples on the stairs in front and a large welcome mat on the floor in the lobby. The office is wide and empty save for two officers, one of whom gets up from his desk to meet me at the front counter.

I explain that I'm looking for someone and hand him the photograph of Mai. He goes to his senior, who takes the photo and scrutinizes it. '*That's* Mai?' he says, and starts to laugh before looking up at me and reverting from amused to the previous implacable. He hands the photo back and shakes his head. The junior officer comes back. 'What's your business?' he asks.

'My business?'

'Why are you looking for this girl?'

'Because she's my sister. I think the *yak*s might be forcing her to work as a hooker.'

The officer flinches. He puts up a hand as if my mention of the *yak*s or hookers has offended him in some way. 'Please, sir, please. I'm very sorry,' he says, handing me the photo, 'but we have no official information to give you about this girl.'

'But, that officer back there—'

'What did you say her name was?'

'Mai,' I'm forced to repeat. 'Mai Fujiwara.'

'Oh yes. Unless you'd like to fill in a missing person report for this Mai Fujiwara, there's really nothing we can do.'

'But how can she be missing when that guy knows her?' I practically shout. 'I *heard* what he said.'

The junior officer puts up both hands now. 'Your conduct is unseemly,' he advises me. 'Please, restrain yourself.'

'Restrain myself? What's to restrain? I'm talking. I'm posing logical questions. Engaging in discourse. All I want is to know how that guy knows my sister.'

'But you're not being polite about it,' he insists. 'If you have any questions for a particular officer, please go through the right procedure. If you'll just fill out this form, I can assure you that your concerns will be addressed.'

I'm nodding. Yes, yes. But I don't really see him any more. My eyes cannot penetrate the odious fug that emanates from crooked officials. He sets about tidying the already tidy pencils in their fancy lacquer tray and I leave in a rage. I'd like to slam the doors but they're electric and close meekly before me. I stand on the front steps, staring at this seedy town where every door closes in my face. I've got to get away, cool down, elaborate a plan.

At the end of the street is a rice paddy, and beyond this the closest of the forested hills that rim the bay. A rough track's been cut through the replanted cedar and I follow it up. The bay shines reliably to my left down the gaps between the cedar rows, but once I'm beyond the cedar the forest is a maze of pathways, all leading in circles around copses of bamboo and camphor tree, or fern-covered knobs of rock. I can't forge my way through the underbrush, but I can't climb the hill by following any of the paths either. I've just decided to head back down when I hear the first of several strange bleating noises, like ships' horns out on the bay or some kind of animal closer by. It's repeated at regular intervals of about a minute, but it reverberates through the canopy of foliage and I can't tell where it's coming from. At the seventeenth or eighteenth interval, a dozen grinning monks wearing white robes and Buddhist phylacteries on their heads emerge from the trees in single file. The leader has a kind of conch that I recognize from one of my father's Flora and Fauna 101 lessons. They bow when they see me. The one with the conch and a coolie hat, an elderly guy sparkling with sweat, stops to talk. He looks concerned. 'You're not looking for the bridge, are you?'

'No. I was just hoping for a good view.'

He looks relieved. (There can be no other country in which a good view is quite so hallowed.) 'Oh, fine then, you can come with us,' he says, 'but as a neophyte you'll have to go barefoot.' This provokes a rattle of laughter from the other men.

I assume it's a joke, but once they've finished laughing they all stand there looking at me expectantly. Only once I kick off one shoe do they start to file away, up the hill. So I follow them, shoes in hand, the neophyte monk.

They're a group of weekend monks, the leader explains. They're just regular guys with regular jobs during the week, and most of them live in Marumachi or the town of Kochiba further down the coast. But every weekend they go on hikes to different shrines in the area. One year they went to Hokkaido, another year to Mount Fuji. 'Our numbers grow every year,' he says. 'More and more men want to spend their weekend afternoons being a monk.'

I try blowing his conch, but all that emerges is an airy soughing.

'It'll take practice,' the monk says.

After half an hour of jovial company, we come to a narrow pass with embankments cut steeply on either side. Beer cans litter the ground. At the far end is a neat, white bridge, its beautifully smooth concrete contrasting sharply with the rough-hewn track that leads to it. It's ten or more metres across and spans a tight ravine covered in *susuki* grass, with what looks like a concrete chute for a giant pinball at the bottom. I ask the monk where the bridge leads to and he makes a raspberry. 'Nowhere. There's nothing up here but an old shrine,' he replies. 'We seek out pristine places. From the other side of this ridge, there's a view over the coastline that hasn't changed since the days of Edo.'

'This view's not bad either,' I say. 'It's pretty generous the government building such a nice lookout.' The concrete is cool beneath the soles of my feet. I drop my shoes and lean on the parapet of brushed aluminium. From the centre of the bridge, the drop must be eight or nine metres to the concrete chute below. Before me is a tidy diorama: the crinkled tinfoil of the bay, the matchstick rooftops of Marumachi to the left, the shining estuary in the middle, and to the right, Amsterdam. I may have been sceptical before, but now that Amsterdam is spread out in front of me, I can't fail to be impressed. The city is laid out in the shape of a giant five-pointed star embedded into the coastline and divided into a dense complex of islands by dozens of intersecting canals. Water-taxis and cruisers cross wakes on a giant lake and disappear into myriad canals. Tulip and lavender fields and truly grass-green lawns lie like festive bunting around the red roofs of the city. From here I can count seventeen white windmills turning. Towers and spires bristle like a cameo against a bright screen of sunlit clouds. To the far right, where the hills sweep round to the peninsula at the end of the bay, is an oval of flattened earth. Yellow power shovels swivel like one-armed insects, dump trucks open their wing-cases, a tiny black car speeds across the plane of earth trailing a greyish plume of dust.

The monk's voice cuts my reverie: 'This is a favourite spot for jumpers.'

'Bungee jumping?'

'No,' he replies. 'Just jumping.' He wipes the sweat from his forehead with a small towel. 'A big *yakuza* boss threw himself off a few years ago. Or got thrown. No one knows. But the bridge got some publicity and now there's a site on the internet with pictures and directions how to get here. It's mostly broke salarymen and pregnant high-school girls. They come down from Nagasaki and other places because it's quiet and has a nice view.'

I'm surprised by the monk's nonchalance. 'You seem to know a lot about it.'

'I'm a police detective,' he says. 'Jumpers, gassers, razors, I know about them all. Too much. Right, I'm sorry but I have to go along with the rest now. Just there the trail leads down.' He points to where the track peters out several metres beyond the bridge at a concrete retaining wall and a profusion of bamboo and devil's weed. A rough staircase leads down through the trees. The other monks have already cut straight up, into the forest, continuing on their way up the hillside. 'Don't trip on the stairs as you go down.' He turns away, and then stops. 'You *will* take the stairs down, won't you?'

'Promise.'

Once the monks have gone, the bridge itself starts to feel spooky. I can't hear the conch any more, only the souls of the dead moaning up the ravine.

the princess michiko

The next morning at ten o'clock, I find myself sitting on the same bench in the pedestrian street again, wondering what to do. A woman in a pink apron sprays the pavement in front of her scarf and hat shop with a hose. A sparrow flits about under the bench I'm seated on, hoping for crumbs from my 7-Eleven pork bun. I try to interest it in a sip of beer but it flies away. (On the Aozoran List of World's Best Breakfasts, the 7-Eleven *nikuman* pork bun rates just above the flatbread and spicy bean dip I once had on a beach in Boracay, but far below the Hard Rock Café's Eggs Benedict and Bloody Mary Special, or the list-leading coriander and scallop won ton nestled in a bamboo steam-basket that I used to eat religiously at 4 AM at Mr Uno's mah-jong parlour, ordered in from a Chinese dim-sum place down the street.) Last night, I spent another 40,000 yen cash advance on my father's credit card in the entertainment district, and there's still no sign of Mai.

I pick up the ubiquitous copy of the free *Amsterdam Blad* that's lying on the bench. *Tulip Parade Today!* reads the headline, with an image of a giant float covered in tulips and two very healthy blonde women carrying milk buckets, and a harlequin with an accordion waving at the camera. Inside there are articles on all things Dutch. There are adverts and coupons and an Amsterdam map. *What's a rollmop? Find out! – Dutch Auction! – Come see the new Spyker at Japan's only showroom! – Experience Dejima Days at Amsterdam! A delegation from the Edo capital makes a special visit today, with Princess Michiko leading the show!* And there she is in the accompanying photo, Princess Michiko, dressed in the kimono to end all kimonos, waving from her seat on a sedan chair. 'Princess Michiko and her entourage.' But forget the caption, the girl in the photo is no more Princess Michiko than I'm Hirohito. I flatten the paper on the top of a trash bin to examine it closer. It's that grin, there's no mistaking it.

With stucco walls, ironwork balconies, red-tile roofs and a campanile, Amsterdam Head Office looks more like a villa in Tuscany than an office block. It's just beyond the pedestrian bridge that leads from Marumachi to Amsterdam, presiding over the vast parking lots from a slight rise to the north. At the centre of the cloistered courtyard is a fountain in a long rectangular pool lined with blue Portuguese tiles. As I walk under the pediment in the archway, jets of water spout around the prancing stallion at the pool's centre and pigeons sweep down from the eaves, their grey plumage flashing blue with the reflected light over the pool. A man in a blue checked shirt and a khaki photography vest, with a pith helmet held under his arm, gets up from a marble bench and crosses the courtyard to a woman in a red-and-yellow summer dress standing in the shade. Beyond the main doors, two girls in white summer hats and red-white-and-blue uniforms await me in the lobby. Have I come to fill in an application form for employment?

'*Er*, no. I need to contact an employee.'

Everything seems clear now. Mai's not turning tricks in Marumachi after all. She's working in Amsterdam. A performer of the public kind. 'Respectable family entertainment.' I'm strangely elated for my father's sake. I imagine his eyes on seeing that picture of Mai in the newspaper. His daughter a princess!

One of the girls makes a quick call, then directs me to a door on the first landing of a wide marble staircase. Mr Hino will be happy to speak with me. And Mr Hino is very happy indeed. It's his job to be happy, it seems. And brisk. This is all turning out to be easier than I expected. He ushers me into an office that could be that of a Mexican governor in a western – terracotta tiled floor, stucco walls, massive, heavy desk, a seat carved out of black wood with red leather upholstery – and takes a seat with a pert little tap on the desk mat. 'Of course, of course,' he says when I tell him I've come to visit someone. 'I can't give you any personal details, I'm afraid, but I could arrange a telephone call. The name?'

'Mai Fujiwara.'

'Fujiwara? Well, that shouldn't be difficult to find. Mai Fujiwara, Mai Fujiwara, let me see here, not a moment.' He types the name into his computer. He frowns. 'I'm sorry, there's no one here by that name.'

'But there's a photo of her right here.' I spread the *Amsterdam Blad* on his desk. 'Look, that's her.'

'Strange,' he says, looking at the picture. 'Her name's not Mai. Her name is Michiko.'

'But that's just a stage name.'

He shifts the mouse on his computer and double clicks. 'Maizono,' he says. 'Her name is Michiko Maizono. Are you sure this is the girl?'

'I thought so.' Or, to be accurate, I hoped so. I look again at the newspaper photo. I realize now how uncertain the likeness is, how blurry and abstract the configuration of tiny dots. How much am I reading into the image? Mr Hino's kind, concerned smile is embarrassing. I sigh and get to my feet.

'Wait,' says Mr Hino, his lips pursed, pensive. 'Please. I think . . .' He places both hands flat on his desk. 'Have you had lunch yet, Mr Fujiwara?'

Lunch? It's not even eleven o'clock.

'Please, let me be so kind as to offer you lunch in one of our forty-two world-class restaurants,' he says. With an air of great magnanimity, smiling like an oil baron writing out a cheque, he takes a book of iridescent red-white-and-blue coupons from a drawer. He signs the top one, tears it neatly from the rest and waves it in the air. 'Up to 3,000 yen! Any restaurant of your choice. Just imagine enjoying the world's cuisine prepared by outstanding chefs while you admire the beautiful canals. Have you purchased an Amsterdam Passport yet?'

'Not yet. Actually –'

'Then today *is* a lucky day, Mr Fujiwara. I have here a coupon for 25 per cent off the cost of a regular one-day Amsterdam Passport, a saving of almost 3,000 yen!' Out comes another book of coupons. 'The parade begins this afternoon at three o'clock.'

'But –'

'Exactly,' he interrupts, handing me the coupons. '"But" is the right word. This girl looks like your sister *but* her name on my computer is Maizono. *But* there's a chance they are still the same person, no? Perhaps she's using two names. I have a feeling, Mr Fujiwara, that Amsterdam Incorporated is not this girl's only employer.' He hands me an Amsterdam map. 'Amsterdam is a wholesome attraction,' he says, 'but Marumachi has attractions too.'

He's too polite to be anything but opaque, but I think I understand him anyway. 'Thanks,' I say.

'Enjoy your visit, Mr Fujiwara. Let Amsterdam provide you with a most exquisite escape!' He pushes one of the buttons on his telephone. 'Miss Tanaka, will you come and see our guest out?'

In the courtyard, the man with the pith helmet is taking snapshots of his wife posing beside the fountain. She's pretty, for mid-thirties anyway, in a creamy yellow summer dress with a pattern of watermelons, and a wide-brimmed cream summer hat. It has a half-sphere crown and a crepe ribbon and looks like a giant fried egg or a 1:120,000,000-scale model of Saturn perched on her head. As I go by, she turns to me. 'Excuse me, sir. I beg your pardon but would you mind taking a photo of us?' She smiles and shows me a digital camera.

I shrug. 'No problem.'

As I take the camera from her and she points out the shutter release, the husband keeps clicking away at her and at me. I frown but he takes five more shots before stopping, then points behind me and says, 'The pigeons. On the eaves of the building.'

I turn to look at said pigeons. Said pigeons are indeed on the eaves of Head Office. Why in the world he should find them picturesque is beyond me. As it happens, when I go to take the snapshot of them smiling beside the fountain, the camera won't work. The memory card is full.

'Oh, that's strange!' she exclaims, and drops the camera in her bag without so much as glancing at it. 'Oh, well. Thank you anyway.' And she and her husband turn around and disappear out the gates arm in arm.

A catalpa-lined driveway – medians laid out with pansies and *Fritillaria imperialis* and the occasional tulip – leads me through a savannah of parking lots to a Van Gogh bridge and the grandiose portal of Arrivaldam. Tourists and schoolchildren and giant Miffy characters handing out Dutch flags emblazoned with *Goden dag!* throng the gateway and the bridge that leads across Amstermeer Lake to the city. Amidst the noise and engine exhaust and the waves of human plankton, I stop to look up at the massive cast-iron gates with their webs of acanthus and gilded fleur-de-lys. After the decrepit shop fronts and uneven alleys of Marumachi, this place shines like a gingerbread palace in a pastry shop. I want to take the bars in my hands to be sure they aren't made of liquorice.

The Amsterdam Passport (with a discount of almost 3,000

yen!) goes on Father's credit card and I spend a couple of hours waiting for the parade to begin, walking through the plazas and pedestrian boulevards and the narrow side streets. Almost everywhere I go the streets look as if a circus has just spilled out from a rent in the big top: there are organ-grinders, balloon twisters, fire-breathers, clowns in two sizes, horses pulling carts full of cheeses, policemen, pretzel vendors, ice-cream carts, double-decker buses. A yellow hot-air balloon decorated with Miffy and her friends, each with a Dutch flag in one hand and the Rising Sun in the other, is tethered by winches and drifts ponderously over the rooftops. And there are tourists, of course, mostly old-age pensioners in groups, or family men with their wives and huge cameras, every photograph an attempt to efface the guilt they feel for not being at work. Amsterdam is very organized. Everyone is very happy.

I'm following the bank of the Nistelgracht Canal from Harry Potterdam towards Bergenstad, guessing at what it cost per metre to build these canals (at a minimum 5 per cent, the kick-backs paid to whoever rigged the contracts must have been stunning!), when I come to the Trattoria Butelli, a small pizzeria stuffed full of diners. Inside are garlic ropes and Italian hams hanging from the windows and rows of straw-wrapped bottles on the windowsills, all basking in the glow of a brickwork wood oven. The welcome mat on the floor at the entrance is a giant map of Italy. I step from Udine to Roma to Brindisi. A young gondolier leads me to a table somewhere in Africa.

The first thing I see on the menu he gives me is this: ALL ORDERS IN ITALIAN. Underneath is a pronunciation dictionary and instructions on Italian etiquette.

'*Desiderate?*'

Initially the waitress scores highly on the Kasane Scale, but I soon downgrade her. Lissom voice and ankles to die for, but *way* too condescending.

'Spaghetti with squid ink and shredded seaweed,' I tell her. An old fave.

She corrects me. '*Spaghetti al nero di seppia?*'

'Whatever spin you want to put on it.'

She shakes her head and puts thumb to index in front of her lips when she speaks: '*Spa-ghe-tti al ne-ro di se-ppi-a. Spa-ghe-tti al ne-ro di se-ppi-a.*'

She gets my seldom seen 'you are obnoxious' smile. 'Thanks for the free lesson,' I say with a sigh, 'but I'm really not interested in taking part.' In anything. Ever. 'Oh, and a bottle of Chianti.'

'*Chianti! Buono, signore. Spaghetti al nero di seppia e una bottiglia di Chianti,*' and those faultless ankles carry the rest of her away.

When I've finished the pasta, I want to order some tiramisu for dessert but can't be bothered to sing *The Marriage of Figaro* to get it. And it's almost three o'clock. On a sidewalk in the Amstelveen, as I'm buying a *gelato* from a short, old, bearded guy with a burgundy-red cart and a green parasol, the entourage I've been waiting for comes parading over the bridge from the Oranjeplein. I hear the drums beating, and soon enough a troop of samurai with palisades of spears and banners and a swaying sedan chair in their midst appears over the hump of the bridge. These swarthy, unshaven types swagger up the Polderstraat in antlered helmets, red lacquer armour and those thick-soled *tabi* rubber shoes that look like penguin feet. I'm assuming that everyone finds these mummers as ridiculous as I do, but the people on the sidewalks are actually gathering round, gazing in admiration. They love it. They love this Japanese stuff more than they love the exoticism of Amsterdam itself. What I assumed, from a distance, was jeering is actually cheering from a long line of fans following the procession. Four heavy-set, bearded individuals in the bulky black-and-red robes of the Ainu tribe carry the sedan chair. (They make it look like they're carrying the chair on their shoulders but the whole contraption's actually supported by wheels concealed beneath a brocade curtain that's flapping open at one of the corners.)

Princess Michiko's sitting high on the brocade chair doing her best effeminate and royal wave at the people on the sidewalk who've stopped to watch. She's dressed like a courtesan in a kimono covered in pink cherry blossoms and cranes and a blue Mount Fuji. At least a dozen layers show at the sleeve. For all the iconic imagery, however, her kimono's not quite traditional: it must be the first one I've ever seen that's cut at the knee and deeply décolleté (I don't remember my sister being so copiously breasted, but then I tried not to pay much attention).

Even in this get-up, I recognize her immediately. As the soldiers jostle past only a couple of metres away, I lean one elbow on the cartwheel and watch her in something like admiration.

'It's a delegation from Edo,' the *gelato* man tells me, sculpting a pyramid of *spumoni* atop a cone with his little wooden spatula.

'Yeah, I read about it in the paper.'

'They arrived in Spakenburg this morning aboard the good ship *Amstel Maru* . . . Well, not really,' he whispers. 'The ship can't actually leave Amsterdam, it just docks in Larsenlaar on the far side of the Rottermeer. They do this every Saturday.'

'I see. And who's the girl again?'

'Her Royal Highness the Princess Michiko.'

'*Ha!*' I laugh out loud. It's too ridiculous, I can't contain myself. 'Royal *High*ness? Get this, my friend – that paragon of femininity up there used to walk around the house in sweatpants cut off at the knee and a "Zero to Slut in Two Beers" T-shirt. She farts like a horse and goes without washing for *days.*'

The guy looks at me agog.

'Oh yeah, no kidding. She considers lemon Calpis and a tube of bean paste a balanced meal. She can watch seven hours of talk show while on the phone, and she once shoved a peanut so far up her nostril that a dentist had to drill the thing to bits to get it out.'

He starts laughing. 'You're having me on.'

'You think so? Watch this.' I cup my hands to my mouth and yell: 'Hey, Mai! Telephone!'

The reaction is immediate. Princess Michiko swings around in her chair, squints at me as I wave, then pulls her veil down over her face. I turn back to the *gelato* guy. 'See?'

Hastily, he sticks a wooden spoon into my *gelato* and wraps the cone in a red-white-and-blue napkin. 'Really you shouldn't, you know. She's acting now. Here's your cone.' I take the candy-bright pyramid he holds out, then fish in my pocket for 650 yen. When I turn back to the parade the whole thing has come to a halt. One of the samurai, short and very elaborately dressed, has stepped up to the princess. They look in my direction, then he nods assent and comes over onto the sidewalk. 'Do you look askance at the Princess Michiko?' he asks me.

At first I'm too alarmed by the guy's appearance to respond – the high ridge on his helmet gives him a dinosaur-like profile and he's wearing a black iron half-mask with fearsome whiskers. One hand rests on his *katana*. 'I say again, do you look askance at the Princess Michiko?'

Though he's ludicrous, I feel sorry for him, having to make a living this way. 'Sorry, but I don't think I even know *how* to look aska—'

'Nonetheless,' he interrupts me, 'I shall protect the Princess Michiko's honour.'

I shrug. 'Sure, whatever.' And I smile my 'that's nice' smile to end our pleasant conversation.

He is not impressed. 'You,' he grunts, 'shall know the steel of my Mitsutada.' He flips up the mask and steps back into the street, pulling the banner from his back with a flourish. I have to say, he plays his part well; he's a ringer for my father's favourite film star, samurai hard-man Toshiro Mifune.

Holding it by the scabbard, one of the other soldiers offers me a sword.

Politely, I decline.

Silently, he insists.

People are staring. Everyone is. 'Really, thank you, but no,' I tell him. 'I don't care for audience participation. It breaks the cardinal rule of theatre.'

But the samurai proffering the sword is stubborn. The *gelato* guy leans across his cart. 'Go on, take it,' he says. 'They do this every day.'

'Why?'

He shrugs his shoulders. 'Why not? For fun. It's part of the culture.' He smiles and points the way to battle with his spatula. 'Go on.'

The crowd's getting bigger and louder, full of anonymous voices. 'Go on!' 'Be a sport!' With a sigh, I pass my *spumoni* to the *gelato* man for safekeeping and draw the sword.

Encouraged by the other pseudo-soldiers, the spectators form a ring and Toshiro Mifune walks the perimeter of it, posturing with his hand on his sword hilt, bowing to the ladies. My *katana* has an elaborate green, cord-wrapped hilt and a brass tang decorated with turtles. I expect to find the edge of the blade dull as a spatula but it's frighteningly sharp. Toshiro must be confident.

After he's satisfied that the audience is geared up for it, Toshiro kneels before the sedan chair of my sister the princess. 'With your permission,' he says. And then addresses the crowd. 'In honour of the Princess Michiko and in the name of the Tokugawa Shogunate and the Sovereign Entity of

Amsterdam and its creditors, et cetera . . . repair the insult brought upon your person . . . et cetera . . . punish this infidel . . . et cetera . . . do my life lay forfeit.'

Enthralled applause.

During his speech, Mai is statuesque, as if none of it has anything to do with her at all. Her head is turned towards me, and though I can't see her eyes through the veil, I know she's watching me.

Toshiro is back on his feet. He takes a stance before me – feet widely spaced, sword drawn and held at an angle across his body. He's either very angry, or very constipated. With the most unbearable sense of my own ludicrous role in this farce, I follow suit. Princess Michiko raises a blue handkerchief. Toshiro leans towards me and whispers: 'You're doing great!'

The handkerchief mushrooms as it falls and then slips sideways, leafing down from the chair to land on the pavement. I think of skewering it with my sword and handing it back to her, to put on a show of gallantry for the crowd, but I don't have the chance. Toshiro lurches forward and steel scythes against steel. With a deft move, he slides his blade along mine, pushes down, twists, pulls up and, in effect, wrenches the sword right out of my hands. It's quite dramatic. There must be a technical term for it. My sword loops through the air in cinematic slow motion and clatters onto the street.

Applause all around. The samurai who owns the sword goes over to pick it up with both hands and scowls at me as if I've just been abusing his only child. 'Try to hold onto it at least,' he mutters.

So in our next exchange, I make a tentative jab in Toshiro's direction. He parries it easily and then disarms me once again. The crowd erupts. 'Hurray!' Everyone is now enjoying the spectacle immensely. A man wearing a pith helmet smiles at the Handycam he's got trained on me; a woman in a wide-brimmed hat jabbers into her mobile phone, probably telling her friends back home how atmospheric Amsterdam is; a dozen or more children are sitting on the edge of the sidewalk eating *churros* covered in sugar; a tour group of elderly women in pastel wool sweaters giggles and claps. The other samurai watch with arms crossed, leaning into one another to exchange commentary. The four hairy Ainu just stand there grinning.

I raise my sword again and again, and each time I lose it. This ritual of swordplay is like the interminable sessions I had necking with Kasane when we first met. We would attack each other's mouths for a short burst, then smile, look around, talk a little, then mash our lips together again, take another break, et cetera, on and on. Amazing how we never tired of it! It's that way with Toshiro, though he's far more skilled than I am and it's obvious he's drawing the spectacle out. He nicks my shirtsleeves, trips me up, juggles his sword and his dagger, clangs his blade off mine and then tells a joke to the audience or some erudite fact about Japanese history. Our blades lock at the tangs in one exchange and he leans in to me, gripping my arm. His jawbone is dripping with sweat. I try to get away but he pulls me even closer and whispers in the most condescending tone: 'Just keep trying your best, sport. You're a real hero today.'

Then he pushes away and yells, 'Saké! Bring us saké! I salute the health and noble beauty of Princess Michiko!' He takes a tiny porcelain cup of saké from one of his compatriots and downs it. 'And please everyone, don't miss Princess Michiko performing "My Heart Will Go On" and other popular numbers from the deck of the historic schooner *Amstel Maru* this evening. This performer is truly a star in the making! The show begins with fire-eaters at six o'clock at the Werf in Spakenburg. Seating is on a first come, first serve basis and everyone is welcome . . .'

As Toshiro's making this public-service announcement, Mai sits there motionless while the Ainu men stand behind the sedan chair talking to one another. I edge over to the sedan chair and lean on one of the poles like I'm tired. I look up at the darkening sky and mutter through my teeth, 'Hell of a place you've ended up in, Mai-Tai.'

She hisses behind the veil. 'This is *not* the time, Ao.'

'Be nice. It wasn't easy finding you.'

'I *am* nice. I'm even happy to see you, but can we talk another time?'

'Sure, whatever. I just wanted to let you know that you're about to take a few days off. I need you to come back to Inaka with me.'

'Inaka?' she guffaws. 'You're dreaming.'

'You're the one dressed up like Sailor Moon. I know those aren't your breasts, by the way. Anyhow it won't take long, and there's cash to be had. Aunt Okane's will just came through.'

Toshiro is now posing for photographs with the other samurai; a semicircle of snapping cameras forms around them.

'Who's Aunt Okane?'

'That's pretty much what I said. Remember the one with the big old house and the dog that had some kind of disease in its ears? Anyhow, apparently she adored us when we were three. She's left us the whole lot, Mai. A *fortune.*'

'Really?'

'Yeah. All you've got to do is come back to Inaka to get it.'

'I'll have to give it some thought,' she says.

This is annoying. It's just like my sister not to understand at a crucial time something as simple as the word *cash.* I try to massage the building tension out of my temples while I speak. 'Thought counts for nothing, Mai. You've *got* to come. I need this money.'

Toshiro comes over to offer me the cup. He winks. 'It's just white grape juice.' I take a sip but I'm losing interest in all this theatrical stuff. I hand it back to him and turn to my sister. 'What time do you finish? I'll wait for you outside the front gates.'

'Ao, please, be patient,' she whispers. 'I'll meet you tomorrow if you like.'

I am now aofficially on edge. Tiny blue sparks are zinging between my grating molars. I should have taken serenity booster shots at the local Zen Buddhist's before leaving Kyoto. How can she possibly equivocate over this much cash? I've got to take a moment's breather to retain my composure. I look past the canal at the windmills and the beautiful peaceful timeless serene tranquil historic hills of Kyushu. Perhaps I should try being more politic, more reassuring, less brotherly?

She snaps her fingers and the Ainu men come forward to take their places at the poles. 'I'll meet you at that sushi place there,' she says.

I groan. '*Sushi?*'

'Fine, that burger place. Two o'clock.'

'But Mai-*chan*, you have to—'

Toshiro leans in to me. 'She's taken.'

Suddenly I understand how Mr Tak felt back in Hiroshima. Suddenly everything in every direction is just Malpeque: an ersatz version of something else and nobody but me seems to feel any contempt for it. I was shocked when he started flinging oysters in that restaurant, but I'm feeling like I could do a lot worse right now.

'Really, friend,' Toshiro continues. 'You don't want any trouble with her employer.'

'Go to hell,' I tell him.

He frowns and takes me by the elbow.

The illustration is of *osotogari*, the major outer cut. Four years of high-school judo did, apparently, leave me with a legacy; the move comes back to me like I've been practising it all my life. Toshiro sprawls across the cobblestones.

The crowd gapes. They don't know what the hell is going on, but before they can even begin to whisper, Toshiro is back on his feet. 'Well, ladies and gentlemen, we have a true combatant here today! Please everyone, a round of applause.' With that, he thwacks me hard on the thigh with the side of his blade. When I go to retaliate, his blade whirs out of nowhere, ricochets off my tang and across my body. My forearm burns. I hold it up and watch as a trail of convincingly red blood worms its way down to the cup of my elbow.

Toshiro tilts his head with a smug, closed-mouth smile as if to say, 'You thought I was joking?'

No, but neither am I. One, two, three – Aozorro slashes at his head. I've got no technique but I make up for it with pure, blind fury. He should be able to deal with me, but when he loses his footing, stepping backwards over the arms of a dray of red cheeses that's parked in front of the Leerdammer shop, I lunge forward with another wild swipe. A spark jumps where my wayward blade connects with a stone wall, but my ensuing backhand meets the hair on the top of his head and leaves his gleaming coif with a towering cowlick. He crawls backwards up the dray as I slash at him again. When he gets to the top his weight makes the whole thing tumble backwards through a display case of plastic hamburgers and potato croquettes in front of the Oranje Burger next door. The crowd goes deathly silent. The only sound in the air is some faraway carousel that I'd like to be on.

The rest of the troop steps in between Toshiro and me. The sword is wrenched out of my hand. 'A round of applause for our actors,' says the Princess Michiko and the crowd finally erupts. Toshiro is on his feet, bowing to the audience as if going over backwards had been planned from the start, but even he can see that the better part of the applause is for me. I duly take a bow. And another. Straighten my shoulders a little. It was a deft move, after all. Poor Toshiro didn't know what hit him. The Ainu pretend to hoist the sedan chair, the drums resume their beat and the procession moves on its way again.

Down the street, two red-and-white Mercedes sedans pull up to the kerb and four officers of the Amsterdam Politie in light-blue uniforms with black Sam Browne belts and shiny peaked caps emerge. I step back into the crowd just in case they want to throw me out for disturbing the peace. An alley leads me out into a large crowded square with a white marble fountain in the centre. There's no line-up in front of the Mind of Escher Theatre so I flash my Amsterdam Passport to the girl at the red velour rope. A staircase leads up, down, sideways, and into the darkness of the theatre. I slump into a seat near the middle. Is it the speakers or is it my brain ticking as it cools down?

Five dizzying *Mind of Escher* shows later, I'm back outside. Night's falling and all through the streets a fine rain veils the fake gas-lamps with a transparent haze and makes the side-walks gleam beneath the lighted shop fronts. The rain in the multicoloured light makes me nostalgic for Kyoto – the cars crackling down the streets, the elevators pumping in their tubes. Storms in Kyoto only make the lights brighter.

Departuredijk is bright and loud. You have to walk through the sprawling gift shop to find the turnstiles and there are employees and old folks and screaming kids everywhere. The Amsterdam parking lots are full of buses and frantic tour guides and private cars queuing up to leave. I join the parade of umbrellas that leads down the promenade towards Marumachi.

mai-tai

I can see why my sister got the role of a princess. She's something else, something *other*. Like twenty-first-century woman among the Neanderthals. This is definitely not the smelly adolescent who used to walk around the house in torn jogging pants and a Von Bitch baseball cap. She's wearing a deep-green minidress and a matching bolero jacket with embroidered roses. Her hair's all done up like some kind of flamenco dancer and she walks through the Oranje Burger with her arms crossed as if to protect herself from all the vulgarity of plastic and Styrofoam around her. Though she doesn't look overly pleased to be here, she slides into the seat across from me and gives me a smile. 'How are you?' she asks.

'Okay. My arm still hurts though.'

'He wasn't trying to hurt you.'

'The guy attacks me with a *katana* and he wasn't trying to hurt me?'

'*Wakizashi.*'

'What?'

'It wasn't a *katana*, it was a *wakizashi*. A *katana*'s longer.'

'Whatever. It was made of sharp metal. It cut my skin. Look –'

'And it was *you* who attacked *him*. You made him lose his temper.'

'*Mmn*, he did go down pretty hard with my major outer cut,' I say smugly.

She lays her huge sunglasses on the table along with a yellow, ostrich-skin Prada and an expensive Vertu telephone.

'So when can you be ready to leave?' I ask.

'That's what I want to talk about.' She sighs and picks up one of my potato croquettes between her shining red finger-nails. She tries to be light-hearted all of a sudden: 'Hey, are you still with Kasane?' she asks brightly.

'Why are you bringing her up?'

'Because she's nice. Are you two—'

'No, we're not. She went to stinking Hokkaido. Forget it.'

'Hokkaido?'

'She's a snowboard instructor.'

'In the summer?'

'No, stupid. Summer she does mountain-bike tours.'

Mai takes a bite of the croquette, careful not to smudge her lipstick. '*Mn! Hot! Mn* . . . Do you – *mn*, god, this is hot.' The cheese is stretching between her fingers and mouth and she ends up spitting it all into a napkin that she folds up and deposits in my Coke cup that's still half full. 'God, Ao, how can you eat this stuff?' She wipes her fingers with a napkin and then checks her lipstick in her compact. 'So do you miss her?'

'Oh, for crying out loud. Stay focused, okay? There's a lot of cash at stake here.'

'And it's going to disappear if I don't come right now?'

'No, but I *need* it now. My bone structure depends on it. Look, you're free today, right? If we catch a bullet train now and meet the lawyer in the morning, you could be back here, fifty million yen richer, by the same time tomorrow.'

'Fifty million?' she whispers, wider-eyed than usual. This is the reaction I've been waiting for. Some vitality, some esprit, some ambition! Something that shows she's got the same good values I've got. 'Wow,' she mouths.

'Yeah. So you ready now?'

She stares at her Prada.

'What?' I ask. 'What is it? How can there be any dilemma about this?'

'Ao,' she says, picking her words, 'singing in the parade isn't my *only* job.'

I can see what's coming. I save her the trouble. 'Yeah, I know about all that, Mai. You don't have to go into it.'

She looks annoyed. 'Whatever you *think* you know, Aozora, I'm not on the game like some streetwalker.' She nods to her left. 'See the car?'

The next row of booths is window-side. On the street outside sits a black Century with darkened windows. 'Those are my *chaperones*,' she says sarcastically. 'Welcome to my life.'

I recognize the car immediately. 'The guy who owns that Century . . . his name wouldn't happen to be Gondo, would it? Fat guy, looks a bit like Kim Jong-il?'

She leans across the table. '*Don't* speak like that about Mr Gondo. How do you know him?'

I shrug. 'He bought me coffee made of cat shit.'

I'm expecting silence or an incredulous *I beg your pardon?* but she says:

'It's called Kopi Luwak.'

I actually smack my forehead in disbelief. 'This is surreal. Am I totally uncultured or what? How is it you know about cat-shit coffee?'

'It's the best,' she says.

'Oh, gimme a break. You couldn't tell the difference between a civet cat and Hello Kitty.'

'But how did you meet him? You didn't say anything about *me*, did you?'

'Um . . . well.' I pick up a croquette. 'Yeah, I might have mentioned your name. I don't know.'

She starts gathering her things. 'I think we better end this conversation. They're waiting for me.'

'But hold it, what's the deal? I thought this stuff only happened to the Thais and the Uzbeks.'

She shoves her telephone and compact into her purse. 'At least I'm not one of them,' she says, perching her sunglasses on her head. 'Those girls take fifteen men a night and then wash the sheets all day. I live here. I've got a tourelle suite at the Vermeer Hotel. The only drawback is them.' She nods towards the car again. 'Gondo doesn't trust me not to leave. Princess Michiko is a *much* sought-after *perk* for his *honoured* business partners.'

I suggest calling the police. 'Seems like a simple solution, no?'

She shoves a finger towards my face. 'You call the police, Aozora Fujiwara, and I become another teenage suicide. You understand?'

'Sure, sure. Take it easy.'

She slumps back against the orange vinyl. 'Oh god, how sad is that? I'm not even a teenager any more.'

That's right. I've forgotten her birthday. Hardly seems like the time to celebrate though. I can't believe the situation she's putting me into here. I try to think of other options. 'This hotel you're in. Can't you just sneak out? Isn't there a window you can hop out of?'

'Ha,' she laughs. 'A convenient window. Just like in the films, right? I've seen things they don't put in films, Ao. I don't want them happening to me. Look, it's not the end of the world. Gondo lets me sing. I know he does it just to keep me sweet, but I don't care. I'm building a fan base. Some day I'll cut a disc.'

'With fifty million yen you could hire a studio and a producer.'

This gives her some pause. The dilemma is heavy on her. She stares at the floor. 'You're making my life difficult.'

'I'll think of something,' I reply. 'Is there any time when your friends out there leave you alone?'

She shakes her head. 'Only on Saturdays. During the parade.'

115

'Okay. Here, give me your number. I'll call once I've got something sorted out.'

She wipes her eyes with the back of her hand and checks her face in her compact mirror again. She glances up. Suddenly she's transfixed by something behind me. I go to turn around but she puts her hand on mine. 'No,' she breathes. 'Just stay.' She gets up from the booth. 'Be careful,' she says, and walks away.

I turn around to watch her go, wondering what the alarm is all about. It's the wrong thing to do. A *yak* with a shaved head and a fancy green tracksuit is standing at the door watching me. Mai has a word with him in passing, but he watches me a moment longer. He puts his sunglasses on and follows her out.

skull and tiger

Now what? I wonder. I need to come up with a plan to rescue Mai from some very heavyweight players. At moments of overwhelming powerlessness like this, when my back is up against the wall and there doesn't seem to be any hope left, I like to get drunk. The tension eases off. Immediacy loosens its claws. The consequences don't seem quite so consequential. I notice the world in front of my eyes again. On an unremarkable street somewhere behind the Oranjeplein I find a Parisian-style brasserie called the Aux Bacchanales. Suits my mood. The August sun is true to form. The silver beer-pumps behind the zinc bar glisten with condensation. For the price of two litres of Asahi anywhere else, the barman brings me a dish of candied almonds, a soft felt coaster and a shapely stem glass of amber-coloured Alsatian bock that I quaff in seconds. I order another.

My table sits at the edge of the sidewalk. There are the omnipresent tourists passing by, and the occasional open-top tour bus. Jane Birkin breathes through speakers behind the bar. The waiters speak in fluent French. I see the attraction of Amsterdam now. I want all my beers to be as atmospheric as this.

Despite the tranquillity of this moment, I suppose it's time to ring my father.

'Aozora!' he shouts down the line. 'Where are you? What's happened? What took you so long to call?'

'Sorry. Is everything all right?'

'Of course. Why wouldn't it be?'

'No reason.'

'Have you found her then?'

'Ah. I . . . Yes. I mean . . . I know where she is.'

'And she's fine?' Father asks.

'She's fine. Don't worry. She's really busy though. I haven't seen her yet. But I'll be seeing her soon.'

'Aozora, you know I'm going into the hospital tomorrow. You'll come visit me, won't you? With Mai?'

'Sure, sure. Of course.'

'Good. Thank you, son. You're doing a good job.'

'Right, better go.'

'Oh and there was a call for you, son. A Mr Uno?'

I cringe. I sit up straight in my seat. 'Yes?'

'I understand he works for a collection agency?'

He certainly *does* collect, that much is accurate. 'You could say that,' I reply.

'He's not the most polite interlocutor over the telephone, is he?' Father tries a chuckle, but it doesn't come off. I can tell he's worried about it. 'If you have some money troubles, Aozora, all you need to do is tell me.'

I am not convinced that his definition of 'money troubles' is quite broad enough to include the sea of hot water in which I find myself. 'It's okay, Dad' – using the D-word is sure to placate him – 'I've got it under control. I'll be in touch again soon. Have a good operation.'

I'm just debating a third beer when the woman at the next table, to whom I haven't paid any attention up until now, turns around to look at me. 'Good afternoon,' she says.

I hadn't noticed the summer hat on the chair next to her. His pith helmet is there too. Camera in hand, her husband gives me a smile, then gets up from his chair and walks across the street to frame up a shot of the Spitztoren Tower. They are the model well-to-do couple on holiday in Amsterdam.

'Hi. Did you get another memory card for your camera?'

'Hm? Oh that.' She smiles richly. 'I don't suppose I could see your Amsterdam Passport?'

I can't imagine why she wants to, but I shrug and pass it to her.

She takes a cursory glance at it. 'There may be a problem,' she says. 'We would consider it a very great pleasure if you'd accompany my partner and me.' What a strange request. She's trying to look nonchalant as she speaks, but she can't quite manage it; her smile trembles with the effort of keeping cool.

'I was just going to have another beer,' I say, 'but thank you anyway.'

'But you've already had two,' she protests. 'Isn't that enough? You really should come with us.'

'Thanks, but, if this is another audience participation thing, I'll pass.'

'Mr Fujiwara' – she emphasizes the fact that she knows my name – 'these people are enjoying their day in Amsterdam. It could be a once-in-a-lifetime opportunity for many of them, something they've been waiting for all their lives. Would you want to be a blemish upon that memory by making a scene?'

I look for a waiter. I make eye contact with the barman, but he looks away.

'Don't worry about the price of the beer,' she says, laying some cash on the table. 'Let's call it a goodwill gesture on our part, shall we?'

Husband comes back and picks up his pith helmet. He looks at his wife and says, 'Such a beautiful view from that side of the street.' He turns to me. 'Well? Shall we?'

I'm still not moving.

But Husband is still smiling. 'Or we could have our friends meet you outside the Amsterdam gates tonight,' he suggests. 'Whichever you prefer.'

He stays where he is until I've stood, then follows behind.

(His camera probably shoots poison darts.) We walk down the street a short way to a pair of red fire doors between two clothing boutiques. The woman goes to an aluminium panel on the wall and checks to both sides to see that no one is watching. Then she swivels the panel to one side on its one remaining screw and touches something inside with the tip of a ballpoint pen. The doors pop ajar with an electric buzz. We go through these, and then another set of doors, into a brightly lit corridor. The two rows of fluorescent bulbs on the ceiling disappear into the distance. I can see now that what I had taken for separate buildings from the street are actually no more individual than shops in a mall, all joined and fed by the same rear service corridor. It's perfectly possible that all of Amsterdam is one labyrinthine building. The doors on my right are on the Willemsplein, those on my left, Heemstraat.

We follow this corridor to a doorway where two *yaks* are waiting. And these are full-on *yaks* like I think I've never seen before – gold chains adorning their gold chains, tattoos where the tracksuits can't contain their muscles, bald and dented skulls, perhaps seven fingers total between them.

There's not much to differentiate them. One's got a skull by Hokusai on his chest, the other a tiger. They don't even look at me. Tiger's playing a video game on his telephone. Skull has his teeth bared at a compact hand-mirror, looking for bits of food to dislodge with a fingernail. Probably human flesh. 'Took your time,' he says.

'When are you going to sell me that car?' asks Husband.

'The grey Skyline?'

'The *white* one. How many times do –'

'Sold it to my niece.'

'*What?*'

The woman intervenes. 'Need I remind you that none of us has any authorization to be here? Can we please go? I have to pick up my daughter from gymnastics in thirty minutes.'

Skull puts the compact mirror away. 'Sorry. How is little Ayaka?' He stretches his hand out towards me. 'Camera phone,' he says.

I hand it over.

He looks at it like it's a cheap piece of crap. Flips it open. 'Password.'

'Kasane,' I reply.

He holds the phone between thumb and middle finger, going through my calls, my address book, the photos I've snapped of Amsterdam. 'Nothing,' he says to the woman. He hands me back the phone.

The couple turn away and go up the stairs. 'If you find another Skyline like that one,' says Husband over his shoulder, 'I want it, remember?'

'Yeah, yeah. C'mon you.'

The two *yaks* take me down a flight of stairs to a tunnel with tracks laid for some kind of train. Massive cables and pipes run along the ceiling and there's an incessant humming of giant fans or high-voltage transformers. It looks like the set for a James Bond film but I'm not overly confident these guys are going to bother with shark tanks or laser beams when it's time to do the business. In an alcove to one side are several rows of white bicycles with woven baskets on the front. Red, white and blue streamers hang from the handlebars. Skull asks me if I know how to ride a bicycle. I'm tempted to say no, but I take the bike he pushes forward and get on. It's way too small and I have to lean forward, doing the praying mantis with my legs doubled underneath me. However ridiculous I feel, watching the two *yaks* climb onto these granny bikes is some solace: the tyres are flattened beneath their weight and they're so bow-legged only their heels touch the pedals.

No matter how far we ride, the tunnel stretches out before us in a shallow right curve. We pass a couple of electricians working on a scaffold and a garbage truck crew emptying a dumpster, but the tunnel is otherwise empty. After a few minutes we come to a stop at an unremarkable set of blue doors.

Beyond these doors, I know, is the trash compactor from the Death Star. They're going to push me in with no Leia.

The *yaks* get off their bikes and lean them against the white concrete wall. I go to do the same but Tiger shakes his torso (his head and body move as one) and points with his remaining thumb across the tunnel at four other bicycles all leaning together.

Now another staircase, this one stained brown and green with humidity. The naked bulbs on every landing flicker and crackle like there are frantic insects trapped inside. After climbing fifteen delightful flights we come to a green steel door. Tiger jams what looks like a chisel between the lock and the doorframe and gives it a shove. There's a flash of blue sky and foliage and I can smell fresh air again. We're high on the hillside overlooking Amsterdam. I recognize the beer cans and devil's weed immediately.

They take me by the arms and lead me onto the bridge. Built for no reason, utilized only for evil. How many of the 'suicides' on this bridge were forced? I wonder. How many 'pregnant high-school girls' were uncooperative girls like my sister? The concrete is so damn white it's blinding. Skull takes a small digital camera from his tracksuit. 'Hold it,' he says, and steadies me in front of the railing. Takes a snapshot. Why? For his *yakuza* boss? For the newspapers? For the photo album he'll show his little *yakuzinis* when he's eighty and they all come clamouring around his armchair for tales of the bad old days? 'Now in profile,' he says. 'Doesn't he have a funny nose?'

'Lemme see,' says Tiger, and spins me around. He takes a step back. 'You're right.'

Their visceral reaction is recognizable as laughter. 'He's the human cleaver,' says Skull.

'The what?' asks Tiger.

'Cleaver. One of those long, pointy cooking knives.'

Tiger snorts with laughter. 'Oh yeah, like that. A human knife.'

Skull puts the camera in his pocket and spits over the rail of the bridge. He points at me. 'Never come back here, Mr Fujiwara.'

And I think, would he bother telling me not to come back if he were about to kill me? I almost drop to my knees with relief.

'Or should I say,' he continues, with droll timing, 'don't *crawl* back here.'

They pick me up under the armpits and seat me on the railing at the centre of the bridge. I want to grab for a hold but they've got my arms held tight in front of me. If they let go, I'm gone. Straight back. There's a lot of airtime between myself and the concrete chute below.

Pertinent Fact: The human body accelerates thirty kilometres an hour for every second it is falling. I have no idea why this is, nor why I know it. But I can guess that I will be in excess of the local posted speed limit when I hit the bottom. The blood throbs in my fingertips and toes.

On the same railing a few metres away is a wagtail. A citrine wagtail – I can see the yellow underside. I'm fixated on the bird for a moment, thinking about my father and how he'll never know I knew the difference between a common wagtail and a citrine. He would have been proud. I snap out of this reverie and start pleading. 'I've got *money. Lots* of *money.*'

They look at me like I'm a child offering a saliva-dripping rattle.

'Hokusai!' I yelp. 'You like Hokusai, right? That skull on your chest is a work of art. Absolute genius. How about *Red Fuji*? I *love* that one, my favourite of all time. Do you know

Eizan? Very important artist. Very important. I can get you some of his prints. Cheap.'

One of their mobile phones rings.

They pull me back and I slump to the ground. Skull flips open his phone. 'It's me,' he says, and listens for a moment. 'What, you want me to put it in writing?' he says. 'I told you, if I find one, I'll sell it to you. Yeah, no matter what colour. *Hm*?' He puts his hand over the mouthpiece. 'You interested in selling yours?'

Tiger's nose wrinkles in a frown.

Skull puts the phone back to his ear and shakes his head. He snaps it shut and they both reach for me again.

'No, that's totally wrong!' These guys have no idea of a reliable cliché. That call was supposed to save me. 'That's not the way it happens!' But I'm yanked up and placed on the parapet again.

Tiger asks Skull: 'Did Mr Gondo want him to go over here or there? We got in trouble when that guy's head broke.'

'*Mn*,' Skull grunts. He's thinking. He bares his teeth and picks at something in his canines with his fingernail again. 'The middle of the bridge is for treason. That end of the bridge is for misdemeanours,' he says.

Tiger frowns. 'Huh?'

'Just shut up. Okay, Mr Fujiwara, your lucky day.' They pull me off the edge and march me to the other end of the bridge. 'You get to jump.'

I stare down. From here, it's a four- or five-metre drop into brush and *susuki* grass, but the banks of the ravine are steep and odds are I'll roll down to the concrete chute at the centre, and from there, if it's as slick as it looks, slide right down to the giant rusting steel grate at the bottom. It's not exactly a playground ride.

'Climb up, climb up,' says Skull impatiently. Tiger kindly lifts me up.

I crouch on the railing, holding on with both hands, my fingers aching like they're on ice. I figure the further left I can project myself, the shorter the fall will be, but I've hardly got time to plan my leap. Skull gives me a nudge. My balance is gone. In that moment I push off from the railing, aiming left, but the soles of my shoes slip on the sheer aluminium and all I can do before the ground speeds up to meet me is – nothing.

I am stationary. In darkness. My breath is gone, my lungs purged of air. A halo of pain surrounds my body, but I can't determine yet where it will localize. There's grit between my teeth and the taste of mould. I inhale slightly and a sharp green smell brings me back with a jolt. Coughing and heaving for breath, I lurch up towards the fresh air, away from the grass and soil that's mashed beneath my face. The air can't get into my body fast enough, but with every breath now the pain comes on faster and faster, oxygen to the fire. I roll over onto my hands and knees. Is there a phone ringing or is it my skull? Spectacular red pain is bursting out from the dull, vaguely orange-tinted shock like spurts of fire from a lava pool.

'Mr Fujiwara?'

I try to spit the soil out of my mouth, but it only dribbles down my chin. I roll back into the grass. Above me are the beautiful beautiful blue blue sky and the two downturned faces and four hands of Skull and Tiger who are staring at me from the bridge.

'Mr Fujiwara!'

One by one, each section of my body submits its fresh report of pain to Aozora Head Office. Both my ankles are sprained – already they're swelling and tender to the touch. My head is not sitting right, like a juggler's ball wobbling on a stick. You know, you'll never realize you even have a coccyx until you almost break it.

'Mr Fujiwara, can you come up here again?' It's Skull. He actually sounds conciliatory, if that's possible. 'Just come up there through the bamboo, will you? We threw you off too soon. Mr Gondo wants to speak with you.'

My breath slowly returns to normal. My wagtail friend flits from the parapet and disappears somewhere behind me.

'Please, Mr Fujiwara.' Now it's Tiger calling down from the bridge. 'We'll get in trouble if you don't come back.'

Even in this state, I could make a break for the bottom of the ravine, sliding down on my butt. Those two bulls would never catch me.

Although, assuming they have guns, they could just shoot me.

And where would I go on my swollen ankles anyway?

I turn and crawl back up the hill.

brand recognition

The Rathskeller is a dingy bar down a white stucco staircase in Marumachi. Peanut shells lie inches deep on the wooden floors and the tables are covered in what look like Turkish rugs. The only light in the room comes from the orange, candlelit hurricane lamps flickering on each table. Behind the dark-wood bar are dozens of bottles of absinthe lit up by pale-green lights.

It's the classic shadowy corner-table rendezvous. The gangster with his back to the wall. The only strange thing is, Gondo's sitting there with a pile of coffee-table books of foreign cities: Florence, Buenos Aires, Rio, Vancouver. I hobble over and ease my joints into a chair. He swivels one of the books around. He slams a pudgy index onto a two-page spread. 'Recognize it?'

'Sydney Opera House,' I reply.

'Brand recognition,' he says. 'Eiffel Tower, Buckingham Palace, Colosseum' – he slaps an open palm for each one – 'Taj Mahal, Statue of Liberty, Golden Gate . . . Well, maybe not the Golden Gate. Nobody's impressed by bridges any more.'

I could beg to differ.

'I want to get into theme parks myself,' he says. 'I may have missed out on investing in Amsterdam itself, but I saw the opportunity it created and single-handedly turned Marumachi into what it is today.' He says this as if it's something to be impressed by. 'Now I've got the capital, the friends, the connections – everything I need except the right idea. What's the next place, *ne*? London, New York, Paris? Everyone's already been to the original ones.' (I'm reminded of a chapter from

Golden Pavilions titled 'Clean Investments for Stained Money'.) Now his fingers are splayed across his wide forehead. He rubs his left eyebrow beneath his glasses and stares at the Red Fort of Agra. 'India's a possibility, *ne*? The fear factor works in my favour. Nobody over forty dares go to the real India. You following this, Mr MOC?'

Like I have a choice. 'New New Delhi?' I say.

'That's it. But New New Delhi . . . big problem. Imported actors cheap, Taj Mahal 100 per cent recognition, people like the food . . . What's the problem?'

'Is there one?' My mind races. What do I know about India? Ganesh and funeral pyres and train wrecks and curry and Gandhi and coconut palms on white beaches. None of which you couldn't recreate for a paying Japanese clientele, though you'd have some trouble growing coconut palms. 'Climate?' I venture.

'*Ya-ta.*' He slaps the table. '*That's* why you didn't end up at the bottom of the ravine.'

'Um, in fact –'

'People who ask too many questions get punished, *ne*? Just like in school. But then I thought to myself, Kyoto University? This kid might be useful.' He straightens his glasses. 'So who wants to go to India in the cold? Only place hot enough is Okinawa but there's no land there. Not until the Americans leave. So what's the next place then? Repeat visits, *ne*? That's what I need. What'll you drink?'

'Kopi.'

He orders two Kopi Luwaks and the bartender has them on our table in sixty seconds flat. 'Disneyland has a film industry. Constant source of updated gimmicks. I don't have that. So what is there that people can't get enough of? Sex and gambling, of course, but there has to be the family, old people, feminine element too.'

I pour the cream into my coffee and watch it go all slinky

and sexy before it clouds. After my near-death experience, this is going to be the greatest coffee ever.

'I'm building a racetrack,' he says. 'You seen it?'

'Not really, no.'

He slaps *A Day in the Life of India* shut and pushes back his chair with a screech. 'Come with me.'

I have the cup in my hands. I'm raising it to my lips.

'I said, *come on.*'

The interior of Mr Gondo's Century smells of leather and cigarettes and the slightly sour odour of the shrink-wrap plastic on his dry-cleaning – at least fifty shirts are piled in the back window. There are two drop-outs in the back seat – the usual blond hair, black clothes, spiked chrome wristbands, and total disregard for planet Earth while their headphones are on. How long they've been sitting there I have no idea.

The massive car swoops down the uneven roads of Marumachi, though Gondo's control over it is frighteningly nonchalant; apparently there are other things to do at the wheel than fret about direction. He lights up a Dunhill and flips through channels with the remote control pointed a hand's length from the television screen. The blue smoke from his cigarette stretches out lazily through the cabin while houses and telephone poles and billboards and garden walls flash by my window. I'm feeling car-sick. I play with the seat controls to take my mind off it. I have a hell of a time getting comfortable in most cars, but the Toyota Century merits the official Aozoran Seal of Approval. The heated seat and Electronic Masseur ease my orchestra of aches.

When we pull into the yard of a concrete factory, piled high on every side with concrete in various shapes, Gondo barks into the back seat: '*Ja,* ready to work for once in your lives?' They're obviously not used to answering in the positive but one of them pulls off a fairly convincing 'yes'.

'Course you are,' Gondo grunts. 'Work on tetrapods today. Need someone to scrape aluminium moulds. Go see Yarimizu.' The drop-out kids shrug and get out.

Gondo drives me back into Marumachi and we stop to buy up all the unsold pastries at three different coffee shops, including the Pêche Délice. Gondo explains that he's the town's best customer. There's iced Kopi Luwak and enough cheese croissants, *brioches au bacon* and *pain aux raisins* for the French Foreign Legion. Gondo tells me to take what I want and then puts the rest into the trunk of the car.

At one of the traffic lights, a woman in a yellow reflective vest and matching cap steps out in front of us with a stop sign and ushers a flood of primary school children in pink and blue caps across the road. Gondo sips his coffee and points with half a brioche. 'Japan's their future,' he says proudly, and pushes the rest into his mouth. 'Or is it, they're the future?' His lips actually smack. (Until this moment I had always thought that was just a turn of phrase.) 'That's it. They're the future of Japan,' he says very slowly and clearly, as if practising for a speech. He looks at me. '*Ne?*'

Just then I'm about to take a bite of *pain aux raisins* and somehow manage to inhale the powdered sugar on top. I go into a coughing spasm. Gondo takes this as a comment. 'Something wrong with that?'

'Nothing,' I choke. 'Nothing.'

The woman with the stop sign bows and retreats from the road. 'Good,' he says as we accelerate away. 'Watch the crumbs.'

When we arrive at the racetrack site, we don't get out of the car but recline in our seats and watch the TV with our cold coffee. Most of the channels are showing the same thing: afternoon talk shows with segments for news and cooking, local travel, and the weather. Three tourists shot in Sri Lanka, crab cakes Creole, an old Christian church that's now the first bed-and-breakfast on Hirado Island. Clear skies tomorrow, chance of a light covering of cirrostratus later in the afternoon, high of 36 degrees. Gondo thumbs through the channels on the remote control until he comes to a rerun of the *London Boots* talk show that I saw months ago. SexMachineGuns, my favourites, are playing mini-golf on an Astroturf green shaped like a woman's body: tee-off from her forehead, natural bunkers, a shapely green. Pink golf balls. The lead singer makes a hole in one. The studio audience erupts. The host raises his eyebrows for the extreme close-up and makes a comment about the hours of practice necessary for such good aim. Gondo roars with laughter, but when the group begins a live performance of 'Wash It, Please' he switches stations to a nature programme – red, green, yellow and blue macaws ruling a pristine forest canopy.

He grunts with approval, but I preferred SexMachineGuns. I know without a doubt that glam-rockers exist in the wild; I can't say the same for macaws or beluga whales or red pandas or blue morphos.

Outside, a man dressed in yellow rubber boots, hiking pants and a green checked shirt emerges from a mobile office. Were it not for the drawing board in his hand and a camera around his neck, he might be going fishing.

'So, that's Choso,' Gondo says, pointing with the remote control. 'Head of the archaeological investigation. University of Nagasaki. If everyone would ignore what he says we might get finished before the new year, *ne*? Slow boat academic. Doesn't have any idea of a schedule. Every day is another day's gambling revenue lost.' The macaw show ends and there's a preview of tomorrow's episode, the life of the big crow butterfly. '*Hmph*,' says Gondo dismissively. 'I've seen plenty of those.' He kills the TV. 'Let's go.'

Between where we stand on the plateau and the cluster of spires that is Amsterdam, sprinklers click across a wide plain of freshly turned earth that will soon become the Happy Way Racetrack.

'The bay is a bowl, holding energy,' says Gondo, waxing suddenly geomantic and holding the bay with his outstretched hands. 'This side of the bay comes under the auspice *Toi*. Pregnancy, *ne*? You don't know any Chinese? *Toi* represents optimism and ongoing luck. I had the best feng shui masters from Hong Kong come here last year.'

Yellow bulldozers comb the back straight, a crane lifts Japanese maples and sago palms from a flatbed truck. There's a centrepiece fountain surrounded by copper dolphins and, at the back of the track, two brick towers with white-shingled steeples and rooster weathervanes and, between them, an immense JVC screen. 'Largest of its kind at any racetrack in the whole of Japan,' says Gondo. The grandstand site itself is graded into steps and marked off with white sticks and pink string and the blue tarpaulins weighed down with sandbags.

More drop-out kids like the ones Gondo took to the concrete factory are ferrying buckets of earth away while elderly farmer types, most of them women, do the actual excavating. Gondo stops one of the boys on his way past. He's dressed in a shiny black Adidas sweat suit and his head looks like a piebald fox. He's a thousand miles away with his headphones on and he comes to reality with an obvious jolt. 'Sorry, Mr Gondo!' The sudden deference is a surprise; these kids don't show respect to anyone.

'Something to tell me about?' Gondo asks.

The kid nods to his left. 'At the back,' he says. 'They've found something.'

Most of the workers are in twos or threes, but at the back of the dig, closest to the cedars on the hillside, five or more women are clustered together with Mr Choso watching them closely.

'*Mn*,' Gondo grunts and starts away. 'And where's Shinji?'

'I think he's sick,' the kid replies. Gondo stops and looks over his shoulder. The kid quails. 'Or else, maybe, surfing, Mr

Gondo. Sorry, Mr Gondo. I think maybe he might have gone surfing. In fact, I'm sure of it.'

Gondo grunts again. 'I've no end of jobs for these kids but they don't want to do them. I hate idlers,' he says to me. 'Even gamblers do *something*.' We continue along the grassy edge of the cut earth.

'Something wrong with your legs?' he says to me as I stumble behind on my softball-sized ankles.

I shake my head. 'No problem. I'm fine. Bungee-jumping accident. Forgot the bungee cord.'

Gondo frowns and continues. He shows himself around with perfect ease, stopping to speak with the men and women, always commenting positively on the progress and never once getting someone's name wrong. A pair of women scraping the soil with trowels and piling it into blue plastic buckets straighten up as he approaches. 'Ah, Councillor Gondo, good morning.'

'You look busy,' Gondo says.

Mauve bows in gratitude.

'So we are!' Fuchsia pipes up. 'Busy, busy, busy! May I ask, Councillor Gondo, but you are busy too, Councillor, so busy, but if you have the time, may I ask, forgive me, will it be a good rice crop this year?'

Gondo winces. 'Been a while since anyone asked me that, Mrs Hiraki,' he says slowly.

Fuchsia turns to me. The wrinkled face and haphazard dentistry form a weird contrast to the bright yellow helmet. 'I'll bet you didn't know that Councillor Gondo is an expert when it comes to predicting the rice crop,' she says.

'Really?'

'Oh yes,' Fuchsia continues. 'When he was just the height of that wheelbarrow, Councillor Gondo cut the first stalks in the harvest ceremony and that year was the best harvest ever. Isn't that so, Mrs Kawai?'

Mrs Kawai nods vigorously, smiling to reassure me that it's true.

Gondo laughs a great laugh, probably just to shut Fuchsia the hell up. 'If you must have a prediction then, Mrs Hiraki, it'll be a good one. A harvest to meet someone's best expectations.'

The two women are very impressed. 'Is that *so*,' says Mrs Hiraki, nodding and pressing her lips tight. 'Is that *so*.'

Gondo bows slightly. 'Work hard,' he says in parting.

Of the group at the back, one woman is daubing with a wet sponge at some sort of shattered ceramic embedded in the ground, while the other three clear the soil away from the sides with paintbrushes. Gondo crosses his arms and plants his feet wide.

The excavator looks up from his sketch. His face is narrow and his hands are the size of a child's. He looks at Gondo with something approaching trepidation. 'Good morning, Councillor Gondo.'

'What's this?' Gondo asks, pointing with his cigarette at the shattered ceramic the women are working on.

Mr Choso tilts his head with the faintest indication of a smile. '*Yaaa*,' he sighs. 'It's a burial jar. Yayoi Period.'

Gondo's nose wrinkles. 'What? Mean there are bones in there?'

'Yes, but only tiny fragments. Nothing you would recognize as a human skeleton.'

'Good grief,' Gondo mutters and turns away to fling his cigarette into the grass.

Mr Choso turns to me. 'Hello. I'm Choso.'

'Fujiwara.'

'Oh? A very old family.'

'Yeah,' I say. 'I'm a living national monument.'

He laughs. He's about to say something else but Gondo interrupts him. 'Are there more of them?'

'Oh, there's only one for the moment,' Choso says, looking

back lovingly at the jar, 'but if there are many more, it could be evidence of a settlement much larger than I first predicted.'

'So what does it mean?' Gondo asks.

Mr Choso doesn't seem to understand. '*Mean?* I don't know what it means. What do *you* mean?'

'Is it going to slow down the excavation?'

Mr Choso's eyebrows meet. He tries to smile. 'Councillor, the excavation doesn't slow down or speed up for the sake of an artefact. Our work continues at the same rate be there one artefact or a hundred.'

'A hundred!' Gondo barks, and begins to cough.

Mr Choso puts his notebook down and climbs out of the trench. 'Honestly, Councillor, I'm only making a guess.' Gondo's flanks ripple with the coughs thudding out of him. 'Mr Yokota! Go over to the mobile and get something for Mr Gondo to drink. There's Pocari in the fridge.'

'No, no,' Gondo protests, 'Fine, I'll be fine. *Hrrrgh!*' He coughs into a Burberry handkerchief. 'History's all fine, Choso, but I think you need to understand something about the urgency of this project.' Mr Choso is alarmed by the tone and tries to motion Gondo out of earshot of the women at work in the ditch. 'These workers,' says Gondo, 'they're just farmers, of course, but how do you feel about them?'

'They're excellent, Councillor, by all means,' the excavator replies quickly. 'A farmer is one person who is practically never blasé. I don't know why you should question –'

'I *question*, Choso, because it's *these* people you're messing around with.' I'm impressed. It is not the same Gondo as I heard on the telephone, or speaking to the drop-outs or even to Fuchsia. He sounds like a politician. He's gone from *yak* boss to Uncle Gondo to Councillor Gondo, future politician, in several minutes. 'Marumachi has a big future with developments like this, Choso. You understand? It's *these* people who need Happy Way. It's for them and for their children.

You don't know how important it is, coming from the city. This place used to be a backwater. Now look at it.'

Mr Choso's hands are clenched together and he stares down at them, trying to wring out an earnest answer. 'I understand you, Councillor Gondo, but please consider: if there is an important settlement to be uncovered here – which I'm still doubtful of, I assure you – such a discovery makes the region an even richer place. Look what they've done up in Yoshinogari, they've turned their discoveries into an attraction.'

'*Attraction?*' Gondo begins to heave as if the coughing attack's returning. 'Some spearheads and busted pots amount to an attraction? Two hundred yen entrance and a country craft fair selling home-made pickles?' Mid-cough he pulls out his cigarettes and sets about lighting one. 'Business not your area of expertise, *ne*? Where's that Pocari?' Mr Choso makes a gesture as if to lead the councillor to the mobile office but Gondo refuses. 'No, no, Choso, continue as you were. *Hrrrgh*,' he clears his throat. 'I'll sort this out myself.'

Gondo drives me to the station. I want to fall asleep in my drowsily undulating seat, but after several minutes he barks at me: 'So?'

So? I sit up. So what? 'Um, nice track,' I say.

'Nice track, sure, but I still need an idea for a new city. I can take care of the sex and gambling, *ne*? That's easy. But what about the broad demographic? I need families and old folks and twenty-five- to forty-year-old single females. So you tell me, Mr Kyoto University, what's the future?'

Why he thinks I should have any clearer idea of this, I have no idea. Does he think there's a 'White Elephants 100' component of my syllabus? Like we go on field trips to DisneySea or Mount Rushmore Tochigi? I read the articles in the papers about the declining fortunes of theme parks with the same morbid disinterest as everyone else. I certainly have never considered what to *do* about the problem. If such it is. It wouldn't matter to me if they all went belly-up tomorrow. But this is not exactly what Gondo wants to hear. I try to buy some time by repeating what he's already said: 'The India idea is a good one, but climate poses a problem.'

He takes the cigarette out of his mouth and stares at me like I'm an idiot.

'So. Brand recognition. Something everyone already *knows*, but *can't* actually *have*. Or at least, not *cheaply*. Or *easily*' – I stress the words like I'm speaking some very abstruse legalese. 'Something they're *familiar* with. Something they're previously *acquainted* with in some form. Something they're *comfortable* with. Or would be *comfortable* with if they only had it.'

He has not taken a drag in, oh, easily a minute. We're flying down the Marumachi bypass but he's looking dead straight at me, very annoyed.

'So the answer is . . .' I say.

'Go ahead.'

'The answer is . . . you'll be pleased with this . . .'

'So?'

'So the answer is . . .'

Across the rice fields, the top of the red *torii* gate I saw earlier peeks above the rooftops of Marumachi. And I think: *Japan.* This is brilliant! This is genius! Japan! Not the ugly cramped bureaucratic well-mannered nightmare you and I have to live in day to day, but the one you see in your mind's eye, the one in carefully cropped or staged photographs, the one you'd try to show a tourist.

'Japan,' I say.

Gondo's head tilts to one side. He rubs his neck. 'Explain.'

'Well, everyone's got this idea of what Japan is, right? But where is it? It's all . . . it's all kind of mixed up now, you know?' The idea is so eloquent, why can't I express it? 'What

I mean is, it's an exotic setting, but everyone's already familiar with it too.'

He repeats my words with dry humour, only without the humour. 'It's-all-mixed-up.'

'Um. Yeah.'

'And that's your *learned* insight: "It's all mixed up." You're proposing that I charge people 10,000 yen to visit a place where they, in fact, already live.' His chin juts out. His upper lip is poised to snarl. I am not, apparently, a genius after all.

'Well, the idea's fresh. It's still . . . germinating.' I point ahead. 'That . . . that's the turn-off for the station, I think.'

We pull into Marumachi Station. He stops the car, cranks the three-on-the-tree to Park and turns to me, speaking very slowly, very succinctly, so I won't miss the drift. 'It makes me fearful that this idiotic idea of yours is the product of a top university education. I thought I was being kind to you for a good reason. I was plainly mistaken.' He presses a button on the console and my door pops open.

I'm supposed to get out of the car obviously, but I haven't even brought up the object of my whole enterprise. It is not the ideal moment to bring it up, but there never will be one. 'Actually, Mr Gondo,' I stammer, 'before I leave, I was wondering if I could have another word about my sister, Mai? I take it she's an employee of yours?'

Both wrists lie on top of the wheel, his hands hanging limp. He sighs, clearly irritated by my continued presence. 'Mai is a good worker. So the answer is no, we can't talk about her.'

'But she's got money,' I tell him. 'Whatever her debt is to you, if you just let her come with me, she'll be able to pay it off.'

'Don't care what kind of money she has,' he replies. 'I let her sing on the side as it is. She has a valued clientele. I value them, they value her. It's a matter of hospitality, not money. You're being a good brother. I respect that.' He puts the gear lever to Drive. 'Don't worry, *ne*? I'll put her back on the straight and narrow the day she turns thirty.'

I'm still half in the car, but he floors it and I have to side-step away to avoid being crushed by the rear wheels.

hibiki

My rucksack is lying on the front desk of the Nishiki next to a large brown paper bag and a ball of white string. Mrs Nishiki hears the door rattle open and shut and emerges from the mysterious nether regions of the house carrying a pair of old black scissors and some tape. She stops dead. 'Ah, Mr Fujiwara,' she says in surprise, then blushes with obvious embarrassment. She indicates my rucksack with both hands. 'These . . . these are your things. Please take them.'

I do as she asks. 'Can I go up to my room?'

'Ahh. The room.' She opens the book in which she makes the reservations and goes to the elaborate length of scanning down the list. 'I'm very sorry, Mr Fujiwara. We have no vacancy for tonight.'

'But I never checked out.'

'Oh. That's right. That's so.' She's practically hiding behind the desk now. She's one of those people who simply can't come up with an expedient lie when it's necessary. I actually feel sorry for her.

'Let me guess. Someone called to say I wouldn't be coming back?'

She looks up and then bows to me several times over. 'So. That's it. Yes. I wasn't expecting you to return.'

'And now you've promised my room to someone else. And the inn is otherwise full.' (The Nishiki Inn is empty and echoes like a cave.)

She grabs at my every generous word. 'Yes. Yes. I'm so very sorry. Promised the room to someone else.'

'A-ha. In which case, I don't suppose you could recommend me another place to stay?'

The 210 highway is tortuous and narrow. Large convex mirrors on orange poles adorn each bend in the road and the bus driver has to brake and accelerate constantly. On his creaking spring-loaded seat, he takes the precipitous corners with the casual insouciance of a character from Dr Seuss. At times he slams the bus to a complete halt as a car coming in the opposite direction reverses to give the bus enough room to make a tight corner. Then the engine starts hammering away again and we speed out from the cedars onto viaducts of dazzling white concrete or bypasses with concrete honeycombs sloping up the denuded hills on either side. From a spectacular suspension bridge that looks as if it's been misplaced from Yokohama Bay, I can see Nakadori Island far out to sea and, to the left, the scalloped coast that leads to the grassy slopes and white lighthouse of Cape Satori, now glowing pink in the setting sun.

Twenty-five minutes up the coast, a stark, black, high-rise broods at the end of a wide bay. The bus driver soon pulls up onto the gravel and, according to Mrs Nishiki's instructions, I get out. Unless I could afford to pay Amsterdam prices, she said, the only option was the Hibiki. 'I've heard it's quite nice,' she said.

Two teenage employees of Amsterdam's Oranje Burger, wearing bright-orange uniforms smudged here and there with grease, and the smell of fried meat on them something terrible, lead me up to the hotel. The driveway's blocked by yellow and black barrels full of sand so we walk down a narrow gravel lane through a glade of bamboo. They tell me a little about the Hibiki. Officially it closed years ago, but it's since become a squat for anyone who can't afford the rent over in Marumachi. A lot of surfers stay here too during the summer. It's not the Taj Mahal, but the rooms are fairly clean and electricity's free.

When we come into the open, it is at one edge of a huge overgrown lawn planted here and there with sago palms and a giant kind of aloe. The Hibiki Hotel looms before us.

'Quite nice' doesn't exactly describe it. It doesn't even *vaguely* describe it. 'Quite vast, concrete and wrecked' comes closer. It might have been an elegant and imposing resort at

one time, but now the concrete is discoloured, the fire escapes are rusted, the dining room above the porte-cochere has most of its windows knocked out (and reminds me of a bucktoothed Chinese character in an old cartoon). I could probably go on at length, but these snapshots I took do the place a kind of vigilante justice.

I follow the Oranje kids into an old service corridor by a rear doorway. Just inside, there's a corkboard covered in pegs and keys, a white wooden box on the wall with a slot in the side, a notepad and some envelopes. I have to write my name and place of work on the paper (I put MOC on the line) and put it in an envelope with 500 yen per day plus 1000 yen deposit for the sheets.

'You got your choice, man,' one of the kids says, pointing at the board.

It's divided in half, with blue keys on the right for boys and pink ones on the left for girls. Each of the rooms is named after a flower or tree: Peach, Wisteria, Hydrangea, Anthurium, Cherry, Camellia, Hibiscus. I take one of the keys to Anthurium and follow the kids deeper into a shadow world of foyers and corridors lined with outdated video games, drink machines and candy dispensers. How many times did I drink Lassi Milk when I was a kid? I don't remember when it disappeared but I haven't seen that little blue elephant in ages. Same for Sugus fruit chews, Haw Flakes, Vessel in the Mist chocolate.

We come out of the corridor into a stadium-like lobby. There's a white mezzanine and the hulking presence of a mod bronze or copper chandelier silhouetted against the tall arched windows. The windows are all smashed out and deep blue acrylic curtains are torn and ragged, flapping back now and again to reveal their sun-bleached reverse. The rings on the curtain rods click and the wind hums like a special effect for a ghost town in a western.

On the curving staircase to the mezzanine the wet carpet squelches beneath our feet. The roof of the porte cochere is almost entirely caved in. Piles of charred furniture and old appliances cover the floor, waterlogged or rusted beyond all recognition. I follow the trail through the junk and we enter another corridor on the far side. From what I can understand of the hotel's geography, this one leads to the back of the hotel. With windows along one side it's brighter here than the nether regions of the hotel and the smell of the old *washi* paper window screens is, oddly enough, vaguely comforting, reminiscent of Inaka. The two Oranje kids direct me down the hall and take their leave at Peach. On my way past, I find the door to Cherry open and can't help but take a peek inside. In one corner a large girl in sunglasses is sitting on a futon playing *Ico* for PlayStation on a huge TV. She may be totally engrossed in what she's doing but the only sign of life is in her thumbs. Another girl is lying on a futon facing the blushing windows, reading from what looks like an English-language exercise book. She's leaning her head on one elbow, the neck of her T-shirt open across her shoulder to reveal a slender mauve bra strap. Even from this vantage point, I can see that she has Kasane's clavicles and her sex appeal (which may as well be the same thing).

She looks up.

`Error. A fatal error has occurred.`

The Kasane Scale – the pop-up on the screen of my vision – is not functioning. The girl *is* Kasane.

Or could be.

I stand there dumb, waiting for her to speak, waiting for her to commit herself to her identity with a word, a flick of her hair, a languid blink.

'Hello,' she says, not challenging, just inquisitive. 'Are you looking for someone?'

Yes! Someone *very* much like you.

'Oh, no, not really,' I mumbulate. 'I'm just . . . I'm going . . . I'm staying here for a while. In Anthurium.'

She nods and turns back to her book. My heart sinks. What did you expect her to do, Aozora, leap for joy? 'Well then . . .' I make a vague hand movement that in my confused head is meant to facilitate an elegant and friendly parting, murmur something unintelligible and shuffle down the corridor muttering, 'She is. No, she's not. She could be. She possibly is. But probably isn't.'

Anthurium is a two-room suite with tatami floors and floor-to-ceiling glass doors onto a balcony that gives a magnificent view of the bay. There are four futons on the floor, all of them vacant. I drop my tired body onto the one with the least evidence of a recent orgy and/or bludgeoning.

She can't be Kasane because . . . I don't know why. Because she didn't recognize me. *She didn't recognize me.* Now, finally, the multicoloured bar graph of the Kasane Scale appears before me, climbing, climbing, climbing through the spectrum . . .

My heart wants to give her a 10 on the scale, but my rational self can't allow it. I limit her to a 7.5; the intensity of my present emotions has not been supported by my typically close scrutiny. How can she possibly merit a 10? Have I seen her walk? Have I heard her laugh? Have I smelled her hair, her breath? Have I watched her roll *kappamaki* without once getting a grain of rice stuck to her fingers? Have I watched her play designated spiker in the Kyoto Collegiate Volleyball Championship, in sleeveless shirt and those shorts, slamming the ball down with all the grace and violence of a samurai lopping off his master's head? Have I been destroyed by her in chess? Have I seen how her lips subside inwardly, closing around my fingertip as if it were the beginning of a process that would see her whole body curl into an armadillo-like ball? Have I seen her naked, kneeling above me, easing herself down, her mouth opening like a pink galaxy for the Aozorium Falcon?

Enough. Enough! For now, 7.5 is enough.

joyfull

The following morning I catch the 210 further up the coast.
The next stop is Shirahama Beach, the only place to get food
without going back into Marumachi or Amsterdam.

My mobile phone rings. I recognize the number right away.
I put on a cheery voice. 'Hi, Ishikawa. I was just thinking of
calling you. I'm wondering what kind of card Mr Uno might
like.' I know this is doing me no good whatsoever. I'm perfectly aware that just keeping my mouth closed is the wise
option, but the temptation to be a smart-ass is just too great.
'Do you think he'd prefer a Hallmark card, or something more
traditional?'

'Huh. Yeah, you're really funny on the phone. I can't wait
to meet you in person.'

Suddenly the nasal public-service voice on the overhead
speakers announces: *'The next stop is Shirahama Beach.
Shirahama Beach. Shirahama Beach, if you please.'*

I snap the phone shut. Damn! Could Ishikawa have heard
that? Does it matter? How many Shirahamas are there in this
country? Probably hundreds. Still, if I wasn't already squirm-
ing like a *tanuki* in a trap, yeah?, I am now.

'Shirahama Beach, if you please,' says the voice again, and
goes on to explain that there have been many deaths by
drowning in the prefecture. *'If you are tired,'* the voice
advises, *'please rest before entering the water. If you are
drowning, please call for help.'*

I press the red STOP button on the pole.

Shirahama Beach is one row of tumbledown houses, a gas

station, a 7-Eleven, and a spic-and-span outpost of the Joyfull Family Restaurant chain. I take a bright-orange booth near the door and order the Joyfull Breakfast: omelette with rice, pancakes with maple syrup, sausages and unlimited coffee. Which is terrible, cheap Vietnamese coffee that's been quick-brewed and left in an aluminium pot for hours. I have to ladle in the sugar to kill the metallic taste. The waitress in her brown uniform arrives with my breakfast seconds after I've ordered it.

'Is this bacon really Canadian?' I ask. (Though my body aches, I'm feeling perky.)

'I'm sorry?'

'Never mind.'

The omelette is undercooked, the rice underneath all gooey with egg white. Still, I gobble it down. As I'm attacking the pancakes, I hear the whine of motorcycle engines from the highway. It grows louder and louder until a bling Toyota station wagon followed by twelve members of a *bosozoku* speed tribe swarm into the parking lot like a bunch of movieland Red Indians. The bikes are standard *bosozoku* – deep purple or metallic red, with café racer fairings lifted on steel poles a metre or more above the engines, the riders peering out from beneath the headlights. Almost none of the tribe are wearing helmets; those few who do have them, wear them on their elbows. They're all dressed in shredded jeans or overalls and their hair's dyed blond, old gold or chestnut brown. They park in the handicapped spots and come in through the doors spewing really bright adjectives for such a calm blue morning. I recognize several of them from Choso's dig site.

I go to cut myself a wedge of pancake and when I look up again she's there – the 7.5K from the Hibiki. It takes me by surprise because I would never have guessed that she could hang with such a crowd. She doesn't look like one of the other speed tribe girls (i.e. no tartan miniskirt or shredded

Levi's jacket). She looks like she shops at the Gap. Her one concession to her companions' sense of style, it seems, is a tiny silver skull around her neck. Probably a gift. What's worse than the general company she keeps, she's holding hands with the guy I ran into in the tetrapods with the towering green Mohawk. They sit down in the next booth. They're obviously a couple, though I'm happy to see that she's not demonstrably affectionate with the guy in any way. She sits crossways on the bench seat with her knees up: Kasane's habitual posture (though the cigarettes she takes from her purse cost her something on the scale: Kasane hated cigarettes).

Mohawk, meanwhile, not a minute after he's arrived, decides to animate the regular proceedings of a Joyfull morning routine.

He stands on the table. From under his leather jacket he pulls a huge silver handgun and trains it on the waitress coming down the aisle. '*Anybody moves and I blow away every last one of ya!*' he screams out in English. '*Boom! Down! Boom! Down!*' The accent and tone are perfect – pure vehemence. He must have practised it in front of the television for ages.

The rest of the tribe go crazy. They're all banging on the tables, whooping up and down, yelling, '*Yeah! More! Freeze! Make my day! Boom! Down! Boom! Down!*'

The waitress hesitates only momentarily before walking past with perfect disdain, shaking her head. (Do they do this all the time?) The tribe are all on their feet, chanting, '*Boom! Down! Boom! Down!*'

'*Boom, boom, boom!*' Mohawk cackles with laughter and slumps into his seat. He slams the handgun flat on the table and looks around at his friends, deeply satisfied. The tribe slowly returns to tribal calm, each of them taking turns admiring the gun, blowing their friends away, the hammer mechanism going *click, click, click.*

'Sweet piece, man!'

'Deadly iron.'

'Full chrome Sword,' Mohawk explains. 'Romeo and Juliet official replica.' He points out the engraving on the butt and barrel.

The girl digs in her handbag and checks the messages on her phone. She looks up, deep in thought, and stares straight at me. After a moment she blinks and recognizes me. Smiles. Rolls her eyes when Mohawk starts shrieking like a Mohawk again.

My pancakes are finished long before they leave, but I stay there drinking the liquid rust because I can't bear to leave before she does. She doesn't fit with the *bosozoku* and I'm wondering how she found her way into this crowd. When they all finally get up to leave en masse, I sit very patiently for nine seconds before following them out.

Just next to the Joyfull, where the 210 meets the coastline at a bamboo glade, is a parking lot surrounded by banana palms, a row of concrete toilets and a billboard advertising local blowfish. Dozens of surfers are gearing up: grommets, softies, Bettys, highballers with their guns, Hang-Tens with their eggs. (I know the lingo. The sport's got cachet for picking up a certain kind of girl.) Meanwhile, the speed tribe mill around the parking lot, checking out each other's machines. Mohawk and the 7.5K are pulling surfboards and wetsuits out of the bling Toyota wagon. The entire car is pure white except for these soulful words in English stencilled on the side.

SOUL

We are Mellowguys who were
Born and grew up in this hood.
Our pride is always withus.
We are Passing through the
Narrow load in Japan with
Righton hip hop. I love the Pride.

149

I'd like to walk up to Mohawk and say, 'Shakespeare?' but I only go as close as possible without posing a threat. Mohawk takes a dismissive glance at me, but the girl's eyes are steady enough to fillip my already throbbing heart.

From the highway, a narrow path leads down through the bamboo. It's perfectly straight, well worn, and passes through a concrete tunnel, past some empty concessions, to a wide and surprisingly busy beach. Close to the water, the wet sand is bevelled like fancy glass. Happy waves rush to the end of their leashes. Thirty or more surfers are bobbing up and down beyond the break or paddling down the waves like salamanders in a frying pan.

I'm sitting on the sand watching them when she passes by with a boogie board under her arm. I'm instantly drawn by the red bikini.

Red? No. It's not really red. Or pink either. What is it? It's not lilac and it's certainly not purple or hot pink. Fuchsia? Magenta? Burgundy?

Burgundy is the word. This distinction is important, because it is not a cute colour. Kasane was *never* knowingly cute. There are no flowers or pretty patterns on this bikini. The material is sheer and shiny and the colour is feminine and intense and regal and numinous with an unsettlingly sexy suggestion of blood.

She walks past me with another girl (pink-and-black one-piece, 4K at a glance) and I can hear Mohawk coming along behind, talking surf with someone else. The girls stop to attach the Velcro bands around their wrists before wading into the white water. She merits every point on the scale, and progresses with every instant of my scrutiny. The ever so slight bunching of her flesh behind her arms when she bends over. That vulnerable hollow of her cleavage. The curvature of her lower back. The rondure of her ass (what word will ever be elegant enough to do these orbs some poetic justice?).

The concave line along her spine that begins between her shoulder blades, deepens as my eyes descend, and feathers out where my eyes must stop at the cruel elastic of her bottoms. And here, just here, is a telling feature. Just where the lower back becomes her bum – at the soft nadir of this inward curve – is a fuzz of black hair spreading out several inches to either side of her spine. It could be mistaken for a very faint tattoo if you didn't know better or weren't looking closely, a broad fleur-de-lys or the sword-like wings of a descending swift. According to the criteria of the Kasane Scale, this feature is very desirable, yet it is not one much prized in a more widespread aesthetic of the female. To make my point clear, how many models, actresses or sportswomen do you see with hairy backs? I'm not touting the universality of the scale. As undesirable a feature as the 7.5's coconut fuzz may be to the general public, it gives me a hot frisson like the onset of heatstroke. The girl disappears into the surf and reappears again at speed, careening down the slope of a wave only to disappear into the white water again. The current carries her and her friend down the beach. When she emerges glistening from the water in an hour's time, Mohawk is leading the way and I have to watch her leave the beach from afar.

nami

I'm forced to wait another day, but eventually the girl comes
to me. I'm lying on my bed, trying to broker a deal between my
coccyx, my still-rattling ribcage and my ankles, brainstorming

ideas for rescuing Mai, when she appears at my door. She
leans against the doorframe with her exercise book open in
front of her. 'Do you speak any English?' she asks.

'Um, sure' – getting up from the futon – 'I used to study it,
sort of. And I went to Manitoba for eight months when I was
twelve. *How's it goin', eh?*'

'Manitoba? I thought that was a kind of dolphin.'

I am dumbstruck. She has Kasane's knowledge of geography

too. She flips a couple of pages through her book. 'What's the difference between *lighted* and *lit*?'

'A-ha . . .' I say. Apparently we're beyond *This is a pen.* 'Is it going to affect our relationship if I tell you I have no idea whatsoever?'

She frowns. But pleasantly. In that way she always had – that way *Kasane* always had when it looked as if she was evaluating me, putting files away for future reference. 'Not in a bad way, I suppose.' She stands there staring at me still. 'I'm Nami.'

'Aozora.'

Silence. Right. Now that we have that much accomplished . . . I'm about to question her on her English when she says: 'Want to see some frogs?'

Yes! With you, anything! Pond frogs. Tree frogs. Desert frogs. Poisonous frogs. Gigantic red man-eating frogs. Name an amphibian.

Poolside at the Hibiki is not what it used to be. I imagine there were once myriad bottles arranged behind the bar and a field of umbrellas leaning at haphazard angles like so many giant wilting poppies. Cinzano (red and green), Orangina (orange and blue), Marlboro (red and white), Matsuya (green and white). There were Adirondack chairs and patio sets, and the lifeguard's chair featured bronze statuary in morning and afternoon showings. A luminous swathe of turquoise water went into choppy fits with children's laughter. But where there were concrete pineapples there are now bent stubs of re-bar sprouting from chipped pedestals. The pool is an olive-green mass of algae; tiny frogs live on islands of woolly green scum. And the sporadic traffic on the 210 only hems in the silence.

She lies down on her front and I sit down next to her at the water's edge. She's wearing a crocheted cream blouse with a see-through lace back. Her thick white bra strap stretches and retracts with her breath, the catches at the centre easing away from her skin when she exhales. On her upper left arm: the shiny pink roundel of a wonderfully successful vaccination – it's a tiny wound, a tiny chemical burn that I would kiss better if only there weren't small talk to get through.

'Good pancakes?' she asks.

'Can't say it was a *joyful* experience,' I reply, and toss a chunk of concrete into the pool. 'Watching your boyfriend was certainly entertaining though.'

She covers her eyes and shakes her head. 'I'm not sure if boyfriend is the right word.'

'Oh?' I'm hoping for an explanation, but she's not ready to give it. 'What's his name?' I ask.

'Shinji.'

'And what does Shinji do?'

'This and that.'

She's not exactly forthcoming. I turn away. I want her to think I think she doesn't trust me. (This moment when the girl weighs her own reserve against the possibility of damaging my sensitive feelings is always a crux.) I toss another desultory rock.

'We're both from Miyazaki,' she says.

I grin, then turn to her with my 'I'm a good listener' face.

And she tells me about their common past, together since they were fifteen. They came to the Hibiki over a year ago because Shinji was in 'some kind of trouble' in Kumamoto. They were supposed to get away from 'all that', but it hasn't been a great success. Nothing much has changed.

She pokes at the algae with a stick. Shinji's working for the *yakuza* these days, doing who knows what. Otherwise he just surfs and smokes weed.

Once she's begun, Nami doesn't seem at all inhibited telling me about her past. I imagine what I might represent to her – a thoughtful and sensitive 'kindred soul', so unlike the macho children of her current crowd. I'm rather pleased by this; it's not my usual self-image. She's working in Marumachi herself, she says, but wants to become a flight attendant. She has an English exam in a week.

I am inept enough to ask what she does for a living.

'Dance. Serve drinks. You know, right?' She looks up at me quizzically. 'Or maybe you don't.'

I do. 'I don't think I do,' I reply.

She smiles. 'Right answer. Though I don't believe you.' She tucks her hair behind her right ear and I want to volunteer to do the other side. 'I do lap-dancing and hostessing at the G-Spot.' She looks for a reaction but I'm deadpan about it. You can't get judgemental this early on. 'And what are *you* doing here?' she asks. 'You don't look like the usual type to come live in the Hibiki.'

I'm about to fabricate my own honest-sounding reasons for being there, when we hear the whine of motorcycles coming from the 210. It's strangely melodious from a distance, warbling like violins, but growing more and more clangorous as they approach.

'That'll be Shinji and his crowd,' she says.

From the pool we can see across the lawns in front of the Hibiki. The speed tribe comes swarming up between the aloes with the white Toyota behind. Shinji emerges from the car – green Mohawk, red leather jacket, purple clamdigger shorts. He's got a burlap sack over his shoulder and is walking with a definite swagger, like a hunter who's bagged game. When he comes down the steps to the pool, Nami gets up and introduces us. I'm a little worried he's not going to take kindly to me, but he just grunts and continues on his way to the cove and its perfect crescent beach.

'What's up?' I ask.

Nami shrugs. 'He did something for Mr Gondo last night, that's all I know. You know who Mr Gondo is?'

I don't want to admit to this; it's clear from her expression what she thinks of Gondo. 'I've heard of him,' I say.

'He's *yakuza*,' she says. 'He owns most of Marumachi.'

We walk along the edge of the pool terrace to where it overlooks the beach. Shinji's next to the water. He drops the sack on the sand, unties the knot at the top and reaches inside. I'm expecting it to be full of hashish or stolen watches, but instead, he pulls out what looks like a terracotta tile. Strange though, it's not in the least symmetrical. He turns to the cove and flings it in a long Frisbee-like arc. Then another and another.

Nami turns away. 'Don't ask me,' she says.

I don't have to. I recognize those shards of ceramic pottery. Burial jars. Yayoi Period. Evidence of a settlement. A vision of Mr Choso surrounded in a halo of afternoon light appears. For his utter devotion to a trifle and his steadfast belief in the value of both the esoteric and the common good, he's the kind of guy my father would refer to as 'a good Japanese'. I stand by watching as months of his labour gets destroyed.

When he's thrown all the large pieces in, Shinji dumps the remaining shards onto the sand and kicks them away.

Nami calls to me from the other side of the pool. 'I've got studying to do. See you later?'

Once Shinji is gone, I go down to the beach myself. The sack is slowly soaking through and sinking into the shallows. There's some reddish dust left where he dumped it on the sand, but the largest of the fragments is only a few centimetres across. Still, I gather what I can and pocket it.

mr choso

If I were organized and assiduous enough to keep a regular diary, here's what I'd write for Wednesday, the 22nd of August:

Still don't have a plan. Mr Ishikawa, acting on behalf of Mr Uno, yeah?, has called three times now. Think they might be trying to trace my phone. Is this possible? Can mobile phones be traced? Could they pinpoint my location using the cellular network and some high-tech GPS system? I can just imagine Mr Uno on the phone to Mr Ishikawa: Call in an airstrike!

At least Nami and I are on. Definitely ON! She's free for the party tomorrow night, a once-a-month bacchanalia for all the local low-life. She made a special point of telling me she'll be there. Yes, Aozora, you are soon to witness an apotheosis. There can be no doubt – once her clothes are off, she will attain a perfect 10 on the scale. She will become Kasane.

Hold it. Stop this foolishness. Am I so feeble-minded as to think that this relationship by proxy will bring me any lasting satisfaction?

No. But, at the very least, for the four minutes I normally last, I will be one with Kasane again. My penis will enter a parallel universe. Time's essence will dissipate and disappear. Instead, I will close my eyes and breathe Kasane's eternal perfume –

Stop again. Stay focused. Money and death, both mine, are presently at issue. How in hell do I get Mai out of Amsterdam?

The tunnels that Skull and Tiger so courteously guided me through are the obvious escape route. All I really need is a ballpoint pen to pop the wiring on the first set of doors and a chisel or crowbar for the final set that gives onto the bridge. But this plan is not without a daunting set of possible glitches. What if Mai gets tailed after her show? How do I know my fingerless friends aren't still waiting for prey down in the guts of Amsterdam? Ideally, once we're out, we'll catch the 210 bus north, all the way to Karatsu, and from there a train to Hakata. But from the exit near the bridge on the hillside, we'll have to trek through the forest to get to a bus stop. Considering my sister's love of hiking and her probable choice of footwear, it'll take us all day. And how long before Gondo notices she's missing? The more I think about it, the more I think I need a back-up plan. I need to get into Amsterdam to do some serious reconnaissance, but this brings up another problem: how do I get in there in the first place? Not only is there no simple way *out*, there's no simple way *in*. That couple will be haunting around. At best they'll deny me entry at Arrivaldam. At worst, Skull and Tiger will show up and drag me back to the bridge for a second narrowly death-defying leap.

I am loath to admit this, but what I need is some help. With the Yayoi fragments stuffed in my pockets, I set off for the Happy Way.

The yellow bulldozers are still snorting and chuffing, and the fountain with its copper dolphins and flowerbeds is almost complete. Three men in blue overalls are adjusting the water jets; every now and again they retreat behind the dolphins and four nine-metre spurts go off at wild angles. The archaeological dig site, however, is empty. A new addition to the pink string and blue tarpaulins is a section near the back squared off with yellow-and-black police tape that swings in the light breeze. With some trepidation, I go up the stairs to knock at the yellow door of the mobile office.

'Mr Choso?' I lean over the railing to look through the window into the shadowy room. 'Mr Choso?'

There's no response.

'Mr Choso, it's Fujiwara. Remember? With the blood of old Japan in his veins? A living national monument?'

The door flies open. Choso has one hand on the doorknob, the other on the doorframe, and he's staring at me like Superman cutting solid steel with his laser eyes. Every atom in his body is quivering with anger. 'You came here with Gondo,' he says.

I do the quick nod/bow that means 'affirmative' (thirty degrees short of the forty-five-degree manoeuvre that demonstrates great respect and which I have not once accomplished in my entire life). And I suddenly realize why he's so upset. He thinks *I'm* the one who took his jar. It's a natural assumption: a stranger shows up with Gondo one day, the jar goes missing the next. I'm blind not to have seen this coming. 'It wasn't me,' I blurt out.

He's unmoved.

'But I know who. That's why I came.' I take one of the shards from my pocket and hold it out to him. He practically leaps at it. He grabs my wrist and plucks the shard up, then goes scurrying back inside to get his glasses.

The mobile office is in a state of total disarray. (I recognize similar handiwork to that which took my room at the university residence apart.) Choso's standing at the window, holding the shard up to the light. 'Is this all you have?'

I empty my pocket onto the table beneath a giant site map that's covered with string and pins and multicoloured notes. Choso examines each piece, one by one, and finally turns to me with a sigh. 'Coffee?'

He stands over the steaming electric kettle and spoons Nescafé into two chipped mugs, brings me the new orange-

and-white Yomiuri Giants one and takes an old, cracked Ski Furano one to a chair by the window. The coffee is deep black, with a brownish sludge of undissolved Nescafé at the lip. I take a brave sip and put it on the desk. 'Gondo did it.'

'*Pah.* I guessed that much already,' he replies.

'It was one of his minions. A guy named Shinji with a green Mohawk.'

He digests this information a moment. 'What's a Mohawk?'

'Spiky hair.'

'Where is the jar now?'

'Bottom of Komura Bay.'

He leans forward on the chair with his hands on his thighs and rocks back and forth. He gets up and stands at the window, looking out at the dig site. 'You saw the tape? The police put it there. It's what they call a crime-scene investigation. *Investigation.* They don't know the meaning of the word. This Shinji with the green hair, he tried to cover up his tracks by breaking the dyke just above the site so the creek ran in and filled up the trench. He thought he was being subtle. Like anyone would believe the creek broke its bank by itself and washed the jar away.' He laughs bitterly. 'I've been looking at cuts in the soil for fifteen years; I could probably tell you what kind of spade he used. But the police didn't want to know. I offered them my help but they said they'd *take care* of it.' He's gripping the mug tight enough to break it. 'I showed them the office. They said they'd send for a fingerprint specialist, but I've yet to hear back from them.' He picks up an empty red filing sheath that was once full of drawings and photographs. Tosses it in the trash.

'I know where the rest of the pieces are,' I say. 'They're not far offshore. I could tell you where.'

He looks at me and smiles. 'Marine archaeology?'

'But I need your help first,' I say. 'I need to know how to get in and out of Amsterdam.'

He listens to my whole crazy story with perfect seriousness, then sits in silence for a while. He spears me with a question. 'Can't you just call the police and get them to free her?'

'The same police who did such an effective investigation here?' I reply.

'Of course, of course. How stupid of me. What about the police in Nagasaki or Kumamoto?'

'Not their jurisdiction. They'd just contact the police in Marumachi.'

He leans back in his chair with his cup of coffee. He blinks a lot, which makes him look especially humble and simpleminded, but I know he's thinking. 'I've never been to Amsterdam,' he says. 'I was thinking about pulling some weeds tomorrow, but I could take the day off.'

mr choso's excellent experiment

So the next morning Choso and I are having breakfast on the steps of the mobile office, looking out across the city that he will soon be entering as a spy.

'Impressive, isn't it?' he says to me.

I'm surprised he feels this way. 'I didn't think you'd be the type to be impressed by Amsterdam. I thought you'd be disgusted.'

'Not at all. But perhaps I see it differently than most. Whenever I come across a large building or development, all that really interests me is its potential for a ruin. I see that' – he opens his arms to the vista in front of us – 'and I think: What a period! I envy the men who will excavate it.'

'All I see is a prison,' I tell him.

'Well. Yes.' He takes a deep breath. '*Yosh!* To work!'

I can see he's nervous as hell. I have to remind him that he's not doing anything illegal. He's just going to look at the sights, take in a show, eat a greasy meal, just like a million other tourists every year. A ride in a balloon, a tour around a clean and modern city, some authentic imported products for souvenirs: such luxuries are the pay-off for years of selfless devotion, no? With your smart shirt and your cap and your camera, you'll fit right in.

'Yes, of course. Yes, of course,' he says, but when he climbs aboard his moped, the sweat's still popping in fully formed drops out of his forehead.

*

'So Fujiwara. It's Ishikawa, yeah?'

Everyone should have an Ishikawa. I'm getting used to receiving his threatening calls. He's like my very own memento mori. And this gives me an idea. A potential money-maker? It's a little electronic skull about the size of a Tamagotchi that you could hang around your neck. At unexpected moments, the eye sockets would start flashing red and a piercing, synthesized Ishikawa-voice would screech: *Death is at hand!* Or *You can't escape!* I can just see myself sitting in a quiet boardroom, or necking with a girl in the back of a car, or sleeping on the beach and suddenly being jolted back to consciousness of my mortality by Ishikawa's cackling. Since he's started calling me, I feel like I'm living life to the fullest.

Anyway.

'Yes, I know who you are,' I reply.

'Good, yeah. So, like, I'm calling to tell you that Mr Uno is just amazing. He's an amazing man.'

'Yeah. Sure. Sure, he's amazing.'

'No, listen. I think we should just find you and hurt you, yeah? But Mr Uno, he's like, no, let's just get the money. Life's too short to waste time on scum like Fujiwara. *Was that it?* Right. So here it is. You get the money into this bank account, listen, yeah? Daiwa Kyoto 4674523. Did you get that? You get the 12 million in there by Tuesday, yeah? And for that little bit of – *What did you say?* – overdue courtesy, Mr Uno forgets what happened to his eyebrow.'

Wow. I'm surprised. I wasn't expecting amnesty, but if it's being offered, I'll take it.

Suddenly it's Mr Uno yelling down the line: '*But if I ever see you again, Fujiwara, I will kill you, you hear me?!*'

'Yeah, yeah. Never again. Twelve million ye—'

'Twelve million yen. Daiwa 4674523, you got it?'

'By heart, Mr Uno. By heart. And I really am sor—'

The line goes dead.

I was going to wait for Mr Choso in his mobile office, but by ten o'clock it's far too hot to stay inside. I take the 210 bus back up the coast to Shirahama. Nami's not around, so I decide to go for a therapeutic swim. For the first time since I put the light bulb into Mr Uno's eye, I'm feeling like I might actually have a future. The current on the surfing beach is too strong so I walk around the point to a small island lying just offshore. It's low tide and the island is connected to the beach by a slender bridge of sand. On the other side of the island is a small cove protected by a reef. I drop my things and dive in. It's the first time I've had any exercise in weeks and I tire quickly. I take a nap on the sand. By the time I wake up and get back to the other side of the island, the tide has come in between the island and the mainland. I'm standing there wondering if I'll have to swim across with my clothes on my head when I notice someone approaching, a tiny human silhouette that quivers against the glare. I watch as it materializes – an old farmer woman walking blithely across the strait that I now realize is only knee-deep. Her green plastic sandals dangle in one hand and she holds a bag of what looks like fruit in the other. As she approaches the beach, I hear noises behind me. At least a dozen perfectly silent monkeys have appeared on the rocks. They sit there patiently, picking occasionally at their fawny fur or their small tufted ears. My presence doesn't seem to faze them or the old farmer woman in the least.

'Hello,' she says. 'Have you come to feed the monkeys?' she asks, holding up the plastic bag full of cherry tomatoes. 'I'm Kakinoki. You're very welcome to feed them with me. It's so pleasant when people take an interest in my monkeys.'

'*Your* monkeys?'

'I'm the only one that feeds them,' she replies, handing me several tomatoes. 'They almost got taken away, you know. There were researchers from Fukuoka University here several years ago. They told me the monkeys were telepathic. I'm not sure about that, but they do like to play games. I hide a tomato under my hat or behind my back and they always find it. The young ones try to climb all over me to find it but the older ones just point now. They're very smart. I come out to feed them their lunch every day. In the morning I scrape aluminium moulds for concrete retaining walls. It's all grannies like me. There are eight of us. We wear bright-yellow helmets. In the afternoon I work my fields. Do you like bracken? I have lots of bracken if you want some. It grows wild in the hills above my house. Butterbur too. And some tangerines. And radishes.' The monkeys reach out with tiny hands and pluck the tomatoes from her palms. 'Good *daikon* radishes. I used to grow tea, corn, cucumbers, and mulberry for silkworms too. You can see my field over there on the hillside. My son gave me a hundred old CDs to frighten the bulbuls away.' Above the plane of water stretching across the bay to the north, a square section of the hillside mimics the water's shimmer.

I help Mrs Kakinoki feed the monkeys. After giving them a few tomatoes, I eat one myself when Mrs Kakinoki has her back turned. The monkeys eye me down. I won't be intimidated though. I like cherry tomatoes. I stare right back at them, hold up another tomato and pop it in my mouth. The goddamn monkeys go bananas.

'Oh, they're excited today,' says Mrs Kakinoki. 'They're not used to extra visitors. And what is your name, if I may ask?'

'Oh, sorry. Fujiwara.'

'Ah, *Fujiwara*,' she says, impressed. 'From Kyoto? Such a beautiful city, Kyoto,' she says.

'Really?'

'All the gardens and temples.'

I smile. Old people, especially from other parts, have the most nostalgic ideas. (If she went to England she'd expect to find all the men in bowler hats and the women twirling parasols.) 'Yeah, they're really beautiful, those gardens and temples,' I say, wherever they may be.

Mrs Kakinoki takes out another tomato and tosses it underhand along the beach. It rolls in a long red arc across the rippled sand and disappears behind the rocks. Two monkeys scramble after it. 'They like to race,' she says. 'It's one of our little rituals.'

For a first date I rarely ever take girls out to dinner or a film. The zoo is my spot. I pretend to be rapt by the animals and offended by the cruelty of their captivity. Why this strategy is so effective deserves an anthropology research paper. I can't explain it, but I've certainly ended up sleeping with a lot of girls, and I guess I've learned a lot about animals in the process. These are Japanese macaques, for example, virtually the same monkeys you see with snow on their heads in postcards from Nagano. Watching monkeys isn't the same without the sexual edge, but now I notice things about them that I never did before. Instead of having to act out 'Aozora watching monkeys', I just watch monkeys.

The macaques finish the tomatoes in Mrs Kakinoki's bag and we start back across the bay. The water's knee-deep and warm, and the refraction of sunlight through the ripples on the surface makes a net-like pattern of light waver on the sandy bottom. (It reminds me of the backdrop to a Smashing Pumpkins concert I went to in Tokyo.) As I'm admiring it, I notice other shapes moving on the bottom: pale, pinkish, hand-sized crabs. They're almost invisible against the sand until their silhouettes part from the background, almost under your feet. I stop walking. 'Um . . . Mrs Kakinoki?'

'Yes?'

'When will the tide go back out?'

'Oh, by morning. Why? Is something the matter?'

I shake my head and fall into step behind her, being very, very careful to walk right in her footsteps.

Totally oblivious to my unease, Mrs Kakinoki talks on endlessly. 'If you're a tourist, you must have visited the theme park. Now just you think, before Amsterdam was built, Komura Bay was a bit like this one, a tidal flat covered with mud and reeds. And Marumachi? It was like a village from a tale. At low tide the fishermen used to go across the mud on sleds and pull up mudskippers with curved bamboo sticks wherever they saw air holes. You could just imagine Urashima Taro coming ashore in such a place and asking where his house had gone! Dear me, imagine him finding a row of windmills! My how poor it used to be here. But I suppose small-town Kyushu's not of much interest to you. Things are better now that Amsterdam is here. It makes people like you come all the way from Kyoto for a visit. I've never met anyone from Kyoto before.'

Halfway back to the mainland, we come upon a signpost of perforated aluminium with a crossbar and two large shards of bent steel screwed to it. It stands out of the water at a slight angle and its lower edges are fringed with gold-green seaweed. Mrs Kakinoki stops and turns to me. Her chin and her eyes and the rim of her hat are shining a weird green in the light reflected from the shallows. Really weird. She just stares at me. It's like some mystical-historical *déjà vu*. I get the feeling she's not actually a kindly old lady leading me back to shore at all – more like a demon gatekeeper blocking this infidel's path back to the Sacred Land.

She chuckles. 'No feeding the monkeys.'

I run the last few steps onto the safety of the beach.

'If it's not too far to walk, you're welcome to come back to my house for that bracken,' says Mrs Kakinoki, 'and perhaps I've got some more tomatoes too. You seem to like them.'

Her 'house' on the hillside isn't much of anything – just a shack with a thick, high-pitched thatched roof sitting in the middle of a few terraced rice fields and vegetable plots. Mrs Kakinoki lives there alone, scrapes moulds in Marumachi in the mornings, feeds the macaques, bathes outdoors in a wood-fired cedar tub, and sells her rice to the local co-op. She could be a one-woman tourist attraction. If this place were just slightly more sanitary, people in Kyoto or Osaka would pay big cash to live so close to the earth for a day or two, soaking up the lifestyle of their ancestors.

She seats me on the tatami in one of the two rooms in the house and feeds me a lunch of home-made pickles, fish cake, garlic stick and her own rice in old white-and-blue bowls decorated with the insignia of the Japanese Navy – which hasn't been in existence since the 1940s. After the size and grandeur and organization of Amsterdam, there's something reassuring about Mrs Kakinoki's meagre little place. It's obvious she's not used to having anyone around; she chatters on and on.

'There are twenty-seven monkeys,' she says from the end of the room that serves as a kitchen. 'There used to be over fifty, but researchers came from one of the universities several years ago. They needed lab animals, I think. That's what my son told me. He owns a little jazz club in Sasebo. He said they probably couldn't get enough dogs for their experiments. One of my neighbours came running to tell me. "Quick!" he said. "They're taking away the monkeys!" I had no idea what he meant, but I just went running down the hill, full speed. He followed me and said, "Slow down! You'll hurt yourself," but I just kept going. When I reached the beach, I saw my monkeys all lying in a row on the sand with their arms and legs bound up with orange plastic. They were hard to recognize, lying there with their eyes closed, even the young ones. I went to them to make sure they were alive, each one of them. They were all still breathing. The men had left food with tranquillizer out for them, and those that hadn't eaten it they were prodding with darts. They had green nets and they'd driven their truck right across the flats.'

'What did you do?'

Mrs Kakinoki looks at her apron, picking at a thread. 'It's embarrassing. I wasn't as polite as I could have been.'

She goes on for a while longer, telling me about the history of Komura Bay and how all the towns have emptied and the industries died, except for Marumachi and Amsterdam. Gradually she quietens down. Eventually she too just sits and looks out the open doors at the bay and the massing cumulus. Once I've promised to come back, she loads me up with tomatoes and waves from the top of the road until I'm out of sight.

Mr Choso's already back in the mobile office by the time I return. He's brought gifts: a quarter of Leerdammer, a box of sugared doughnuts, a four-pack of assorted Dutch beers (still cold!), a collection of Van Gogh fridge magnets and a half-dozen Amsterdam maps. We take a seat on the front step of the mobile. The heat of the afternoon is just waning now. 26°C. A little altocumulus above the hills. Mr Choso hands me a frigid bottle of Oranjeboom. 'Well?'

He tilts his head and sucks his teeth. 'It looks like a Christmas decoration from here,' he says. 'But then you look around with a different object in mind, and you see how tight it is.'

This is not overly optimistic. 'But?'

'But. Yes, there is a "but". Come.'

He leads me inside and spreads the largest, most detailed of the maps across the inclined drafting table and clamps it down at the top. 'I've established the exit points on the maps. I rode the entire perimeter on a White Bike, checking each one for possibilities.'

'And?'

'There are none. So I went back to the maps and, using a highlighter pen, I traced the whole canal system, the pedestrian exits, the service roads that lead in and out.'

'And?'

'Nothing.'

I've finished the Oranjeboom and reach for the Grolsch. 'May I?' (The little lever that releases the stopper is worth as much as the beer itself.)

'Just looking at it,' Choso continues, 'I saw no solution. But when I had put the maps away, and was just staring at the swans swimming against the current, something occurred to me. The current itself. The water for all of Amsterdam comes from the Chikuho River, just here.' (I follow his finger across the map. We are unshaven mercenaries in *The Guns of Navarone*.) 'The river splits near the bypass and this branch flows past Marumachi, the other one directly into Amsterdam. It's obvious enough where it enters the Amstermeer Lake through Arrivaldam, but it's far less apparent where the water leaves the system. All that water has to flow out into Komura Bay *somewhere*, but it's impossible to tell exactly where from any of these maps. So I went on another tour and found it . . . The Kempinski Grand Hotel Vermeer.' He strides like a general to the open doorway and points at Amsterdam. 'There.'

Beyond his outstretched arm, on the southern skyline of Breukelen, a tall, black, hip-gable roof juts out from the profusion of red and ochre rooftops.

He does a volte-face back to the map. 'The Rijkscanal leads right up to the front entrance and then, *blinko*, disappears beneath it. There's more than enough room for two swimmers or even a small boat to pass underneath the archway, but it's the passage beneath the hotel that's worrisome. I could see clearly enough where the water went in, and – once I walked through the lobby of the hotel to the bay windows on the other side – I could tell just where it came out. But I couldn't see anything at all in between. My biggest worry was the presence of some kind of overhanging grille or steel mesh meant to keep flotsam from entering the bay.'

Hence:

Mr Choso's Excellent Experiment

Equipment: Four two-litre bottles of Pepsi and a roll of Scotch tape purchased at one of the 7-Eleven *conbeni* stores in Breukelen for the sum of 1200 yen.

Laboratory: A public WC.

Method:

A. Lock oneself into cubicle.

B. Open two bottles at a time and, one in each hand, let them chug into the toilet. (NB This process, Mr Choso assures me, is surprisingly loud and crudely suggestive and may occasion unwanted attention upon one's exit from the cubicle.)

C. Bind bottles together with entire roll of Scotch.

D. Drop this jerry-built raft into the canal directly in front of the tunnel. (Again, this may draw unwanted attention.)

E. Behind a palmetto next to the high windows in the lobby of the Kempinski Grand Hotel Vermeer, wait calmly.

Result: In three minutes and twenty seconds, the *Choso Maru* bobs out onto Komura Bay in perfect condition.

Which seems to give Mr Choso some confidence that the plan he outlines for me will actually succeed. It's totally half-baked but I'm up for it, 100 Aozoran per cent. Clint Eastwood swims away from Alcatraz. Papillon hurls himself into the sea on a sack of coconuts. How half-baked was that?

'So how do I get into Amsterdam in the first place?'

He smiles a very strained smile and sucks his teeth. 'Arrivaldam is busy, but if they've got your picture, there's too great a chance you'll be recognized.'

'Why don't I just swim across one of the canals in the dark?'

'I thought of that too but it won't work. There are ha-has beside every canal, full of razor wire. You can't see them when you look across the fields, but if you cross the tulip beds to get up close, you can see how deep they are. You'll have to go through the employees' entrance.'

'How?'

'In disguise. You could dress like me. Perhaps you could wear a pair of my old reading glasses too? And I could give you a haircut. Or even a colour change. And perhaps you could bend your knees a little when you walk, to look shorter?'

We talk the plan into shape and I give Mai a call to tell her the good news.

'Be ready to go on Saturday once your song is over,' I say. 'I'll come pick you up in a boat.'

'A boat? How are you going to get a boat?'

'That's privileged info, Mai. Need-to-know basis.'

'This doesn't sound good, Ao. Maybe we should think about this some more. In two weeks would be better. I'm singing a new song this Saturday and –'

'No way, Mai-*chan*. No cold feet.' I try to rationalize with her. How long before she gets pregnant, infected with AIDS, tortured by a psycho, murdered, or some lamentably unoriginal combination thereof? I'm sure we could Google the life span of the average indentured prostitute.

But it's not like she's unaware of any of this. 'I still think we should wait until we've come up with a solid, *reliable* plan.'

'There's no *time*, Mai-*chan*.' I'm desperate now. 'We've got to be back by Tuesday.'

'Why?'

I search for a reason. 'Because . . . because Dad's sick.' It comes to me. It's beautiful. It reminds me of how lucky I am to be Aozora. And it's not even a 100 per cent lie, that's the respectable beauty of it. He *did* say he was having surgery for something or other. What was it? 'I've just been on the phone with Inaka Regional Hospital.'

'*Dad?*' she repeats. 'Is this my brother on the line? First it's Mai-*chan*, now it's *Dad*? Since when did you start calling him *Dad*?'

'Since he got old and feeble.' I speak slowly now, as if I could crack up with emotion at any moment. 'I didn't want to worry you with this before but . . .' (The unfinished sentence gives the impression I'm distraught.)

'But what?'

'He wasn't feeling well when I saw him last and now it looks as if he has cancer.'

'Cancer?'

'Yeah, of the . . . spleen. And thereabouts. It's spreading.'

'So what does that mean?'

'It means he walks around like he's perpetually cramped. It means he eats nothing and shits blood. It basically means he's dying, Mai. And I know he wants to see you.' The last bit is true too; and it's this that concerns her most.

'Did he actually say that or are you saying it for him?'

'*He* said it. He said, "Give Mai my love. Tell her I made a lantern for her." He made you a paper lantern for *o-bon*, Mai. We went to the shrine together to pray and we had to leave your lantern at home.'

She's quiet for a while. 'I prayed too,' she says finally. 'For Mom.'

'Then come pray with me,' I tell her. 'For Dad.'

'It's too weird hearing you call him "Dad",' she says. 'Like you were close or something.'

Maybe more than I realize. Whatever. 'Good then, just keep your mobile phone on you and do your regular routine. Wear some sneakers in case we have to run.'

'I can't wear sneakers with a kimono!'

'All right, all right. Look, I'll let you know once I've got a plan.'

'Is this supposed to be confidence-inspiring?'

'Think of Dad. The important thing is, you're with me, right?'

There's quiet on the line. I can see her spinning the telephone cord around a finger, eyes closed. 'Be ready, little sister,' I say quickly. 'Just be ready.'

shinji

Made up entirely of old files and documents from the Hibiki reservations department, the bonfire on the beach sends papery embers wafting over the cove like tiny zeppelins. All the speed tribe are here, the surfer crowd, the workers from Amsterdam and the concrete factory – probably the region's entire population of under-twenties. There's a lot of cannabis and music and chasing through the gardens with torches like some drunken, friendly scene from *La Dolce Vita*. Shinji is out getting stoned in the cove, drifting around with a dozen other kids on an armada of surfboards. Nami's sitting with a girlfriend on the sand. The girl is short, has punky hair, and is wearing jeans and a jean jacket that could have been made for just about any biped. She's a 3.5 at best and I'm hoping she'll go away. In fact, she gets up and leaves almost immediately, a very good sign that Nami has been talking about me.

We take a six-pack of Salty Dogs from one of the garbage bins full of ice and go back into the Hibiki to sit together in one of the banquet rooms upstairs, hanging our feet through what used to be a balcony and is now just an open doorway five floors up. Below us, wavelets appear from out of nowhere and meet the shore in tidy white curlicues. With sky and sea and twilight around us, the party going on underneath, it's like being on a Ferris wheel. I can't hear the sound of the waves, but I can hear Nami's breathing, which is the perfect overdub. Every now and again, Shinji's strident voice reaches us from the cove.

'So what's your sister's name?' Nami asks.

I've been telling her the more or less honest account of why I've come here, though I haven't mentioned the money. She seems impressed.

'Bet she's pretty,' she says. Her cigarette is making slow figure eights that I'd catch with a slow shutter if my phone camera were more advanced.

'Yeah,' I reply. 'She's pretty.'

'Worth rescuing.'

True again, I have to admit it.

'You must miss her a lot.'

I do, come to think of it. It must be the beer but I'm starting to reminisce. Pretty soon I can't tell if I'm saying what I'm saying because I want Nami to believe it or because I truly believe it myself. 'I relied upon this idea of the future that never materialized. I never imagined we'd *always* be belligerent with one another. It was just a game. Though I enjoyed playing it more than she did. Or took it less seriously. I don't know. I thought one day there'd be time to do things together, go shopping or have coffee and a doughnut.' She's watching me intently. If Kuwahara and the other guys from the res could hear me now they'd say I was a real shark. Probably take notes. 'But things never calmed down,' I say. 'There was never any time to devote to my sister.'

'All hail Gondo!' Shinji starts a chant somewhere below us. He is now back on the beach, it seems.

Nami puts her hand on my cheek. I should stop talking. Now's the time to strike. But I can't. Not yet. 'You know, the times when we were closest, Mai and I – back when we were kids listening to cassette tapes of *Grease* in the attic or stealing gum from the tuck shop or hyperventilating on the lawn –'

She laughs. '*Hyperventilating?*'

'Yeah, sure. We used to kneel on each other's backs until

we passed out. It's a good memory.' As good a memory of any intimate, breathless contact I've had with a woman.

'All hail Gondo!' Dark savages spin around and through the fire. The chant rings through the cove. 'All hail Gondo!' It looks more like *Lord of the Flies* down there now.

'Why's he going on about Gondo?'

Nami frowns. 'It's Gondo who paid for all this alcohol. He was happy about what Shinji did for him.'

Shinji's leaping through the fire now; you can see his silhouette perfectly. 'What a freak.'

'Please don't call him that.'

'Am I wrong?'

'He wasn't always like that,' she says disconsolately.

Suddenly I'm feeling like I've been sent to this earth solely to disabuse this trusting, compassionate, well-meaning girl of her naïve notions. 'No, he was a perfectly adorable little foetus, I'm sure. And now he's a freak. Why don't you find yourself someone normal?'

She bites her lip and looks the other way. I should be touched by this. It's pretty obvious by now that I'm that someone normal she's aspiring to. Instead, I'm feeling angry and omnipotent. I put my hand behind her neck and pull her in to me. Her breath falters when my other hand finds the elastic of her panties – her heart interfering with her sensible lungs. I should want this experience for its own sake; she's as close to Kasane as I'm ever going to meet. But all I can think of is how much it will anger Shinji if I sleep with his girl. Some kind of revenge for the destruction of Mr Choso's jar.

Minus the Mount Fuji, this is more or less what happens:

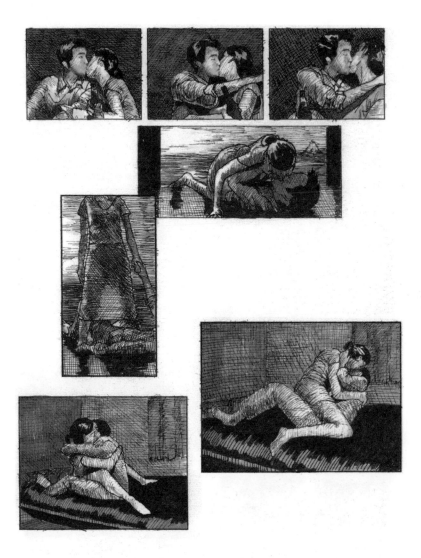

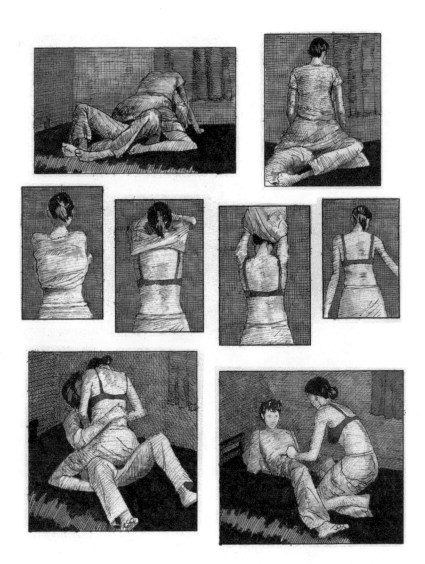

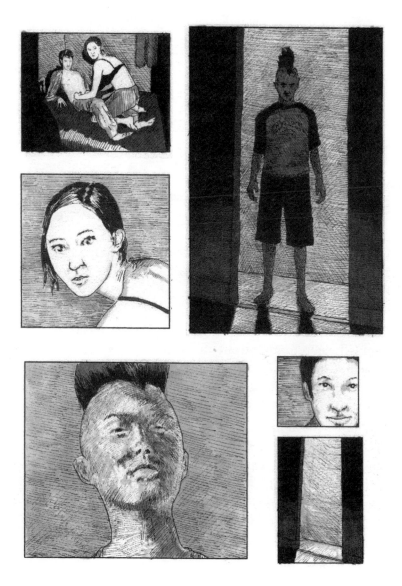

I shrug and look at Nami. 'Think he's upset?'

She's hardly even breathing. '*Mm-hm.*'

'How upset?' I'm wondering whether I'm going to have to employ my now world-famous major outer cut again.

'Enough to go and get his gun.'

'Has he got one?'

'Didn't you see it in the restaurant?'

'What,' I scoff, 'that replica thing? The Romeo and Juliet special?'

'It's not a replica.'

I grab my jeans from the floor and ask if there's an ironing board around; I'd like to press them before fleeing.

'Go straight down the hall,' she hisses.

'So long. I'll come see you at the G-Spot.'

I'm out the door and down the hallway in no time. My ankles may still be the colour, size and consistency of over-ripe aubergines, but I feel like Ben Johnson. As I'm coming to the corner, the window at the end of the hall goes white with a network of a thousand tiny cracks. If this were all, I might actually stop to investigate this strange phenomenon, but a fraction of a second later comes the report. *Clack clack clack*, like the teak rhythm sticks that monk was knocking together on the street in Kyoto, only a hundred decibels louder. The windowpane folds, disappears altogether. Night air rushes in. But I'm not hanging around to compose haiku. I'm through the chicane and down the stairs, out into the moonlight in the wrecked porte cochere, slaloming through the obstacle course of overturned tables and kitchen equipment. The rhythm sticks *clack* again and there's a thud as a bullet smacks into a refrigerator beside my head.

And then come the stairs.

– Let's watch this in slow motion. Fujiwara's the first to come around the corner.

– He looks intent here.

182

– Does he ever, but he's approaching with unrealistic speed for such a technical feature. His hand is on the handrail when he comes over the top but you'll notice in the replay he's not holding on tight enough to be able to arrest his forward movement when his feet eventually lose grip.

– He practically tap-dances down the first portion of the stairs!

– That's right. This section of The Stairs gets direct sunlight through the wrecked roof of the porte cochere and is comparatively dry. But watch what happens when Fujiwara gets halfway down, into what I like to call the Gambit of Perpetual Shadow. His right foot meets a two-centimetre thick patch of moss and slips to the next step, and the next, and the next, and the next in rapid succession.

– It's incredible!

– Fujiwara's no surfer but look at this, he *surfs* to the very bottom.

– Incredible. It's difficult to say what he's doing with his arms, though.

– It looks like an attempt at a Full Windmill, but they're just flailing too wildly.

– Not enough synchronized motion?

– That's right. Not enough composure. He's taken the term 'free-style' too literally. It's less a practised manoeuvre than just an acrobatic fight for balance. But what he loses in points for artistic interpretation, boy oh boy, does he make up for it on the clock!

– And the landing?

– Seven. You'll see his left knee connect [painfully] with the concrete there.

– Ooh.

– Crunch is right. Let's hope Fujiwara can limp out of the Hibiki before Shinji terminates him.

*

The light of the bonfire on the beach flickers red through the bamboo as I stumble down the lawns of the Hibiki. The spiny spectres of aloe leap at me out of the darkness. Three cars are sitting at the far end of the drive with engines running, tail lamps burning red in the darkness. Just when I'm getting close, the two nearest cars pull away with a chirrup of tyres and head down the highway in the direction of Marumachi. The tail lamps contract like evil pupils until they disappear one after the other around the bend. The last car, a white Skyline GT-R, burbles in the shadows, the windows open. I go straight to the passenger side and lean in. The interior smells of leather and vanilla and there's piano music on the stereo. A girl in the driver's seat is speaking on a mobile phone. There isn't much light but in the red glow of the myriad gauges across the dash and the warbling blue LED wave on the stereo, I can just make out her uninteresting features. It's Nami's friend from the beach. 'Hi. Can I catch a ride?'

'Just a second,' she says to the phone. 'Who are you?'

'Friend of Nami's, remember? I need a ride.'

'What am I, the taxi service around here?' she says. 'Get in then, I'm late.'

I slide into the shapely red seat and slam the door. She shoves the shifter into gear and we accelerate violently onto the highway, the whole car jerking to the right when the tyres grab the pavement. 'What's your name?' I ask.

'Mash.'

'What are you late for?'

'Pachinko.'

'You work at a pachinko parlour then?'

'What is this, an interrogation?'

'Just curious. I'm Aozora.'

'Congratulations.'

'Nice GT-R, by the way. Is it yours?'

'You think it's my boyfriend's, right?'

'Yep.'

'Typical. You want a ride or not?'

'Sure, don't get upset. It's not every day you see a girl in a car like this.'

'It's not every day you meet a girl like this,' she says.

She's got the pedal to the floor and the fog settling on the road where the 210 winds up into the hills doesn't slow her down a bit. Road signs and barrier reflectors glimmer like trinkets underwater, only they're not sinking – they burst to the surface, glaring in the headlights, and Mash is wrenching on the wheel to avoid them, giving only the barest contours to her concentration. I'm groaning. 'Slow down,' I tell her, already feeling in my mouth the bite of rising Salty Dog. But still, she attacks the curves through the mountains as if you couldn't drive a car any other way. 'Do you always drive like this?'

'What's the point of owning a Skyline if you're not going to drive fast?' she asks, hanging on the wheel as the car glues itself to another corner. I stick my head out into the cold rushing air and feel like Saint-Exupéry for a short pleasant moment before vomiting down the door of the car.

'What are you doing?!' she screams.

'Your fault,' I moan.

She takes me to a pachinko parlour somewhere on the outskirts of Marumachi, a bright neon palace called Tyranno-X with the predator itself towering above the parking lot. 'Amsterdam's that way a couple of kilometres,' she says, pointing to the west as she gets out of the car. She disappears through the revolving doors. Great. Insects swirl through the night, cook on the lights, corkscrew down onto the parking lot pavement. All around me, the rice paddies recede into darkness. I start plodding in the direction of Mr Choso's mobile office.

g-spot

I hide out in the mobile all day while Mr Choso takes pictures of the scene of the theft and speaks with one of his colleagues who comes down for the afternoon from Nagasaki. He disappears for a while and then returns around seven o'clock with take-out *sukiyaki* from Hoka Hoka Tei, a lot of beer and saké, and a home peroxide kit. We spend the evening going over plans for the escape one more time and preparing my disguise. My hair is the colour of burning magnesium and neatly parted on one side the way my father used to like to see it when I was ten.

We sit on the steps of the mobile eating and drinking, watching the amber and silver lights of Amsterdam slowly presume upon the sunset. The night view attracts a lot of visitors. The Amstermeer could be a miniature Hong Kong harbour for all the lights streaming back and forth upon it. All the vanes on all the windmills are rimmed with lights and the Spitztoren Tower changes its colour constantly from red to purple to blue to green to yellow to red. But in my present mood, I am less interested in these window dressings than in the sliver of multicoloured neon just visible in the town of Marumachi beyond. Chantilly Lace. Superpussy. G-Spot. Come Bar. I'm drunk and still thinking about Nami. The lights of Marumachi, they beckon.

'I think I'll take a little walk down into Marumachi,' I say. 'To see the lights.'

Mr Choso doesn't think much of this. 'That's crazy,' he says. 'You want to avoid Mr Gondo, not walk into his hands.'

'Last place he'll expect to find me,' I reply. 'Besides, look at my disguise.'

She's there on the catwalk that runs between the tables in the G-Spot, dancing lazily in yellow lingerie, silver high heels and a silver necklace with a large pendant number 9. Seeing her now, in the flesh, she's very close to reaching 10. By the logic of the scale, she *becomes* Kasane, which is ridiculous of course, but so long as the two girls remain apart in time and space, there is no problem. I knew Kasane there, then. I know Nami here, now.

And besides, I'm a little bit drunk.

She sees me when I come in, I know, but there isn't the slightest flicker of recognition on her face.

There's nothing subtle about the system. A topless waitress comes over and I order a bottle of Veuve rosé champagne and a Number 9. The number comes up at the bottom corner of the TV screens playing MTV around the room and Nami brings the bottle to my table.

'Only the best for our valued clientele,' she says with a wink. She sets the glass bucket on the table, lifts out the cold bottle and wipes it down with a cloth. 'What did you do to your hair?'

'Disguise.'

'Ha! Are you all right?' she asks.

I nod. 'You?'

She holds the cork and twists the damp pink bottle until they part with a *thpp!* Thumb inserted into the hollow at the bottle's base, she pours until the foam just reaches the lip of my glass before bubbling away. 'Have a glass yourself,' I tell her. She pours a thimble measure, tastes it and sits down next to me in the same posture as all the other girls with their men, leaning back, legs crossed, 'chatting' with winsome smiles.

'I'm fine. He's funny, Shinji. He wants to kill *you*, but he could never do anything to me. He started crying, you know? Saying it was his fault. Which it is. He's cheated on me lots of times. I know all about them. But we've forgiven each other.'

I'm incredulous. I didn't necessarily want her to fall in love with me, but I didn't want her to go back to him either. My opportunity to sleep with a 10 is disappearing fast. 'So you're just going to stay with him?'

She shrugs. 'This isn't the first time something like this has happened. You understand, right?'

No. Is she giving me the shove? Is she actually in *love* with the guy? Am I merely the comic foil in this love triangle? She looks over towards the bar. A host in a white tuxedo is ostensibly mixing cocktails, but his glance is running the entire place. 'I'm supposed to be giving you a lap dance now,' Nami says. 'Shall I get one of the other girls?'

'Nope.' I pour myself some more champagne.

'Really?' she asks, through that inexorable smile.

'Sure, why not?' I say. I don't mean to be thoughtless or crass, but I suppose I'm not exactly charming her either. 'It's more or less what we were doing last night, isn't it? It's just a change of setting.'

She looks at me with some fairly palpable distaste, then reaches past me to turn over the hourglass on the table. Her weight upon me, she's just as I imagined. Just as I *remember*. She straddles my lap and begins to shift, rubbing herself against me in a circle from my knees to my crotch.

'I'm going to buy the night with you,' I tell her. 'I'm going to put you on my credit card.'

'Oh, it's the Special you want, is it?' She puts on a moue and runs a finger down my temple. 'Were we having a long looong day at the office? You look like you need some *ten-de*rness. Working so hard. Wouldn't you like a nice massage?

188

Then, if you like, I'll let you take my panties off. *So slowly.* I just can't wait till you're plunging into me from behind. Over and over. Making me scream. Is that what you want from me, Aozora?'

I hoped, at best, that she'd be touched, happy to transform the dingy act of selling sex into a night of true lovemaking. At worst, I thought she'd be indifferent. But I didn't expect this telephone talk. The vulgarity is not lost on me, but I'm half-drunk and upset. I *know* what I *should* do, but it's far easier just to follow my instinct. To my left, our images are repeated in a mirror, down a murky row that leads all the way to Namba, Nakasu Island, Sakae, Kabukicho – all the red-light districts in the nation. I just want to drop into that mass of maledom and believe, along with all the rest at this very moment, what the woman is saying. Her thighs are so firm beneath my palms, so tender beneath my fingertips! The sand runs out. She steps off me without a word and goes back to the catwalk.

I signal the host over and pour myself more champagne. 'Number 9 Special,' I tell him.

He gives me a bow and turns towards the catwalk. Almost imperceptibly, Nami shakes her head. The host starts offering me alternatives. Number 8 would be very happy to see me. Or perhaps Number 5, in the blue just there?

I toss my father's JCB card on the table. 'I'm a friend of Mr Tak's.'

He spreads his hands. 'I'm sorry? Mr Tak?'

'Yeah, and Mr Gondo too,' I add. 'I'm doing some consulting work for him.'

It takes him a moment, but he relents and picks up the card. Letting me have my way with number 9 is a better option than risking offence to one of Mr Gondo's friends. When he returns, he's carrying the card, a receipt and a key-card to a hotel room on a black tray. There's no price or record of the transaction on the receipt, just 'Hotel Lorelei', a room number and a time.

The green light finally blinks on the lock. The door handle turns. She's standing in the middle of the hotel room, feet spread wide, drinking a can of Sapporo and watching the news on NHK. She looks over at me and sighs. She drains the beer and does that elegant contortion of her arms and shoulders that will unzip her dress. Strangely enough, I'm not sure what to do at this moment. The formality of the room with its expensive furniture and red-gold Chinese lacquer panels above the bed, Nami's obvious anger – I don't feel quite as aroused as I thought I would be. Short of another option, I go to the toilet.

A large black butterfly is battling the windowpane in the bathroom. I capture it easily. It tries to edge out between my thumb and index finger. How often have I held a life in my hands? It's fragile and tenacious and kind of sexy. What if the sexual impulse could be satisfied by insects, butterflies in particular? By the mere *proximity* of their fluttering, futtering wings, like a waking wet dream? I have a vision of butterfly bars and butterfly strip clubs and butterflies smoking cigarettes all across the Kyoto skyline. Sex vacations to Malaysia and Brazil and the Rocky Mountains. If I lived in that world I'd probably fall in love with some Madagascan ornithoptera instead of finding a nice, simple cabbage white. I come back into the room with it cupped in my hands.

Nami's sitting on the bed in the yellow lingerie she was wearing at the club, rolling her pantyhose down into two neat black doughnuts. She looks up at me and frowns.

'Caught a butterfly,' I tell her. 'It's a . . . damn. I used to know the name of it.' I take it over to show it to her but she rolls to the other side of the bed.

'Mmnn!' she squeals. 'Take it away!'

'What's the matter?'

'I don't like butterflies. I'm allergic.'

'How can you be allergic to a butterfly?'

'I just *am*, okay?'

'What is it you're allergic to? A caterpillar can give you a bit of a rash —'

'Everything.'

'That's stupid. If you don't like butterflies — if you're phobic of them just say it.'

'Okay, then, I'm phobic of them.'

'Phobic of butterflies? Look at the thing. It's not going to hurt you. It's not like a swarm of them could attack you or something.'

I take the butterfly onto the balcony and let it go. *Karasu-ageha*. That's what it's called. Big crow butterfly. Hefty moniker for such a pretty thing.

Back in the room, Nami is already naked. She has turned back the covers of the bed and is lying there with her legs spread as wide as they can possibly go, as if she's waiting for a Pap smear or something. She says: 'Forty-eight minutes left of your Special, Mr Fujiwara. Come stick it in.'

candy girl

The Nistelgracht Canal leads past one windmill after another, all turning slowly at the same rate though there's not a sorry sigh of air moving across Kyushu today. It's Saturday, 7 AM. I'm walking along the dusty, overgrown side of the canal sporting my new disguise. Yellow rubber boots, a pair of khaki workpants, a pink shirt, a Day-Glo yellow safety vest, Mr Choso's square black reading glasses, an orange helmet and a clipboard.

I try calling my father to tell him Mai and I are coming home and that he should make an appointment with the lawyer as soon as possible. He's not there. Probably still in the hospital or out with the topiary already. Why the guy can't buy a mobile phone, I cannot understand. 'Enslaved to the devices of our own construction!' I can hear him rant.

The employees' entrance is only several hundred metres ahead. An access road leads down from the highway to a white wooden bridge and a small guardhouse with red shutters, green shingles and flowerpots on the windowsills. I detour from the bank of the canal into a bamboo thicket and pick my way down to within a few metres of the guardhouse. Inside are two Politie in their blue uniforms and black Sam Browne belts, one standing at the Dutch door next to the barrier, the other sitting at a desk reading.

I have hopes that, one day when virtual-reality technology can really do it justice, my trip to Kyushu may serve as the basis for an adult-only video game. It could start in Inaka, where my father would be this Yoda-like figure and Player 1 would get to select an array of personal attributes to customize his very own Aozora.

Then, on a picaresque journey through an urban nightmare to the looming citadel of Amsterdam where the massive-breasted techno-maiden waits to be rescued, Player 1 carefully farms experience points, pitting his virtual proxy Aozora against the evil forces under the control of Player 2: a giant snake called Mr Unoboa, his henchman Ishikawabunga, a gang of *Loli-Goth*s with ninja-like powers, evil old Mr Gondolph and his rocket-equipped Century, a robotic speed tribe and the poison-tipped Shinjinx.

Hiding in the brush, I'm now at that brief moment of repose when the screen goes dark and the disk whirrs as Final Stage is loaded. It lasts no more than two deep breaths and is brought to an end when the tropical foliage and the little guardhouse reappear on the screen and a small yellow delivery van whines down the road to pull up before the barrier. (The graphics are perfectly convincing.) The guard leans out of the guardhouse window to speak to the driver.

Without thinking, I tilt my helmet down and walk straight past the barrier on the other side of the van.

The guard calls out as I go by, 'Excuse me, sir. Sir?'

I look over my shoulder and give him a wave like we're old friends.

He doesn't buy it. 'Sir, stop please. Are you an employee?' He opens the Dutch door and comes out onto the drive.

I hold up Choso's Japanese Archaeological Association Card (the most official-looking document he could find). 'Doing some excavation back there on the hillside,' I tell him. 'For the racetrack, you know. Thanks.'

'But, hold it now. You're not an employee of Amsterdam then?' he asks, shifting his cap.

I'm supposed to tell him that I need to check the water table along the banks of the canals, with some jazz about salinity and subsidence thrown in for confusion's sake, and that if he needs anyone to verify my activities he can contact Mr Choso of Nagasaki University. It's all planned out. I've practised it. But I'm still not convinced it will work as planned. I'll probably get tied up all day with HO and Amsterdam Maintenance and the opportunity will be gone. So I lean in to Mr . . . T. Kawai a little and say: 'I've been digging since five o'clock and the smell of the bakeries has been wafting up from Amsterdam. I tell you I'd love a fresh cup of coffee and a croissant. I can't tell you how long I've been drinking Nescafé, it's killing me, it really is. You wouldn't consider, I suppose, letting me nip in and grab something to eat? Ten minutes at the most.'

Poor guy. He's too polite just to tell me to take a hike. He actually looks sympathetic to my need for a coffee, but he has to do his duty. 'I'm sorry, sir. Anyone who wants to participate in Amsterdam must enter at the main entrance in Arrivaldam. To reach it, it's very simple really. If you go back up this road, then take a right on the main highway, go through the tunnel, and go right before the bypass.'

I can't figure out what gives Mr Kawai the impression I'm driving.

'Well,' he says when I point this out, 'there's a bus stop at the top of the road. The bus will take you into Marumachi, and from there you can catch a taxi back to the main entrance at Arrivaldam.'

I thank him for the advice, but I'll go back the way I came. He frowns, lets the man in the yellow van continue on his way, and turns to the other man inside. 'Mr Narazaki, this gentleman wants to walk along the Nistelgracht to Arrivaldam.' Narazaki looks up and lays down his *manga* on the table. *Pink Parsley.* I catch a glimpse of a girl on her back with her legs in the air and a giant pink hibiscus blossoming between her thighs – '*Mnn, mnn,*' it reads. Mr Narazaki comes to the door and looks me over. 'The canal? You're doing what?'

'Working at the racetrack site.'

'I'm sorry, sir, you can't.'

'But I just did. It's a pleasant walk actually.'

He smiles and laughs as if I weren't serious. 'Pleasant walk, yes, well, you're not allowed to walk next to the canals where there aren't any railings.'

This is the moment in an action movie when the hero loses patience and puts a bullet through the guy's eyebrow. I give him a sincere smile. 'Thanks. Thank you. I'll just walk back along the highway then.'

'But you can't walk,' he objects. 'The highway goes along the hillside and through a tunnel.' He leans inside and consults the wall, taking his time. 'The next bus is in forty minutes. The bus stop is only five minutes up the road.'

There are no more words to be said. I give them what looks like a nice smile but is, in fact, a baring of teeth in a silent howl of pent-up anger at the stupidity of officialdom. I walk up the road until I'm out of sight, then creep back down through the bamboo to the canal and go back the way I came. There's nothing for it now, I've got no other option than to go through the front gates of Arrivaldam.

Across the parking lots, where thousands of cars sit baking in the sun, the spires and gates of Arrivaldam shiver in the heat off the tarmac. I'm within sprinting distance when I see the summer hat among the crowds of people lining up at the gate. Or at least I think I do. I duck low behind a BMW and take off my helmet. A coach pulls up in front of Arrivaldam and obscures the hat from view. There's no doubt Gondo's people are around, but I don't have a second plan of attack. I put the helmet back on. Either the disguise works or it doesn't.

It doesn't.

I haven't gone another five car-lengths before I notice a black roof gliding above the parked cars. It's the Century, creeping along at just the right speed and trajectory to intercept me before reaching Arrivaldam.

An acquaintance of mine was in a car accident once. At the bottom of his insurance claim was an empty box in which he was supposed to draw a diagram of the accident as it occurred, with a blue rectangle marked 1 to represent his car, another marked 2 for the other car, stick figures for pedestrians, and arrows to indicate direction of motion. A large black X was the point of collision. As if none of this couldn't just have been explained. When I saw the drawing he'd done, I laughed. It was not at all the accident he'd described to me. 'Which one's the truth?' I asked.

'Doesn't matter,' he replied, snatching the claim away. 'I've hired an expensive lawyer.'

Please use the box above to plot out the following scene. Let a stylized lightning bolt represent Aozora, a skull and crossbones the Century, and simple rectangles for parked cars. I'm walking straight for Arrivaldam down one of the traffic lanes between rows. The Century approaches at right angles. I run. If I can only get inside Amsterdam I'll have a chance of eluding them, but here in the parking lot I'm finished. The twelve-cylinder engine grunts as the Century surges forward. In a moment it's clear I'm not going to make it. When the Century is within one car-length of me, I turn abruptly right, through the row of parked cars and around behind the Century. Whoever's driving – Skull or Tiger, I presume – hasn't time to stop and put the car into reverse to cut me off. (No need for the X!) I skip across two lanes and avail myself of the cover of a family emerging from their Bongo minivan. I walk just ahead of them and they shepherd me across the rest of the parking lot.

The forecourt of Arrivaldam is full of belching coaches, tour guides waving useless flags, and schoolchildren in identical yellow caps. I step between two coaches onto the pavement and I'm greeted by the sight of my favourite couple standing in front of the ticket guichet with two officers of the Marumachi Police. I remember what Mai said, call the police and she disappears. They're hardly on my side. There's no way they'll let me into Amsterdam. My self-preservation instinct surfaces. I take a sharp left and hurry along the line of coaches towards the bridge that leads to Marumachi.

'Excuse me, sir,' calls one of the officers. 'Excuse me? Sir?'

Stay nonchalant, Aozora. Stay cool. Aozora Takeshi. Aozora Eastwood. Hands in pockets. Out for a brisk stroll.

'Excuse me. Sir? Sir?'

Slightly, oh so slightly, speed up pace.

'Sir!'

I'm half-walking, half-running, starting to panic yet still mindful of appearances, undecided whether to flee or try to get by on nonchalance. It's only once he's close enough that I can hear his boot-steps that I break into a sprint down the wide concrete path that runs along the bay and across the bridge of the estuary. On the Marumachi side are a cluster of a half-dozen or so hotels, all designed with faux-European façades to borrow some of Amsterdam's shine. Ludence, Regent, Monterey, Plaza. The signs bounce in my field of vision. These boots aren't the most comfortable running shoes, but I've got a long stride and a good lead.

At the other end of the bridge I leap a privet hedge and bound across a lawn into the Hotel Primavera. The hall I slide into is all polished marble, console tables, dusky old paintings and massive golden girandoles. To the left is a succession of banquet rooms. On the right are French doors giving onto a balcony. I bang one of them open and slip through, hoping for a crowded Marumachi street in which to disappear, but the white marble stairs lead down to a dock on the bay. Several men and women are boarding a double-decker *bateau-mouche*.

Back in the corridor, the officers are peering into banquet rooms. As I skip across the vestibule one looks up and puts his hands together as if in prayer. The pleading look he gives me is impossible to ignore. I'm sorry for causing him trouble, really, but there's no stopping now. Up the curving marble staircase. Back along the mezzanine. Down a perpendicular corridor. Out an emergency exit, in through another. One frantic preposition after another. I'm no longer certain what building I'm in. In one hallway several men are standing about in front of a table set with coffee and biscuits. Beside the banquet hall doors, a small sign on an easel reads, CIN-CIN MASTURBATION LIFESTYLE. I grab a Fig Newton and enter.

The waiting area set up inside is cut off by office dividers and curtains from the rest of what is evidently a large, ornate banquet hall. The ceiling stretches away in friezes of gilt filled with blue skies and golden cherubim and sparkling chandeliers. Several girls are seated around the waiting area, all wearing the same pink polka-dot minidresses. One's bent over at the water dispenser, her skirt riding high up the back of her thighs to reveal matching panties. Another's reading a novel on a bed made up with a shiny red silk duvet. And two are seated at a desk. It takes me a moment to figure out which girls are real, and which are Candy. I truly believed the day would never come, but I go straight to the desk and ask for a session.

The girls are very sweet, but my yellow boots and safety vest give them cause for a quick glance at one another. Do I have an appointment?

'No . . . not exactly,' I reply, taking off my helmet.

They try to be sweeter. 'If you would like to make an appointment, we have taster sessions available tomorrow?'

'Tomorrow won't quite do. I have a personal invitation from Mr Takamura. Is he around?'

Suddenly I'm the Shogun. Both girls stand at once and make obeisance. One of them comes around the table to take my arm, the other parts the curtain and shows me into a corridor with numbered cubicles on either side. As if he's been waiting there for me, Mr Tak is coming forward with his arms opened wide. Black suit. Burgundy-and-gold tie. Gold Rolex chronograph. 'Mr Fujiwara!' he cries.

'Mr Tak.'

'I knew it! When I saw you, I knew it. Here was a man who needed to masturbate.' That same annoying self-assurance. 'You've missed the coming-out ball but there are still several debutantes left. Come! Come with me. You've deliberated long and hard and now you have accepted that you are a man in need.' We come to Booth 11 and one of the girls steps in front to draw the curtain open for me. 'Yumiko will introduce you to one of my daughters,' he says and bows deeply. 'Please, Mr Fujiwara, I invite you to enjoy yourself.'

And with that, Yumiko takes me in. On one side of the curtained-off cubicle is a table arrayed with various of Mr Tak's sex toys, and a double bed like the one in the foyer. On the other is a blonde Candy Girl in a pink polka-dot minidress identical to the ones I saw outside. She's seated on a leather sofa with a martini in her hand.

'First of all, Mr Fujiwara, none of these items has been previously used,' says Yumiko. 'If you are not satisfied with the performance of any product, you are under no obligation to purchase it. Is there any product in particular that you find tempting?'

No, not tempting exactly, that is not the word. More like . . . morbidly intriguing. But I have to choose. I point at the blonde. 'Her?'

Yumiko smiles. 'Of course, one of Mr Takamura's daughters. Here, why don't you sit down together for a while?' She takes the martini glass out of her hand and puts it on the table next to the sex toys, then reaches behind the Candy Girl. The doll's lush eyelashes part with a tiny whirr to reveal striking grey eyes of a kind you almost never see. Her face shifts into a smile. 'No two Candy Girls are the same,' Yumiko tells me. 'They are all individuals. This Candy Girl's name is Sayuri and she likes to ride her bicycle and swim. She likes all kinds of music too. Why don't I let you get acquainted for a while? Remember, the secret to a happy relationship is never to do anything with Sayuri that you would not do with a real girl.'

There's some commotion in the corridor. If they check through each of the cubicles, they'll be sure to find me. 'Um, can I take her to bed?' I ask.

Yumiko smiles. 'Of course.' She bows. 'I can see you two will get along very well.' She backs out of the room, closing the green curtain behind her. Now I can hear Mr Tak's even, steady voice cutting through the more frantic demands of the police.

Sayuri is damn heavy. I drag her across the room and onto the bed, then peel back the covers and leap underneath with her. The first thing that strikes me is how she smells – just like a real girl. Her skin is some kind of rubber composite, smooth to the touch, minutely spongy and ever so slightly tacky under her armpits and at the back of her neck. In the greeny half-dark beneath the covers, I have the impression she's going to come alive – as if Mr Tak's secret wish will finally come true and the Blue Fairy will arrive in a blaze of light . . . Eyes closed, I run my 20/20 fingers down her body. She's an 8 or a 9. It's amazing. Sayuri could have been created with a wax mould of Kasane's body. The moment takes me. 'Kasane,' I whisper. 'It's me, Aozora.' At this, her body gets warmer and starts to vibrate slightly. Her grey eyes shine brighter and the rubber-and-lamb's-wool apotheosis of Mr Tak's R & D glows with tiny fibre-optics. When my hand drifts down to it, it turns from green to yellow. 'Oooh,' she croons as it deepens to orange.

I spend too long staring at Sayuri but I can't help it. It's like Shakespeare's Hamlet with the skull: I knew you once. On a purely physical basis, she's *way* up the Kasane Scale. What does this say about my criteria? Contemplating the implications of this is – thankfully – cut short.

'Mr Fujiwara? It's Mr Tak. Is this a good time?'

I slip out of bed. 'Yes, come in. I was just admiring your craftsmanship.' He spreads his hands and shrugs as if to say, 'Ah well, it's nothing.' 'Really,' I continue, 'she's very lifelike. Almost better than lifelike.'

Mr Tak beams. 'A-ha,' he says, one finger in the air. 'That is the aim, Mr Fujiwara. That is the aim. Already we're incorporating real biological materials. Did you notice her toenails? They're real. But, enough for now. It seems, Mr Fujiwara, that you may be in a little trouble, no?'

I start to explain. 'The police are crooked—'

But he cuts me off. 'Please, I know what these provincial police are like. It's the other ones you should be worried about.'

'Bald heads? Gold chains?'

'Detriments to a healthy society. Whatever you did to upset

201

them, they deserve more of it. Still, when you leave here, your safety will be in question.'

'I need to go to Amsterdam,' I blurt out.

He smiles broadly and checks his watch. 'Nothing simpler, but you can't stay in Amsterdam for ever.'

I tell him about my plan. He's very amused. 'You have a good spirit, Mr Fujiwara. I enjoy your company. Come with me, though may I suggest you leave the helmet and vest here? Perhaps you can pull your trousers down over your boots?'

He calls down the hall for Yumiko, who comes along and eases Sayuri out of bed. 'All Candy Girls are equipped with heel rollers,' she says. 'You simply lock her limbs, lean her against your shoulder, and walk her anywhere you'd like to go.'

With Sayuri leaning in front of me, I follow Mr Tak to the far end of the banquet hall and down a service corridor full of tables and stacks of dishes on trolleys. Another door leads into the hall I first sprinted through. Beyond the French doors, the sea is a bowl of blinding sun. The *bateau-mouche* is still at the dock. Mr Tak says, 'Hurry, they're about to cast off,' and skips down the steps.

The crew puts down the gangplank again, and Mr Tak sees Sayuri and me on board. 'This is the Bonbon Voyage Luncheon Cruise,' he explains, 'part of our Candy Girl Weekend Holiday. You'll make a short tour around the bay, then have an hour-long stop in Amsterdam. Men only, I'm afraid. They won't let facsimile companions into Amsterdam yet. Then everyone comes back to the ship for a buffet lunch on board as you cruise back. It's a very appetizing buffet, but I understand if you won't return for the second half of the voyage. Goodbye, Mr Fujiwara. I hope we will appear together in another sequel. *Bonbon voyage!'*

*

If you know how to talk cars, you'll know what it's like to talk Candy Girls. They all have different standard features and customized options. Some are more advanced and expensive than others, some have more classic lines, but each Candy Girl has her own personality, a rich patina of original design and individual use. Some men treat their Candy Girls like wives, which means they leave them seated inside while they go onto the deck for a smoke. Others are more romantically inclined, holding hands with their Candy Girl or leaning back with one arm around her neck and a grin of supreme satisfaction. The man seated next to me on the cruise has a striking blonde Caucasian girl dressed in a flouncy French dress. (Considering the range of nationalities available, it's surprising how many of these men have not opted for tall, lanky Finns, muscular black Americans, or imperiously busted Venezuelans. The large majority of men have women like you see every day. Normal height, normal waist, normal breast size, normal Japanese.) He's constantly shifting her hands around for her and adjusting her posture. 'Is this all right, dear?' he asks. When he starts pointing out the sights to her through the window, I've had enough. I get up and join the smokers outside until we approach the 'Port of Amsterdam', two piers and a cluster of clean white '*Douanes*' buildings with colonial-style galleries and mansard roofs. The water churns violently astern and, as if choreographed, the men take a last drag on their cigarettes and fillip them expertly into the wake.

When I go back inside the cabin, there's a very definite tension in the air. The men in their seats glance at me, frown, turn away, shake their heads. The uxorious fellow with the Marie Antoinette lookalike stares at me with obvious disdain.

And then I see why.

Sayuri has slumped head-first to the floor.

I go to pick her up and seat her again, but she only falls forward. So I shove her into place, this time so hard that her head snaps backward and gongs against the window. A murmur goes around the cabin. It seems I have seriously breached etiquette.

'You should lock her into place instead of treating her like that,' says the guy next to me.

'Oh, right,' I reply. 'And how does one –'

He sighs in consternation and puts Marie's hand back into her lap. He puts one hand on Sayuri's shoulder. 'May I?'

'Of course, of course.'

He leans her forward and opens a Velcro flap on her dress, then reaches into her kidneys and pulls some kind of lever. 'There,' he says. 'That's how you lock her into position. She's a nice girl. What's her name?'

'Sayuri.'

'Very pretty. She deserves good treatment.' The censure is unspoken but it's obvious in his voice.

'Sure, yeah. Thanks.' I make for the door.

On the gangway, one of the crew hands us each a Temporary Amsterdam Pass that we swipe past a laser at a row of turnstiles in the empty terminal. Beyond the doors is a cobblestone arcade lined with boutiques, and beyond this Amsterdam itself. I'm nervous. I can't imagine I'm not being watched. I linger at the shops. There's a hair salon all done out in aluminium and bamboo with three customers in the chairs; an empty tobacco shop with two Red Indians in full regalia flanking the entrance – one brave and one maiden – and a very fat tobacconist wearing a burgundy velvet vest behind the counter; a perfumery like a tiny hall of mirrors; a cute umbrella shop called Les Parapluies de Cherbourg; Sphinx Jeweller's; and, the last shop before the streets of Amsterdam, The St Siebold's Carrefour Shoppe, a clothing boutique with leaded bay windows and walnut panelling. I'm searching the reflections in the windows for anything suspicious, but as far as I can tell everything is normal. Business as usual.

The door to St Siebold's jingles as I go in. A pretty clerk

with her hair in a tight bun greets me from her lamp-lit desk. It smells like cloves and the shelves are full of Scottish tartan caps and scarves, Norwegian knit sweaters, tweed coats, plus fours, shortbread, silver whisky flasks ... I slip a heavy Tyrolean camel-hair coat with raglan sleeves and silver coins for buttons off its hanger. The price is astonishing, more than 70,000 yen. I would never buy a coat like this in any other circumstances. But if I'm putting myself in this much danger to bring Mai home, my father can at least participate vicariously through his JCB credit card. I turn to the approaching girl. She's in her twenties, dressed in a white lace blouse close-fitted at the sleeves and a long grey wool skirt with a huge silver clothes pin on the placket. She should be the schoolmarm in a western instead of an Amsterdam sales clerk.

'How does it look?' I ask.

She must think I'm a freak. I should be shovelling dirt in this outfit, not browsing in her boutique, but her professionalism is up to it. 'Superb,' she replies without a moment's hesitation. She steps forward to pull on the shoulders. 'Yes, a nice fit. It goes well with your khakis.'

'And with a hat?' I take a black Kangol from a shelf.

'Very stylish.'

'Do you sell sunglasses too?'

'Of course.'

'And perhaps . . .' I stare down at my yellow boots.

'Of course, of course. Come right this way. A pair of deck shoes from Sebago, I think.'

Once I've got the shoes, she picks up the coat and the hat and takes them to the counter.

'I'll wear it all now, if that's all right with you.'

'Fine, that's fine,' she replies. 'I can see how excited you are about it.'

In order to cut off the tags on the sleeve and the inside of

205

the coat she has to turn the lapel. It's a delicate manoeuvre and she scores highly for her elegant, porcelain hands.

Equipped with Ackermann, Kangol and some free Scottish shortbread in a tartan plastic carrier bag, I enter Amsterdam. All you need is JCB. I finally believe the commercial. I feel valiant, victorious, validated: if I haven't paid the 10,000-yen entry, I've given them seven times that much for a genuine Ackermann Kamelhaar. If anyone asks to see my passport I'll show the sales receipt instead.

geronimo

The *Amstel Maru* comes across the Rottermeer to dock in front of the Van Gogh Hotel and Princess Michiko's entourage debarks with a great deal of fanfare. There's a marching band, flame-throwers, jugglers, a harlequin on stilts, and a huge crowd to greet them. They set off with drums banging, thundering down the Polderstrasse. I have two hours before the troupe returns to the ship to depart, more than enough time to put Mr Choso's plan into action.

First, at the Pedalo-Pedalo on the banks of the Amstermeer, I pay in cash for a rental canoe and leave it tethered to a tree in one of the calmer canals on the outskirts of Nintjedijk. I now have transport. I know my route. Once we're out of Amsterdam, we'll paddle north to Shirahama Beach and catch the bus to Karatsu, another one to Hakata, then catch a flight or a bullet train to Kyoto and rent a car for the drive back to Inaka. We'll be home by one in the morning. All this is straightforward enough, but now that my archaeologist's disguise is blown, there is a missing component: an alibi. For this I summon all my Aozoriant genius and head back to the Port of Amsterdam.

Target? That fat tobacconist's Red Indians.

They're still there, flanking the doors just outside the shop, dressed in their deerskin trousers, beaded moccasins, deerskin vests, and headdresses – towering constructions of feathers dyed a hideous purple with cheap silver beads, plastic bones, and black headbands embroidered with ambiguous red shapes. Geronimo holds out a peace pipe in his left hand

and Pocahontas a plastic tomahawk. I note that both brave and maiden are fitted, just like Candy Girls, with wheels on their heels for easy manoeuvring. The shopping arcade isn't empty by any means, but there's no point being equivocal about stealing a full-size Red Indian. I walk straight up to the mighty Geronimo, lean him backwards and wheel him down the arcade, past several entirely unconcerned shoppers, to a large white door marked STAFF ONLY. I leave him there in the fluorescent corridor and go back for Pocahontas. When the tobacconist turns his back inside the glassed-in cigar humidor, I wheel her away too.

Deerskin is comfortable stuff, like a second skin floating just outside your own on a cushion of air. The front of my vest is open, V-neck, and the back is decorated with an eagle in colourful beadwork. Did Indians not have pockets in their clothes? I'll have to keep my telephone up my sleeve. I'd like to try fitting the deerskin over the Ackermann, but it won't go. The Ackermann, all 70,000 yen of it, goes into a garbage bin with my khakis and the Kangol. I've got no choice. If I'm going to do this, I'm going to look the part. The new deck shoes are my one utilitarian concession – I imagine having to flee on foot at some point and Geronimo's beaded moccasins are worse than useless. Once the Indians are both in the nude, Pocahontas goes down on Geronimo in a broom closet. With the second costume bundled under my arm, I don my sunglasses and headdress – the bones and feathers crackle slightly when I adjust it – and stride through Amsterdam.

Green canal. Swans to starboard. The zelkova trees are perfectly spaced between the curved Dutch pediments. Most of Amsterdam is off limits to the canoes and pedalos for rent on the Amstermeer; when I paddle out of Nintjedijk, it's through a forest of OFF LIMITS signs. Once in the canals, I have to keep to within a metre of the brick banks because of the numerous *bateaux-mouches.* Their speed is much greater than mine and it's clear from the constant horn-blowing that the captains are unaccustomed to encountering slower traffic. Around each bend in the canal I'm expecting to find a battalion of Politie with a net strung across the water. What I do meet, in Leuven, is a police launch. I see it approaching from a bisecting canal and it comes alongside very quickly, a superb Boston Whaler open-decked speedboat with two huge square Mercury V-6 outboards gurgling and smoking in the rear. There are two policemen aboard, one guiding the vessel, the other standing at the gunwale. I thump my chest with a closed fist and start chanting: '*Hey-ya, hey-ya, hey-ya, hey-ya!*'

The one at the gunwale laughs. 'What's this all about then?'

I pick up the tomahawk. 'Geronimo go attack *Amstel Maru.* Kidnap Princess Michiko! I may even take some scalps too. As souvenirs.'

'Nice costume. Have you got your employee card?'

'Do you think I've got any place to put a card?' I ask. 'Geronimo no bring card!'

The policeman at the gunwale consults an electronic notepad. 'There's nothing in the schedule about this. What department arranged it?'

I have no idea what to say. Foreign Affairs? Domestic Affairs? Ministry of Culture? Ministry of Defence? 'Department of Native Affairs,' I reply.

He laughs again. 'No, really. Was it Animation and Events?'

I nod. Yeah, that was it. 'A last-minute arrangement to drum up interest in the Nomadic People's Biennial.'

'That's all right, then,' he says. 'We'll escort you in.'

This won't work at all. 'No *kimosabe*,' I tell him. 'Law man no bring good feeling. Geronimo *hostile.*' I drop my voice to a whisper. 'Get it? I can hardly be hostile with you guys following me. Look at them, for instance.' Already there are people lining a nearby bridge taking photographs. 'People much watching. People no believe in red man.'

The policeman at the gunwale turns to the pilot. He shrugs and then they both give me the thumbs up. I wave goodbye with my tomahawk as they ease back and turn sharply down another canal.

Across the Rottermeer is the *Amstel Maru*. To its right, where the pier meets the wide expanse of the Oranjeplein, is a large crowd. I can't distinguish Mai exactly, but there's a thicket of banners where she must be, carried along at the centre of the parade. At first I think of giving her a call to prime her again for the escape, but I decide against it: better not give her a chance to think too much about it. Things never work out when she does that. I slide in among the boats at the private marina to wait. The walkways are totally deserted and the pristine yachts and shining white cigarette boats are as static and perfect as models in a showroom.

The show begins with two sailors swinging down from the boom of the *Amstel Maru* with red-white-and-blue banners unfurling behind them. Then the band starts up a Nami Amuro number and I can see a little purple Mai mount the dais at the rear of the ship. I have to give her some credit; though her choice of tunes is terrible, her voice is something else.

After almost half an hour of Top 40, at the last dying gasp of 'I Will Always Love You' the crowd goes nuts. Mai bends down at the edge of the dais to pick up flowers, then descends into the ship to her dressing room. A moment later, one of the dark portholes on the ship's flank turns amber. I push off from the hull of a huge yellow cigarette boat and start pulling as hard as I can, sending the canoe surging forward across the expanse of water. It would have been better to wait until the crowds of onlookers had fully dispersed, but we've only got a couple of hours before Mai's friendly chaperones begin to wonder if she's left the dance. I head as far from the Oranjeplein as possible before cutting back at an oblique angle, using the bulk of the ship to shield me from the crowds still on the pier. When I'm within five metres of the ship, a sailor dressed like a schoolgirl in white and blue comes out of the control room on the bridge and stands at the gunwale watching me. 'What are you doing?' he asks.

'*Hey-ya, hey-ya, hey-ya, hey-ya,*' I yell. 'Raping your daughters. Scalping your sons. Pissing on your decks.'

The guy tries to smile, but can't quite manage it. 'Have you got permission?'

'Of course I do.'

'From whom?'

'Animation and Events.'

He frowns. 'Wait there,' he tells me. 'I'll go check with the captain.'

The moment the door to the control room closes, I make for midships and stand on the seat of the canoe, trying to reach the lighted window.

'Mai!'

No answer.

I'm tall, but I can't reach the porthole standing on the seat of the canoe. From a more stable platform I could jump high enough to catch the window ledge and pull my face even with the porthole, but the canoe will surely drift away and strand me if I try it. Keeping the canoe beneath me as I lean against the sheer side of the ship is already a balancing act. I reach up with my paddle and tap at the window with it. No response. The pane of glass has to be ten centimetres thick. I tap harder. Still no response. I'm about to give it a solid whack when it swings open and Mai's head and shoulders appear in the gap. 'Oh my god, Aozora. What are you wearing?'

'Here, put this on. You Pocahontas. Me Geronimo. Get it?'

'We're escaping in a *canoe*? This doesn't sound like much of a plan.'

'It isn't,' I reply. 'But it'll be fun. Just like old times.'

She reaches down with a frown. 'When was that?'

I shrug. 'Come on, Mai, please. Hurry up!'

The current takes us down the Rijkscanal and out of Breukelen in short time. On the Dolce Vita dining pontoon, the white-aproned waiters with their small zinc trays pause between guests to watch us go by.

'Put the headdress on too,' I tell Mai.

'Where did you get this stuff?'

'Habana Cabana.'

Mai cracks up giggling. For the first time in a very long time, I am responsible. She looks pretty in her embroidered armband. 'So they're just standing there naked?' she asks.

'They're doing a rather prudish sixty-nine in a closet.'

One of the diners aims his camera as we pass and I brandish my plastic tomahawk. Two officers of the Amsterdam Politie pause at a parapet to watch as we pass beneath a bridge. The current moves faster now and the hip-gable roof and ironwork faux-balconies of the Kempinski Grand Hotel Vermeer ease ahead of the surrounding neighbourhood until they're towering above us. What I feel at that moment, with Mai finally in the boat with me, leaving this gingerbread kingdom, is a kind of euphoria, like the effect of cocaine or what characters in books call 'romance' or 'adventure'. My chest is tight, my breathing fast, my head icy clear and my arms and legs so pumped they're light as helium balloons. I can feel the cartilage and tendons and muscles in my shoulders and arms all working together like titanium and Teflon componentry. I've got a fantastic hunger coupled with the delicious sensation that everything in the world is edible, that it's all just confectionery. I want to scream out with the pleasure of it as I lap up Pepsi-Cola from the river, chew the jellied tulips, crunch the windmills' brittle arms. Guests lean from their balconies on the massive façade, watching us, and I watch them right back, proud as a brave, until the gaping archway of the tunnel swallows us in.

It's cool and dark and the light recedes behind us until there's barely a glimmer on the water. Our voices echo down the corridor. I was expecting to see the other end of the tunnel immediately, but all there is before us is darkness and a sound like one infinitely long sheet of paper being sheared in two.

I yell at Mai: 'How you doing?'

'Scared!' she calls back.

Me too, I think. 'Don't worry!'

The noise gets louder as we're sucked down the tunnel. It feels as if the walls are closing in, the current getting faster and faster. I can just imagine what Mai's thinking, sitting at the very bow of the canoe: we're probably headed for the blades of a massive, bone-grinding, sluice-driven turbine and she'll be the first to be chopped in two. I paddle as hard as I can now. The current is too strong to go back. If we're going to die, I want it to happen quickly. The volume builds to a roar.

'Heads down!' I yell.

And at the deafening metallic crescendo, when I'm expecting the canoe to be crunched like a celery stick, I smell tempura. *Ebi* shrimp tempura, to be exact, and possibly sweet potato as well. We're enveloped in a hot wash of air and a miasma of frying oil. What can only be kitchen ventilators pass by noisily, harmlessly overhead.

'My god!' Mai yells.

'Damn!' I'm laughing, because she is too. 'Damn, Mai-Tai, if we get out of this alive, I'm gonna appreciate my next *ebi-fry.*'

'Aozora, I thought we were going to die!' She hasn't spoken to me with such feeling since we were twelve, jumping into the Kurokawa River in the middle of winter.

From the front of the canoe comes a flicker of amber light from Mai's lighter. It disappears quickly, then reappears, sustained this time. The tiny flame makes the walls of the tunnel warble like something organic. We're a tiny bubble of greenish light drawn down a long tube. In a moment we'll be reborn into sunshine and warmth and freedom. But this trance comes to an abrupt end.

The canoe slams to a stop.

I'm pitched forward onto the floor. I reach up to grab the gunwale as the canoe swings around and then shears along the concrete wall, pinned there by the force of the current. The knuckles of my right hand are ground to paste. I slump to the floor again. The canoe jerks and turns and there's a sliver of light ahead and I hear Mai moaning and it's all mixed up with my own fresh pain like butterscotch swirls in ice cream that's too damn cold for your taste buds to function.

Mai's silhouette emerges before me. 'Think I cracked my skull,' she whispers, and slips sideways, halfway out of the canoe. We ship some water before I can crawl down and pull her back in. I run my left hand over and around her head. 'No blood,' I tell her. 'Can you see straight? How many tunnels are there?'

'Two?'

'Good. You're fine.'

Myself? A rapid Aozoran physical. Head? Intact. Face? Intact. Torso? Wet deerskin clad. Legs? Carl Lewis. Phalanges of right hand? Bloody, painful. The archway is approaching at speed and is now dazzlingly bright. I'm dazed but I get the canoe righted in the stream and we slide out from the tunnel into the sunlight of Komura Bay.

mrs kakinoki

'He was almost fifty and really prim, like an Englishman or something, with a burgundy-red paisley cravat. And when he comes into the bedroom – imagine this, Ao, *I* had to wait for *him* – when he comes in he's dressed in sky-blue pyjamas with navy cuffs, and he steps into bed and pulls the covers up to his chin. He was really tentative about it. I think his wife was dead or something.' I never thought Mai'd actually answer my questions about what I euphemistically term 'her career path', but she's talkative this morning, running high on a mixture of elation and fear. 'Anyhow, I thought, what's the difference between this and getting drunk at a club and meeting some guy and going home with him? I mean really, which is the worse of the two situations? At least I don't wake up with a hangover or any less money than I had the night before.'

'Yeah, I'm sure it's like sleeping with Prince Charles every night.'

'You're such an ass.'

'Well, stop rationalizing. You sound like a spokesperson for the trade.'

'No, they're not all like that. That's exactly why I *do* rationalize.'

I toss a pebble over the edge of the cliff. The water is stretched like cling wrap between the island and the mainland. Another speedboat churns past in open water to our left. Four times already this morning boats have come down the coast: the long hulls of *yakuza* cigarette boats driven by guys who look like they're auditioning for *Miami Vice*. The island is thick with vegetation and we've pulled the canoe far back into the trees. It took us longer than I expected to get here and we missed the last Karatsu bus. We spent the night beneath the canoe and now we're sitting in our underwear, waiting for our deerskins to dry, investigating various insect bites, getting hungry and arguing about what to do. We can't continue by canoe with the patrols going past, and Gondo's men will be all over the 210 highway by now.

Characters in films have fear in their eyes, but I can see it in Mai's fingers. Perfectly unaware of what she's doing, she nips at the palm of her left hand with the glossy pink nails of her thumb and little finger. All I've thought about up until now is what I have to gain, but I take a moment for imaginative investment in Mai's situation. She's damn scared. She'll be beaten if they catch her. Locked in some dingy room in Marumachi. Forced to work like the foreign girls work.

'I'm going to miss Amsterdam,' she says.

Right, there goes my empathetic state of mind. Risking my life to get Mai out of there, I'm not overly pleased to hear her wax nostalgic about it. 'The place is a sham.'

'I was popular. I had fans. Did you hear me sing? Those are the first real audiences I've ever had.'

In droll monotone I address the assembled audience of bugs and trees: 'The Princess Michiko will now lecture us on what is real.'

'Okay, you lecture me then, Mr Kyoto University. What's real in *your* life?'

It wouldn't be like me to let her get the upper hand in a conversation by actually considering something she says, but my life back in Kyoto's a haze of mah-jong, nightclubs, video games, all-night drinking parties and casual sex-friends. I don't know if I've learned one useful thing in university. All I've really achieved apart from a record score in Sega Rally is to lose my girlfriend and get my only friend pulped. 'Don't know,' I say. 'Don't know.'

Mai doesn't quite know what to make of my reflective state of mind. 'Well, that's nice to hear for a change,' she says. 'Oh, how's Father? Have you talked to the hospital again?'

'Ah, yeah. Yeah, sure did. They said that we'd better come as soon as possible, but that maybe there's a chance of remission too.'

She looks down sadly at her neat red toenails. I wonder how she's going to react when she finds him happy and healthy back in Inaka. He'll be up a stepladder in the garden when we arrive, I know it. In his damn baseball cap. And he'll invite us in for percolator coffee and Fig Newtons.

Morning becomes noon and we still have no clear option. I propose that we walk back through the hills to Amsterdam and get help from Mr Choso. He offered to do anything he could. They won't be expecting us to stay close by. We could stay in the mobile, Mr Choso could get a car and drive us out by night. But Mai is sceptical. She doesn't want to go anywhere in the direction of Marumachi.

'Look,' she says.

Someone is out on the water.

Mrs Kakinoki. We watch as she crosses the reach and the monkeys emerge from the trees. I'm hungry. I stare at the bag, trying to make out whether she's brought cherry tomatoes or persimmons. I get up and start down the hill. 'Come on. She's a friend.'

Our sudden appearance and unorthodox clothing don't faze Mrs Kakinoki in the least. (When you wake up one morning with a full-size Amsterdam next door, a couple of Red Indians in the bushes is nothing.) 'Hello,' she says. 'Have you come to feed the monkeys again?'

I introduce my sister, then we go through the same routine of feeding the monkeys as before. Afterwards she invites us

up to her hillside hut for lunch. My sister's height and posture aren't so surprising outdoors, but in the cramped interior
of Mrs Kakinoki's house, Mai's like a peacock in a rabbit
hutch. She sits there on the tatami rigid as a Bodhisattva,
almost as tall seated as Mrs Kakinoki is standing up. Despite
herself, Mrs Kakinoki gazes as she makes tea, unable to
believe the progress between her own generation of gnomes
and this athlete/pop star/princess. She serves us rice and
pickles in the Navy bowls, then goes out of her way to make
us *mochi* cakes burned with a five-petal plum-blossom pattern. 'Not as good as you could have in Dazaifu,' she says.
Mochi's pretty bland no matter what, but I'm content sitting
on the narrow veranda beside the sliding doors, watching
the ships far out on the sea and another of the cigarette boats
making a tiny white cursor on the calm bay. The magpies
scout around for goods, sparring with the CDs that turn and
flash in the breeze. She opens the grill and taps out the steaming *mochi*.

While we're eating our rice and pickles, I hear what sounds
like a mosquito buzzing somewhere nearby. But it's not. It's
coming from further away. I stand up and walk out into the
open.

'Speed tribe,' says Mai behind me.

They're probably just on their way up to the Hibiki, I think.
But I'm not convinced. The sound of the bikes keeps getting
louder.

Mrs Kakinoki comes out with the plate of *mochi*, a quizzical look on her face. 'That's strange,' she says, coming out
onto the veranda. 'They're coming up the track.'

'*What?* Coming *here*?'

Mai sees my alarm. 'What?' she asks.

I run back inside and put on my shoes. 'Mrs Kakinoki, it
was very pleasant, but now we have to go.'

'What's the matter?' she asks.

What's the best way of putting this? 'Mrs Kakinoki, do you remember telling me the story of how you saved those monkeys?'

'Of course.'

'Well, Marumachi, you know, it's a big laboratory. And my sister, she's one of the monkeys. [Predictable facial expression from my Mai.] She's out of her cage, and I'm pretty sure whoever is coming here wants to put her back. Do you understand my meaning?'

It's the wrong question, of course. For her to admit to understanding me would insult her guest, Mai. But she's not stupid either. She knows exactly what I mean. She's a dear old bird, but that crumpled face of hers gives me a sharp look that says, 'Are you totally uncouth?'

'You haven't done anything wrong?' she asks.

'Think of your monkeys,' I reply. 'Totally innocent.'

'I'll take you into the hills then,' she says. She gets up and dumps the plate of hot *mochi* into a brown paper bag. Then she starts stuffing plastic sacks of butterbur, huge black aubergines and Tupperware containers of who-knows-what into a green cotton sack. 'Do you like aubergine?'

'Love them. Love them.' The motorcycles are getting louder. 'I really think we should make a move.'

'I have some of the little white and violet aubergines out in the garden,' she says. 'They're very tender.'

Once the excruciating process of putting together a seven-course picnic is done, Mrs Kakinoki leads us out of the house and between the rice fields. The tussock is narrow and muddy and Mai slips into the rice paddy. I go back to pull her out and the vegetables and the bag of *mochi* spill out of the sack over my shoulder. Mai goes to pick them up.

'Leave them!' I yell at her. 'Come on!'

There's no doubt where the speed tribe is headed now;

their engines are reverberating through the bamboo like a squadron of Zeros at Pearl Harbor.

'Go,' says Mrs Kakinoki. 'Run up the path to the Jizo statues, then go left. There's a big stone there you can hide behind.' She turns back.

'What are you going to do?' Mai asks.

'I'll make them some *mochi*. Oh, please don't disturb the moss on the stone. It's very old.'

I had expected the Jizo statues to be a long way up into the hills, but they're only several metres up the path through the bamboo. Moreover, the huge stone is the most obvious hiding place possible. It seems Mrs Kakinoki doesn't have much experience at clandestine operations. We race around the moss-covered stone and tumble into a panting heap.

The bikes roar as they come out across Mrs Kakinoki's fields, then one by one the engines stop. Suddenly it's eerily quiet in the feathery green light. A common crow barks hoarsely and disappears into the foliage, wings soughing loudly in the calm air. We could be in one of those gardens that tourists somehow find their way to in Kyoto. Several years of fear-time pass. I wish I had a Game Boy.

The motorcycles roar back to life. Mai looks at me like I should know what the hell to do. I play it cool and shake my head. 'Could be a trick.'

Finally Mrs Kakinoki calls to us from the pathway. 'I'm afraid your *mochi* is ruined,' she says. 'Don't worry though. We'll get you something to eat when we get there.'

'Where's "there"?' I ask.

But she's already set off ahead and doesn't seem to hear me.

For an old bird, Mrs Kakinoki makes her way through the forest with incredible speed. She's not exactly agile, but she seems to know instinctively how to avoid anything that might constitute a barrier to her forward progress. I know enough to follow along behind her, but my sister is gawky, upright, not paying attention, and constantly walking into/tripping over/getting entangled in things. At least once every thirty or forty metres she stops to do a frenzied dance with spiders' webs in her hair.

'How much *longer*?' She is the whingeing child in the back seat.

Mrs Kakinoki has no conception of time precise enough to suit my sister. She knows the geography perfectly; she tells us what ridge we're on, what valley we're heading for, which path will take us where, but the nearest approximate ETA she can give us is 'before night falls'.

Mai checks her watch. 'That's *hours*!'

'Oh yes?' Mrs Kakinoki replies.

I do my best to keep up with her and inquire about our destination. She's been so focused that it hardly seemed necessary to ask her at first. I assume we're going to someone else's farm higher up, an old boar hunter's shack, or even a shrine.

'We're going to Yoshii,' she says. 'But we'll stop in a ghost town first.'

I'm in a Haruki Murakami novel now. I'm certain of it. We're going to meet eternal World War II soldiers and singing skulls and find an entrance to a real Netherland. 'And there are . . . um . . . *ghosts* in this town?' I ask.

'Of course. But no more than anywhere else.'

Of course. Far be it for me to suggest otherwise. I'm glad Mai's too far back to pick up on our surreal conversation. I can just hear the remonstrations she'd be making. Because *I'm* the one who got us into this *mess*. She didn't *have* to leave Amsterdam today. We could have waited and come up with a *better* plan.

'It's called Takayama,' says Mrs Kakinoki, leading us across a clearing where tiger fritillaries burst from the field grass and the leaves of aspens glitter like the bay far below. 'Everyone left when the pulp mill closed.'

I try calling Dad, but for probably the first time in my life, I'm too far from a cellular tower for a signal. The baby antenna on the screen extends to adult size for a short flicker and then disappears completely.

The fields of Takayama High School are windswept and empty. The front office is empty. The main corridor is empty. So far

then, there's nothing to distinguish the school from the rest of this sometime town. We walk down the drive and across a courtyard to the front office. Other than bulbuls bickering over loquats, the silence is complete. The front door is unlocked. 'I thought we could stop here for a rest on our way to Yoshii,' says Mrs Kakinoki. She takes off her shoes and goes straight to a dark-wood desk to sign her name in a heavy green book. She insists we do the same, and has us clip yellow Visitor's Passes to the collars of our deerskin tunics.

Strangely enough, the school is in perfect shape. The windowpanes look as if they've just been cleaned and the linoleum floors are polished to a luxuriant shine. Mrs Kakinoki leads us along the second floor to a set of sliding doors with a small card on the wall that reads, DR NOGUCHI. 'He lives in Kagoshima now,' says Mrs Kakinoki, 'but he still comes here once a month to look after the place. It was his school for many years.'

What most impresses me on entering Dr Noguchi's room are the towers of books leaning in from the walls – biology textbooks and workbooks and lab manuals from 1972 to 1999. They form crags and arêtes and I have the impression I'm walking through a canyon. The four desks in the centre of the room have been inundated by more books, as well as telephones, coffee mugs, coffee and biscuit and tomato-salsa jars full of mould, a television, beer cans and an empty hibiscus pot. In one corner is a large glass cabinet full of lifeless beasties – scarabs, sparrows, horseshoe crabs with legs all broken and scattered, a once ferocious and now almost completely denuded ferret casting a shadow of brown, white-tipped hairs, a beaver's skull, and numerous other fragments of animal matter – wasp and butterfly wings, fish bones, spiders' legs, still iridescent blue flies – all shored in small drifts against the glass. The remaining space in the room is taken up by a refrigerator, a small gas stove and six cycling machines that look like they came from a Soviet gulag.

'Sit down, please,' says Mrs Kakinoki. 'Would you like tea?' Apparently her definition of tea includes coffee because she sets about prising open coffee cans with a bent butter knife to find one that's not empty.

I pull a chair into the one crack of sunlight escaping the drapes.

I'm reminded of my father's office. He worked in the National Revenues office in Inaka for twenty years before it closed down and he turned to topiary full time. We were never allowed to go there on weekdays, but on the odd Saturday or Sunday he would let Mai and me go to the office for an hour or two in the morning. It was at a sun-shot window just like this that I found the skin of a newly moulted snake hanging from a drainpipe, swaying in an imperceptible breeze. At first I had thought it was a metre-length of toilet paper or translucent plastic hanging there; it was only when I had reached out to tug it away that I saw the yellowish filigree of scales. It was, to quote my father, 'a fine specimen'; the eyeholes in the head had been perfectly intact. I had pulled it in gently and laid it on my father's desk. When he returned, I told him it was an *aodaisho*'s skin

(a mere guess), and he said what a wonderful botanist I would make. We all took a turn stroking the snakeskin for good fortune.

Mai looks at the piles of books. She peers at the spine of one near the bottom of the pile and reaches out, but then thinks better of trying to remove it. There's no way that book is coming out without the whole Guinness World Record attempt coming down on top of her.

Mrs Kakinoki brings mugs of coffee over and sits across from me in a seat that screeches in agony. Every time she shifts her weight I can feel my molars cracking. Mai stares at the books along the walls. The desk I'm sitting at has a clear rubber surface protector. Absent-mindedly I pick up a pencil and sink the lead into the soft rubber, making a circle of small, blackened holes. I almost finish the circle before I even realize what I'm doing. 'This Dr Noguchi,' I say, 'he thinks this school will open up again some day?'

Mrs Kakinoki sucks her teeth. 'I doubt it.'

'Then why look after it? Why not just let it go?'

She smiles her crooked-toothed smile. 'Oh, who am I to say?' She gets up from her chair. But I think she could say more. I think she understands just why he doesn't give up on Takayama High School, and is leaving me to figure it out myself.

She leaves the room and comes back a few minutes later with new Takayama High School tracksuits, still in their plastic wrap. Mai's is light blue, mine navy. 'There,' she says, 'you'll be more comfortable in these.'

I lose track of all the mountains and ridges we've walked over since we left Takayama, but at around seven o'clock we emerge into a clearing on the top of a ridge. Far below is a village in the valley. It's almost night by the time we cross the last of the rice paddies and kiwi vineyards to arrive at the main road. There's a bus stop glowing fluorescent yellow up ahead, but Mrs Kakinoki hails a taxicab from the rank instead, goes to speak to the cab driver, and then motions us inside. 'Go on, go on. He'll take you to Karatsu. From there you can catch a train or a bus.'

We both go to thank her but she waves us away.

'It's nothing,' she says. 'Nothing. Please remember to send the tracksuits back, or else pay for them. Some day they might be needed by students at the school.'

I doubt this highly. But I promise. I bow to a full forty-five degrees and hold it.

I had envisioned the journey back to Inaka fraught with danger, full of high-speed chases and cliffhanging adventure, but the public rail system works with perfect boring efficiency. A bullet train takes us back to Osaka within four hours. We pay for four hours in a karaoke parlour near Umeda Station and fall asleep on the benches. The next morning, we're on our way back to Inaka on the single-car diesel.

inaka

Do you remember this commercial? Departing taxi shivers as it dwindles down a hot tarmac road. The hero slings a sack over his shoulder and starts walking away from the station. Sweat streams from his temples. The sun screeches like a beginner's violin. Desert birds wheel. He slows. Hand goes to brow. The heat is too much. The bag drops to the road. He drops to his knees. The end is near. But hold it, what's that? In the distance a smudge of blue appears, getting larger, warbling as it grows. Is it a mirage? With a blast of rock and roll, a blue Jeep full of beautiful girls and cans of Asahi on ice pulls up. Snowflakes fall all around. The can cracks open in a cloud of spray. *Ahhh!*

But this is Inaka. All that corresponds to the cinematic vision is the taxi, Inaka's only one, disappearing into the heat waves.

There's still no answer when I ring the house so now we're walking. It's too hot for Mai. It's too humid. It smells like swamp gas. There are too many insects. God, she'd forgotten about the insects! She can't walk in these shoes. Aozora, you have no idea! The snakes come out as the sun rises; a large blue *aodaisho* crosses the road ten kilometres ahead of us and she leaps onto my back, blubbering. By the time we're passing Inari Shrine she's lagging far behind, sulking because I won't 'wait up!' I'm hot and thirsty and dreaming of beer in the fridge.

The driveway is empty. The Proudia is nowhere to be seen. Everything looks much as it did the last time I was here, though the ground beneath the topiary is desiccated into one immense, impossible jigsaw puzzle and the box elephants have yellowed. The front door slides open with ease. (My father was always very proud to explain to anyone from the city that he had not once in his life locked the front door of his home.) The anteroom is still lined with bottles and smells of stale saké, though there's a whiff of old cigarettes from a coffee cup full of cigarette butts on the shelf.

My father doesn't smoke. Never has. Then again, he never used to drink much either. I continue through the next set of doors. The house is in deep shadow. A miasma of cigarette smoke hangs in the foyer. The orange tip of the offending cigarette glows in the semi-darkness in front of me.

I could, I believe, defend myself from a major outer cut if I saw it coming. But not in the dark. My body slams into the floor. The sliding door crashes shut.

'Finally!' a man shouts.

I roll over but my face is pressed against the floor and what I assume is someone's knee jams into my spine.

'So, we were just about to leave, yeah?' continues Ishikawa. 'Really, Fujiwara. Another day and we'd have given up. We thought you weren't going to show.'

The lights go on, but all I can see from this position is the far wall of the corridor and two tennis shoes. My dad did a good job with this floor; the grain of the wood has been brought out by careful sanding and years and years of polish.

I think of Mai. She's trudging into a trap. She must be approaching the drive by now. I yell as loud as I can: '*What do you want?!*'

'Whoa, whoa. What's the commotion?'

'*I'll call the police!*'

By the hair, my head is gently lifted from the floor, then replaced with considerably more force. Twice over. My cheekbones are not used to this treatment. They feel as fragile as bird bones.

'You going to keep it down?' I still can't see anything but Ishikawa's K-Swiss.

'*Okay!*' I croak as loudly as I can. 'I'll do what you *say.*'

'Damn it, is he deaf or something?' The shoes retract from my field of vision, then reappear directly in front of my face in frightening perspective. He is now standing directly over me. With a raised *katana*? This may be my last conscious moment. The vast kaleidoscope of my life contracts to this? Or, no, what was it called?

A *wakizashi*.

'Ah, Mr Uno,' he says. 'So, it's Ishikawa. I have someone here who would like to say hello, yeah?' Ishikawa squats down in front of me. Khaki cargo shorts. Black T-shirt. Long hair. Goatee. Nose ring. An armoury of earrings. Lennon glasses. I vaguely remember having seen him in Mr Uno's bar. 'Say hello,' he says, and puts a telephone to the side of my head.

It is a fuzzy connection, as they always are in Inaka, but I think I can hear Mr Uno breathing on the other end of the line.

'Hello, Mr Uno. How are you today?'

There is no response.

'Um, I almost have your money. We agreed on Tuesday, remember? Daiwa 4674523, I know it by heart.'

'Heart?' he says finally. 'Heart?' He really is breathing hard. 'Put Ishikawa back on.'

The phone is taken away. 'You want us to bring him to Ikoma?' Ishikawa asks. 'Yeah, it's quiet. Ah, probably. Nope. Good idea. Yeah. Okay.' He snaps the phone shut.

Something's moving in the anteroom. A bottle clinks. My hopes fall. Now Mai's going to be mixed up in this too.

'What was that?' says Ishikawa. 'Go check.'

The knee comes off my back. A pair of Nike Airs go to the door.

I try warning her again: '*PLEASE! Don't kill me. I'll pay you the –*'

Ishikawa's knee comes down hard on the back of my neck. 'Listen to me, yeah? I've got to keep you in presentable condition till Mr Uno gets here, but that doesn't, like, mean it needn't be a painful wait.'

I had never imagined that, when being throttled, it is less the lack of oxygen that one finds alarming than the sheer pain – multicoloured cables of it bundled into my crushed neck. He gets up. 'What was it?'

The other man steps back into the foyer. 'Land crabs. Eating the cat food.'

'Crabs?' says Ishikawa. 'What the hell are crabs doing here?'

'They're *kawagani*,' I whisper, though my speaking apparatus seems to have a crimp. 'Freshwater crab. Live anywhere there's moving ground water.'

They haul me up from the floor and push me down the corridor, into the tearoom. They have a bag of plastic bands that my father uses for the topiary and they use at least two dozen of them to bind my hands to my feet. Then they push me back onto the tatami.

'Take it easy,' says Ishikawa. 'Mr Uno wants you fresh.'

The second they're gone I try to move, but the bands cut into my skin. There's no way I'll get free. I'm tired. It's nice to lie on the fresh tatami and look out the windows at the ornamental garden. I like this room now. I'm glad it's empty and quiet and full of light. I should have thought about death a little more before, it's the only way to appreciate things. A white-eye lands on the veranda, then skips across the garden in several short bursts of flight. I close my eyes. If I fall asleep, I'll wake up with Mr Uno's face in mine, but I can't help it. I always thought I'd fight, that I'd never give up. But we don't all have to be Saigo Takamori, marching to the sea through a

231

super-human barrier of pain just to go out honourably. It occurs to me that most people die without any honour at all. You can just lie down. You can just go to sleep.

'But I'm a fighter,' I tell myself, and repeat it. 'I'm a fighter. I'm a fighter. I'm a fighter . . .'

The gunfight begins in my dreams. It's clear and dramatic – in vivid colour and very loud. So it's something of a disappointment to wake up and find, once the first flash of fear has subsided, that I have very little idea of what's going on. There's someone crashing around in the anteroom, screaming and smashing bottles, and from somewhere else in the house, perhaps the kitchen, comes the sound of gunfire. *Clack clack clack bang bang clack clack.* I thought a gun going off would be like a thunderclap, a rent in the atmosphere, but these guns sound tinny. Like castanets. *Clack clack bang bang.* The windows break with a pitiable *tinkle tinkle.* It sounds like my third-grade band, a little louder perhaps, but just as discordant. It doesn't come close to living up to the film versions I've seen; there are no special effects or choreography at all. It's certainly no ballet with guns. The *clack clack bang bang* moves outside. The screaming stops. A car engine roars.

I'm still lying on the tatami just where I was an hour . . . two hours ago? The door to the TV room slides open behind me.

Mai's head peeks through.

'Mai!' I yell. 'I'm here!'

'*Shhh,*' she hisses. 'Come on.'

'I can't move.'

She's still wearing her blue Takayama High tracksuit. 'They did a good job,' she says, examining the thick plastic bands around my hands and feet.

'They'll slice easily if you've got a knife,' I tell her. 'Or even a pair of scissors.'

Mai starts ransacking the room for something sharp.

'What's going on out there?' I ask.

'Gondo's friends are here.'

'What?'

'I called him. I didn't know what else to do.'

'Why didn't you just call the police?'

She stops for a moment. '*Hm.* Didn't think of it. God, there's got to be a pair of scissors here somewhere. Oh, hey, what about this?' She holds up an adjustable wrench. 'Think it'll work?'

No, but it's worth a try. If both Uno's and Gondo's men are in this house, *anything* is worth a try. She jams the head of the wrench between the plastic bands around my wrists and starts twisting. 'Hey! *Easy*, Mai, *easy*. That thing is useless.'

'Can't you move at all?' she asks. 'Where am I going to find a knife? Do you think I should chance going to the kitchen?'

Yes! Go to the kitchen. Get a knife. Come back and save me. 'No,' I reply. 'You'll get yourself killed. Get me on my feet.'

She angles me off the floor. All I can manage is a crouching frog position. Mai holds me by the sweatshirt while I make tiny hops, pushing off with my toes. Twenty hops later, I've covered about a metre of the three that lie between me and the door to the garden. And once we get outside, what am I supposed to do then?

The cosmic castanets stop. Then start again in earnest. On the wall to the left of us, three perfect holes appear one after the other. *Clack clack clack.* A fourth crashes into the piano in the next room with a jangle of smashed metal viscera. All the photographs and knick-knacks topple to the floor.

I see the piano as I last saw it. 'Scissors!' I shout. 'Mai, on the piano. Go!'

She skips into the TV room and comes back with Mom's tailor's scissors, the ones she would never let us use because she didn't want them going blunt. *Snip* – it's easy! She gets four of the twenty or more bands sliced before silence returns ominously to the house. She pauses. We can hear someone coming down the old floorboards of the corridor.

'Hide!' I hiss.

'Here, use these.' She puts the scissors into my hands, then steps into the darkness of the TV room and slides the door shut just as the door leading to the corridor slides open. Ishikawa's head ducks into the doorway and disappears. Ducks in again. Then a black handgun leads him through. He turns left and right, both arms outstretched, rigid, as if the handgun is charged with several thousand volts and he can't let go.

He sidesteps around the room and, satisfied there's no one else here, drops his arms. He's breathing hard. 'You've got wicked friends, yeah?' He reaches into the side pocket of his khaki cargo shorts and takes out a black tube the size of a cigar. This he screws into the barrel of the handgun.

So this is how it happens, I think. I've been waiting to learn these details for so long I can hardly believe the moment is now. I'm not terrified, just transfixed by the progress of the well-oiled silencer into the barrel, the number of turns it takes to tighten it and the butterfly-like movement of Ishikawa's fingers as he's screwing it in. 'What kind of handgun is that?' I ask.

He puts his fingers to his lips.

'No, really. I'd like to know. And where do you get one of those anyway?'

'You're too much, you know? It's a Beretta, yeah? And as a favour to Mr Uno who is probably like dead now, I'm going to cap you with it.'

And that's what he's about to do. The silencer gets one more half-turn. He points the gun at my guts. The door to the TV room slides open and my sister screams: '*Ao!*'

Ishikawa turns and fires at the door. Mai disappears.

'*Mai!*' I yell.

The darkness in the TV room is pierced by a stuttering flash. *Clack clack clack clack* go the guns and it sounds like someone is playing drums on the wall behind me as it's peppered with slugs. One of them thumps into Ishikawa. '*Owww!*' he cries, stumbling to his knees. He crawls into the ornamental alcove, upsetting the dish and the foxed camellia. '*Owww*, that hurts.'

It's a bit of an anticlimax. I think for a moment that he hasn't actually been shot, even though that squelch as the bullet hit him – though it's the first time I've heard it – is unmistakable. He's holding his side, but I can't see any blood.

'Oh, damn it, that hurts, yeah?' He edges further into the corner, like some more pitiable kind of wounded animal. '*Bas*-tards. Where's my gun?'

It's on the tatami between us, but he doesn't see it. His eyes are clenched tight. The pain's got him gripped. Two men slip through the door from the TV room. With my hands and feet tied, I'm hoping it's very very obvious I'm not a threat.

'*Bas*-tards,' says Ishikawa again, and finally notices the gun that's right in front of him. He goes to grab it. I shut my eyes and turn my head away.

mr kuroda

It's seven o'clock in the evening. Skull is sitting at the kitchen
table, looking at me with a dimwit smile and eating Fig Newtons
for his supper. He's finished the entire pack before Gondo
comes back with Mai. I'm glad to see that her face is intact,
but it's obvious that she's been crying. Gondo is grim. His coif
towers with a laquered shine and his eyes dart about behind
his glasses like riled animals in a cage. Skull gives up his seat
and Gondo sits down, leaning across the table. He starts in on
me right away. 'Aozora!' he barks, and I have to straighten my
shoulders to repress the chill I get hearing him use my first
name. 'You're going to have to learn something, *ne*? You
can keep secrets from the public but *not* from me. They're *my*
currency, *ne*?' He takes out his Dunhills. '*Ne*?'

'Yes, Mr Gondo.'

'I was in the middle of a meeting with Chinese investors.
They want to build a theme park in Shenzhen. All of a sudden
I get a call from Mai. My best girl. Says she's in trouble. So
I call my friends in Kyoto and ask them to come here as a
favour. Then I drive all the way from Kyushu at 200 kilometres an hour only to find this mess.' He flings his hand
around to indicate the house. It's only then I notice there's
blood on the floor. 'And you know what? This could all
have been avoided. Why didn't you tell me your father was
dying?'

The honest response would be: 'Because, Mr Gondo, sir,
it's not true.' But there may be other less perilous and equally
acceptable responses. Such as silence.

'You could have told me. Mai could have told me. I have respect for fathers. Show me the man who's disrespectful to his parents, yet still faithful to his employer. Impossible. Yet, instead of trusting me, you put your lives in danger playing cowboys and Indians and getting mixed up with these small-time hoodlums.'

And that's it for the time being, I suppose. I'm not sure what to say, though he obviously wants a response. If I were wearing a watch I would time the silence. I smile sheepishly. 'What's the Chinese theme park called?'

'SORRY!' he roars.

Everyone in Inaka hears him. I've got my forehead pressed against the table. 'Sorry, Mr Gondo. Very sorry. Very sorry.'

He shakes his head and stubs out his half-smoked cigarette into a coffee cup. He sighs. 'Honestly,' he says to Skull. 'Young people. For them, it's always the "what", not the "how".'

Skull nods like he actually understands a word.

'Terrible, if you'd like to know, Fujiwara. Terrible. Their tastes are puerile, pre-Disneyland. No model for what I want to do at all.'

This is good. He likes this topic. We'll talk about this for a while until he calms down. 'The Chinese will be your biggest clientele in twenty years,' I tell him. 'The Chinese are the Japanese of the fut—'

'I don't care!'

'Sorry, Mr Gondo. Very sorry.'

'I cater to Japanese clientele only. And don't sidetrack me. You want to pay respects to your father? That's good conduct, *ne*? He's in the local hospital?'

'Um, yeah,' I reply because nothing convincing comes to mind. The hospital is twenty minutes' drive away; my life has been reduced to such hard-won increments.

He gets up. '*Ja*, come on then.'

*

237

We're somewhere between Inaka and Kurokawa, heading for the regional hospital. Mai and I are in the back seat, Gondo at the wheel. (Charged, I understand, with unspecified errands related to Mr Ishikawa and Mr Uno, Skull's staying at the house. I don't know any more of the details, and I'm not going to ask.) We drive in silence. And is the Century *ever* silent. It's as silent as a hearse. Every minute that goes by I'm just waiting for Gondo to turn off the highway into the forest and order us out and onto our knees. He turns on the television, finds a nature show.

Mai looks at me. 'What's the matter?'

'Hm? Oh. Um, there's an expression in English,' I whisper, though the jeering of gibbons from the speakers covers our voices in the back seat, 'that suits this occasion admirably. *Out of the frying pan, into the fire.* Get it?'

'No.'

'Dad may not be in the hospital,' I mumble. Her eyebrows flare. 'All he had was some gallstones. It was nothing.' She stares at me uncomprehendingly.

She pulls her hands forward across her face like an android pulling off a human mask, then clenches them into fists and starts pounding me on the chest. '*Idiot!*' she hisses. '*Idiot idiot idiot!* How the hell can you keep doing this?'

'I thought you wouldn't come in time. I owed those guys at the house a lot of money.'

She's about to cry. She slumps over on the far side of the seat, staring at the ceiling like a cadaver. Then she jolts upright again. 'And if they did something to Dad?'

We arrive at the hospital without a plan. Neither Mai nor I can find the willpower to come up with a new alibi. So we just play our roles in the nightmare scenario as it develops. We walk through the obliging doors and go up to the front desk. I ask the girl in the smart uniform which room Mr Fujiwara is in, fully expecting her to frown at the computer, search around with her

mouse, ask me if I'm sure of the name, call someone else over
to help, and eventually inform me of what I already know, that
he isn't there. I'm prepared to act astonished – to wonder aloud
if he's been taken to a different hospital, perhaps in Kyoto. This,
at least, will buy us more time, there being a good hundred or
more hospitals in and around the city. But none of this play-
acting turns out to be necessary. She writes a room number on
a slip of paper and passes it to me across the desk.

'Fujiwara?' I ask.

'Yes.'

'Shunsuke?'

'Yes.'

My relief is only slightly tempered by the thought that Dad
really is ill. I spin around with a grin. 'Mai! He's here!'

Mai grins too, then puts her hand over her mouth and turns
away. Gondo frowns and shakes his head.

Dad's deeply unconscious, but it's probably more comfortable
for everyone this way. Mai gets to cry and hold his hand and
whisper, 'I'm back, Dad,' and other things that I try not to
listen to, and neither of them has to suffer any embarrassment
about it. As for myself, I don't know what Dad and I would
have said to one another anyway. He would have thanked me
for bringing Mai back. He would have asked me if I needed
money. He'd have said something about the prestige of Kyoto
University and inquired again about my 'studies'. He'd have
tried to persuade me not to sell Aunt Okane's *ukiyo-e* prints –
'our priceless cultural heritage'. And I would have shrugged.
So he would have started talking about those damn birds out
there, now stalking around on the eaves of the other hospital
wing. Now, Aozora, which are they, rooks or jackdaws? And
I would have shrugged and said 'rooks' because of the greyish sheen on their necks when they turn in the sun. Dear me,
Aozora! It's no wonder you're not studying zoology. Have I

not taught you the difference? Hand me that pen and that napkin there. Here look now. The beak of the rook looks like this . . .

'He had a stroke during a liver replacement,' a Dr Honda tells us. 'We've been looking for family for five days now.'

'A *liver* replacement?'

'He'd been waiting for a donor for a long time. Finally we got one from a pig. Most people find the idea distasteful but your father was quite enthusiastic about it. A very practical, thoughtful man, it seemed to me.'

We wait for him to die. Mai and I take shifts because she doesn't want to leave him alone. She wants someone to be there with him, holding his hand when he finally goes. I think she's been watching too much TV but I don't make a fuss. I take late nights and early mornings because there are better programmes on TV and the hospital has satellite; she sits with him through the day.

Gondo's presence – and, moreover, *patience* – during this time is unnerving. He seems perfectly content to wait around until Dad dies and he can take Mai back to Marumachi again. Stranger still, he seems to be taking a liking to Inaka. He sits in the tearoom all afternoon, poised as a monk, though in his corduroys and golfing shirt he looks more like somebody's granddad. Skull comes in later and tries to emulate him but his legs won't cross and just lie jackknifed in front of him. I bring them green tea, playing the host.

'Try the persimmons,' I say. 'They're local.'

Gondo sighs deeply. 'I miss this, *ne*? My house in Marumachi, it's all marble and Italian furniture. But I never sit on any of it. Too comfortable. This is what I miss, *ne*?' He thumps the tatami floor. Gondo talks on like this, reminiscing about his childhood in the countryside, then goes outside to water the dying topiary and sends Skull on an errand to get real local food. Where in hell he finds it I don't know, but he comes back two hours later with pickles, dumpling soup, wild boar sashimi, fried okra, stuffed eggplant, devil's-tongue jelly, five kilos of kiwis and eight bottles of local saké.

I'm not sure whether to join in the impromptu feast. I'm not particularly comfortable around Gondo. He's not pleased with me, that much is certain, and he hasn't yet stipulated what form of punishment, if any, awaits me. I make myself useful, constantly running back to the kitchen to fetch things or make tea, avoiding the silence. After dinner Gondo starts sighing a lot and looking bored. There are no nature shows on the TV.

I suggest going for a walk up to the hot springs on the hill, anything to keep him from getting bored.

Albino evening sky with one dying red eye and a perfect eyebrow of cirrus. The swifts are nothing but silhouettes. For all I know, they're as flat as paper cut-outs. Might be nice to spend 90 per cent of your life in the sky, free from earthly obligation and danger. The bamboo hills are minutely detailed in the clear air; the breeze makes slow waves upon their flanks. Even in summer you can see the steam rising through the trees from the clearing next to the creek. The hot springs flow into a small river in the forest. There are rock walls that Inaka residents have built up over the years to pool the water, and at the largest pool the rocks are covered in multicoloured wax from all the candles burnt at night.

An old couple are already there bathing. They do their best to be polite when we arrive, but the sight of Skull peeling off his clothes to reveal an entire phalanx of ghosts in blue tattoo has got to be a strain on their delicate sensibilities. They exchange uncertain glances.

I try to lighten up the atmosphere. 'I'm from Inaka,' I tell them.

'Oh, is that so?' Themselves, they've come out from Osaka,

241

they explain, for a drive in the hills, some real Inaka wild boar and a dip in their favourite hot spring. 'There aren't many places like this left,' the man says.

Skull has his head back on a towel he's bundled on the rock. Gondo makes a menagerie's worth of grunts getting into the hot water, then leans back and stares out through the trees at the setting sun. 'I'd forgotten places like this still exist,' he says.

'Yes,' the woman joins in, 'if too many people knew about this it would be ruined. When you're sitting here, you can imagine everything as it used to be. There were places like this even in Kyoto, I imagine.'

'Back when Kyoto actually looked like Kyoto,' says her husband.

My idea for a theme park comes back to me. And suddenly I'm less concerned by the here and now than the what-could-be. My Japanese theme park has just found a home. Inaka. What place could be better? It has mountains and a river. Hot springs. Four distinct seasons, with maples for the autumn, cherry trees for the spring, deep snow in the winter and eels and fireflies in summer. Most importantly, it's got cheap land, as cheap as it comes. I look across the Inaka Valley and I see temple roofs, pagodas, bridges looping over the river – an entire city straight out of a picture book.

'The whole country used to be like this,' I say to Gondo. 'Back when everything looked like a Hokusai print.'

The old couple's faces light up. 'Exactly. Exactly.'

'Good thing this is a secret though,' I continue, aiming my words at Gondo. 'It would attract *far* too many people if word got out.'

There isn't much to do at the hospital that night. I sleep, drink beer, watch soccer on television and read whatever magazines I can scrounge from the public areas. At times I can hear noises echoing down from the nurses' station, but there isn't much activity at this end of the ward. In the corridor an elderly man in slippers and an intravenous frame come past, supporting each other like two old friends. An even older woman follows an ant in the other direction.

The next afternoon, I go with Mai and Gondo to see the lawyer about the will. Gondo waits, uninterested, in the lobby while we sign all the necessary forms. The buyer from Dubai is ready and waiting to make the purchase, but I tell the lawyer I'd like to stall for a few days. The lawyer can't argue with me, but Mai's at her wits' end. She grabs my arm in the hallway as we're leaving. 'We go through all this so you can get that money,' she says, 'and now you're turning it *down*?'

'I'm not turning it down, Mai-Tai. I've just got another buyer in mind, that's all.'

'Why? Why? Is 100 million not enough for you now?'

'It's not the money,' I tell her, then hesitate. 'Did you hear that, what I just said?'

'The sky must be falling.'

'Yeah. I'm wondering . . . Anyhow, I don't need to remind you that as soon as Dad . . . passes . . . whatever . . . as soon as that happens, Gondo's taking you straight back to Marumachi. Assuming he doesn't lose patience first. But we may just have a little leverage. You trust me?'

'No. But do I have a choice?'

When we arrive at the hospital for Mai's shift, a Mr Kuroda is waiting outside the room. He bows at the doorway and Mai goes over to greet him.

'I know your father,' he says. 'I've come from Nagoya today. I asked the doctor if it would be appropriate to visit.'

Mai invites him in and he hands her a pinewood box with 'From Hokkaido' branded on the front and a gold-and-blue ribbon that reads 'Takahashi Melon'. He's not the first visitor and this is not the first melon. There are nine boxed melons in various stages of decomposition on the windowsill and bedside table already. Three of them are from Gondo, one each day, and the rest from neighbours or business associates or members of the PTA Alumni. For the time being at least, the slight perfume they're giving off is rather pleasant.

'You're kind to have come,' says my sister. She's adept at these formalities, though it is slightly disconcerting to consider why. There could hardly be any better training in customer relations than 'elite' prostitution.

'No, no, it's nothing,' he says. 'It's my duty to your father. He provided my perfume shops with topiary for fifteen years. He was a reliable businessman.'

It will be awkward in the extreme if he stays for very long, but at their age, all Dad's cronies have made so many of these kinds of visits that they've got them perfected to a seven-minute routine of consolation, compliment, reminiscence and self-effacement. He compliments my father's skill and reliability several times over, wishes us the best, gives us his business card and asks if he may call in the coming days to check on 'Mr Fujiwara's inevitable recovery'. We all bow to one another a million times and Mai walks him back to the front door of the hospital.

Once they're gone, I take a look at the melon he's brought. The value is purely symbolic. Actually *eating* the thing wouldn't be good etiquette – and my father's certainly in no condition to eat it – but I prise open the lid to take a look just the same. And there it is, a double-grapefruit-sized, yellowy-green cantaloupe bedded in excelsior with the stem wrapped in gold foil and tied with a red prize ribbon. A tiny black-and-gold card has a picture of a smiling farmer standing in his field holding up two similar melons. It's a pity to let this gastronomic wonder go to waste. I wouldn't mind a slice of Hokkaido melon. There's a plastic knife on the bedside table. I'm sure it's incredibly sweet. I sit there staring at that melon for ever. Eating or not eating the thing is of absolutely no consequence to my father. The gesture's been made; here's the melon. Perhaps we've all just been dulled by politesse. Perhaps the point, way back when people first started giving one another melons, was to actually *eat* the melon. It's full of vitamin C at least, right? I angle the knife into the top, just beside the stem, and saw off a chunk. It's like melon-flavoured candy it's so sweet. I saw off another slice for Dad. He can't eat, of course. His mouth is dry, lips cracked. But I take the chunk and brush the wet fruit against his lips. I'm waiting for the top lip to come down over the bottom, to take in the sweetness, but it doesn't move.

The melon fits back into its excelsior nest, the damage on its flank hidden by the bright ribbon. I pound the cover back on and put it on the windowsill to slowly, ritually rot with the others.

Dad dies on my shift, 8 AM. His breath catches in his throat like he's got indigestion, but it doesn't resume. There's nothing more. His head is turned up at the same angle it's been at for the past three days, as if he's dying of thirst, straining for a last drop of water. A nurse rushes into the room, followed by another and another. One goes to the vital signs screen, the other opens his mouth and puts her fingers in. 'No obstruction,' she says.

I get up from my chair and stand back as they pull the curtain around. And I think to myself: 'No, not any more.'

eulogy

I am silent at the funeral, but in the weeks to come, when I am emptying the house, I will come across these. Drawings by a father for his son. They're as eloquent a eulogy as I can provide.

Fujiwara Shunsuke
1930–2000

みつば　あけび

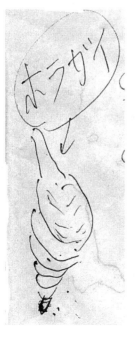

ホラガイ

かめ

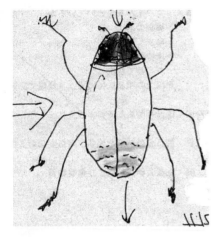

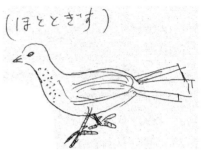

（ほととぎす）

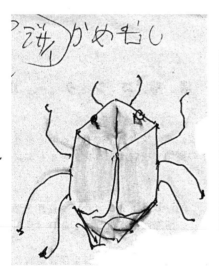

かめむし

15 cm

からすうり

j-land

Kyoto's spread out like all the contents of a toy box dumped onto the floor, the new and the shiny jumbled in with the old and worn. We're on the raised highway, driving in the Century above the billboards and rooftops. Pixelled with rain-drops, the windscreen flushes a rhythmic yellow to the lights overhead, green and red neon flickering in between. Gondo's got clients and concrete to take care of back in Marumachi. Before driving back by night, he and Skull and Mai are going into Kyoto to eat and buy her a Chanel evening gown for her performances. I'm cordially invited to come along.

Mai's wearing black-and-white striped socks pulled up past her knees, an orange miniskirt, a pink T-shirt that says LOVE ME on the front, and earrings that are just the very essence of the girl, these weird, feathered, Indian dream-catcher things in bright pink. It's like she's trying to recapture some youth before returning to the real world.

'So where are we going?' she asks.

'Dunno,' says Gondo.

'I know a place,' I say.

'Let me guess,' says Mai, 'Mos Burger?'

'No, really, I know this traditional seafood place. Great sashimi.'

'Sashimi? Are you feeling all right, Ao? Since when does Aozora Fujiwara eat sashimi?'

Gondo grunts. 'I could eat some seafood.'

Mai looks at me suspiciously. 'Just what kind of place is this?'

'Don't worry,' I tell her, 'there's no dress code.'

The restaurant has a huge façade with a giant crab suspended over the entrance, arms rotating. The interior is one
large courtyard with a glass roof and tiled pools full of a great
quantity of crabs and puffer-fish and other monsters. It's very
classy and hushed and old-fashioned; there's bamboo growing everywhere and a second-floor mezzanine with tiny
balconies overlooking the room.

Mai whispers as we come through the door. 'You've actually been here before?'

Never, but it's on my way to my favourite *ramen* shop.
'Sure,' I reply. 'Lots of times.'

We stand by one of the pools waiting for a hostess. We
don't have reservations, but with someone of Skull's presence
in our party, the matter gets quickly overlooked.

'What's that?' Mai asks, staring down at a number of fat,
grey, penis-like creatures on the bottom of one of the bubbling
pools.

'Geoduck,' I tell her. 'It's a big clam. They can live to 100.'

'How do you know that?'

I shrug. 'I don't know.'

The hostess comes along with our menus and leads us up
a carpeted staircase lined with sepia photographs of old
Kyoto.

'Dad, probably,' I mutter.

The hostess turns. 'I beg your pardon?'

'Oh, sorry. Nothing.'

A corridor lined with ikebana and lacquered samurai
armour leads to the sliding paper doors of our dining balcony.
We lean on the little railing and drink beer and watch the
cooks scoop up fish in their nets.

'Well,' I say to Gondo with a sigh of feigned familiarity,
'foreign places are all right for a change, but this is where a
man can really feel at home, no? We're lucky we got a table.
Did you see their list of reservations? They're packed.'

Mai frowns at me. Gondo just grunts, though the way he's leaning back against the cushions, he looks pleased with my choice of restaurant.

We start with *asupara-bacon* – crackly red strips of Minke whale bacon wrapped around asparagus stalks.

'What a delicacy,' says Mai, trying to be upbeat. I'm impressed by her courage; she won't let her fear show. (If it were me going back to slavery, I'd just sulk.)

'Whale's becoming more and more popular,' I tell Gondo. 'A good traditional Japanese food.'

The second course is a whole live *aji*. The sides are scored crosswise and it's skewered on a bamboo stick to stop it flapping, but it's still very much alive. The mouth is opening and closing, the gills fluttering slightly every now and again. When I look closely at the body between dorsal fin and tail, I can see the blood still trickling through the veins.

Gondo attacks the thing like it's French fries. Though I'm hardly tempted, I do the same.

'I can't believe you're actually eating this,' Mai says. 'I didn't think you liked fish.'

'It doesn't taste like much of anything,' I reply. 'But eating it makes me feel like Vlad the Impaler.'

'It's a very delicate flavour,' Mai says to Gondo making conversation, 'nutty and fruity at once. This Ukiha saké complements it perfectly, don't you think?'

'*Mn*,' he grunts.

The fish's body is half gone but it's still quivering. The waitress comes back and shuffles inside with a tray of black lacquer bowls for miso soup. She puts one down in front of me and I take off the lid expecting a rush of steam. The shiny red insides of the bowl are empty but for a pile of shredded seaweed and several cubes of tofu. Then a tiny movement in the bowl catches my eye. Out from between the strips of seaweed crawls a small grey-green crab no larger than a 500-yen coin. I put the lid back. I'd prefer the proverbial fly. I don't want to embarrass the waitress by calling attention to the crab in case it's there by accident, but I don't want to look uncultured if, by some perversé *must* of haute cuisine, it's meant to be there either. 'She forgot the soup,' I say.

The waitress's pasty cosmetics allow a smile. She goes back into the corridor to get the soup tureen. Mai takes the lid off her bowl and she has an identical crab too.

'House speciality,' I guess. 'The hot soup cooks the crab.'

I stare at my crab. It's now atop a tofu cube trying to escape. It reaches up with two or three legs outstretched but is unable to get a grip on the sheer surface of the lacquer bowl. I'm not sure if I pity the thing or if I'm just feeling subversive, but when the waitress returns with the soup and sets it in the centre of the table, I grab the little crab with my chopsticks and hold him under the table. His legs wave about, but I've got a firm hold on him. The waitress takes the lid from the steaming pot and, with a bamboo ladle, fills the bowls with piping-hot miso broth. The crab in Gondo's bowl shudders and expires with several bubbles around the edge of its shell and a barely audible wheeze. It slowly turns crimson, spinning on the surface of the broth like an autumn leaf before slipping back down into the cloud of miso and *konbu* seaweed on the bottom. While she's serving Mai and Skull, I reach to my left, still underneath the table, and place the crab under the railing of the mezzanine.

The waitress looks for the crab in my bowl before serving the soup. I smile and point to my mouth. She smiles back, though her expression is quizzical. She doesn't know whether to be impressed or disgusted that I've swallowed a live crab.

'Your appetite,' I say, and raise the soup bowl to my lips. On my left, the little crab is trying to hide, edging itself into the narrow gap between the two open *washi* paper windows. I wonder how long it'll live in there. Perhaps it'll make it its home.

'Sad, *ne*?' says Gondo as he lifts his soup bowl. 'Your sister leaving again.'

The silence that follows this tactless comment is a void beyond metaphor. Mai's façade looks as if it's about to crumble. Now's the time. I fish in my pocket for a 10-yen coin and toss it on the table. 'Recognize it?'

He frowns at me. 'Byodo-in temple,' he mumbles with the bowl to his mouth.

'That's called Brand Recognition,' I say. 'Byodo-in, Todai-ji, Nikko, Ise –' I list them off, one after the other '– Gion, Kinkakuji, Mount Fuji. Everybody knows them.'

'So what?'

'So you're still looking for one thing people here just can't get enough of? I already told you what it is. It's *Japan*.'

The words sound like prophecy in my ears, but Gondo's not convinced. 'This again?' He drains a glass of beer and pours himself another from the bottle. 'I told you before, it's idiotic. People aren't going to pay for it.'

I point at the *washi* paper doors and the tatami floors. 'So why are you paying for this then?' I ask. 'What's the point of coming to a traditional place like this? It's not just for the food.' Gondo takes another gulp of beer and unbuttons his jacket. 'Imagine going out the door of this place and finding a whole city just like it. No neon, no video, no loudspeakers, no Western architecture or buildings that look like space-ships. You don't think people will find that attractive? I've thought of calling it "J-Land". Or maybe "Japan City". The name may need some work, but the idea is we build a new Kyoto. A new *old* Kyoto, just the way it looked forty or fifty years ago – all narrow streets and bathhouses and red bridges. Geishas, samurai, with a nearby Mount Fuji thrown in for good measure.'

Gondo's not looking at me. But it's not the usual dismissive nonchalance. With amazing dexterity, he's spinning his

254

lighter on his fingertips, staring all the while at some indistinct point above and beyond me.

'And what's the perfect place for J-Land?' I ask. 'Inaka. Cheap land, hot springs, rail line to a metropolis of 10 million people. The place already needs regeneration. You can practically buy the whole town and everyone in it. I suggest the first things you buy are our prints. All the old museum pieces that are supposed to go to Dubai. And the houses and gardens too, Aunt Okane's and Dad's. You can have the Daihatsu for free.'

He raises his hand. 'Okay, I get it.' He's staring down at his soup bowl. I know he's grasped the idea, but I can't stop. I'm building the future. This conversation is historical.

'How improbable was Amsterdam?' I ask him. 'It was just some marshland and a weird vision was all it was, right? How less improbable is J-Land?'

'I –'

'And for providing you with the details of this vision, as well as agreeing to sell you all the land and the art for a very reasonable price, all I ask is that you let Mai go. That's all.'

Gondo smiles and reaches for the soup ladle. 'I could just take it,' he says, pouring himself some soup. 'What makes you think I need to pay you?'

He has a queasy ability to make his silences stretch wide as crevasses in a volcano. I have to admit, he could just take it. 'That's true,' I say. 'Too true.' With a couple of phone calls he could make Mai and me disappear, take our houses, the prints, the lot. 'But you said yourself it's not the "what" that matters, it's the "how". What good would it do you to start on crooked foundations? If you want a clean place for dirty money, then you'd better keep it clean.'

His eyes flash. He doesn't like the word 'dirty'. 'Enough, MOC, enough,' he says. 'Let me think.'

*

255

The Century is sitting in front with its hazard lights flashing, holding up traffic in the near lane. Skull leans against the hood examining the tattoos on his upper arm, enjoying the commotion of horns and the sideways glances of the pedestrians on the sidewalk.

He steps forward to open the rear door for us. Gondo puts one hand on the windowframe and turns around. He looks straight at Mai. 'My best girl,' he says.

We wait for him to continue but he only sighs and shakes his head. The people on the sidewalk stop before this odd, tense scene and edge around us. 'What's a girl here or there?' I say. 'All that matters is the broader demographic, right?'

Gondo chuckles. 'Mr MOC. You're an angel. You tell your lawyer to get in touch with me tomorrow. Whatever price you've got in mind, cut it in half. And you, Mai, you never come back to Amsterdam.'

Mai's quivering. It looks like she's about to shatter into a thousand pieces of painted porcelain. She bows. And bows again. Gondo ducks inside the car and Skull closes the door after him. He eases his bulk into the front seat and the Century burbles away from the kerb, the street life coursing down its mirror-polished flanks. Like the most prudent innkeeper saying goodbye to an old customer, we watch the traffic long after the Century has disappeared amidst the stream of red tail lamps.

Mai and I walk through the city with no direction at all. I want to laugh, but I'm too tired to manage it. Mai's eyes are glossed with tears. She cries and cries, soundlessly amid the bustle of Kyoto. The stores are all still open. There's a Mister Donut near the Maruzen bookstore on Sanjo-dori. It's busy and bright and you can smell the doughnuts out in the street. Mai has a Perrier and a Honey Dip. I go for a coffee and a Walnut Crunch. We sit in silence amidst the chirruping waitresses, raucous teenagers, and the sustained, aggravating jingle of 'Yum-cha, yum-cha, delicious delicious yum-cha. Mis-ter Donut!'

'It's kind of scary,' says Mai.

'Mister Donut?'

She shakes her head. 'Being left to fend for yourself.'

She's got no more job, no more 'chaperones', no more sugar-daddy. No more Daddy. Not even Inaka to go back to. Even for me, the thought that I won't be able to go back to my old home is harder to take than I thought it would be. I may have disliked the place, but I was still comforted knowing it was there. 'But that's all over,' I say to her. 'With fifty million yen, we won't have to do much fending for a while.'

With her perfect nails, Mai picks away the flaky coating on her doughnut. A tentative smile stretches her lips. 'Can we still go to Chanel?'

She knows exactly where it is. It's up ahead on Heiwa-dori. But before we get there, we come to a giant sports store complex with every conceivable type of sports gear in the two-storey windows – bicycles, hang-gliders, a flower of tennis rackets, a bobsled, surfboards, skis, snowboards, giant nets full of footballs.

'Hold it,' I say.

'Where are you going?'

'Hokkaido.'

'*What?*'

'I want to look at snowboards,' I tell her. 'Jackets and gloves, hats, goggles, that kind of thing.'

'In August?'

'Yeah,' I reply. 'It's about time.'

acknowledgements

The author wishes to thank Sara Holloway, Mark Stanton, Bella Shand, Sarah Bower, Iain Robinson, Chaulam Karen Cheung, Harriet Carter, Gary Kissick, Michelle Remblance, Claire Hynes, Claire MacDonald, Chi-Chi Lai, Mary Allen, Michéle Roberts, Andrew Cowan, Patricia Duncker, Helen Kidd, Don Winslow, Sarah Wasley, Sajidah Ahmad and Jane Barringer. Also Mansho-*sensei*, Yokota-*sensei*, and Joe, for your daily lessons on all things *Nihon*, *arigato gozaimasu*.

Special thanks to Richard Perkins, a meticulous critic, and creator of the manga in this book.

Invaluable in the writing of this book was Alex Kerr's *Dogs and Demons: The Fall of Modern Japan*. (If only it were fiction too.)